Christmas on the Range

Also available from Diana Palmer and HQN Books

Magnolia
Renegade
Lone Star Winter
Dangerous
Desperado
Merciless
Heartless
Fearless
Her Kind of Hero
Lacy
Nora
Big Sky Winter
Man of the Hour
Trilby
Lawman
Hard to Handle
The Savage Heart
Courageous
Lawless
The Texas Ranger
Lord of the Desert
The Cowboy and the Lady
Most Wanted
Fit for a King
Paper Rose
Rage of Passion
Once in Paris
After the Music
Roomful of Roses
Champagne Girl
Passion Flower
Diamond Girl
Friends and Lovers
Cattleman's Choice
Lady Love
The Rawhide Man
Outsider
Night Fever
Before Sunrise
Protector
Midnight Rider
Wyoming Tough
Wyoming Fierce
Wyoming Bold
Invincible
Untamed
The Morcai Battalion: The Recruit

And don't miss

Wyoming Rugged
and
The Morcai Battalion: Invictus

DIANA PALMER

Christmas on the Range

Recycling programs for this product may not exist in your area.

ISBN-13: 978-0-373-78851-4

Christmas on the Range

This edition published by arrangement with Harlequin Books S.A.

For questions and comments about the quality of this book, please contact us at CustomerService@Harlequin.com.

www.HQNBooks.com

Printed in U.S.A.

CONTENTS

Winter Roses

1

It was late, and Ivy was going to miss her class. Rachel was the only person, except Ivy's best friend, who even knew the number of Ivy's frugal prepaid cell phone. The call had come just as she was going to her second college class of the day. The argument could have waited until the evening, but her older sister never thought of anyone's convenience. Well, except her own, that was.

"Rachel, I'm going to be late," Ivy pleaded into the phone. She pushed back a strand of long, pale blond hair. Her green eyes darkened with worry. "And we've got a test today!"

"I don't care what you've got," her older sister snapped. "You just listen to me. I want that check for Dad's property, as soon as you can get the insurance company to issue it! I've got overdue bills and you're whining about college classes. It's a waste of money! Aunt Hettie should never have left you that savings account," she added angrily. "It should have been mine, too. I'm the oldest."

She was, and she'd taken everything she could get her hands on, anything she could pawn for ready cash. Ivy had barely been able to keep enough to pay the funeral bills when they came due. It was a stroke of luck that Aunt Hettie had liked her and had left her a small inheritance. Perhaps she'd realized that Ivy would be lucky if she was able to keep so much as a penny of their father's few assets.

It was the same painful argument they'd had for a solid month, since their father had died of a stroke. Ivy had been left with finding a place to live while Rachel called daily to talk to the attorney who was probating the will. All she wanted was the money. She'd coaxed their father into changing his will, so that she got everything when he died.

Despite the fact that he paid her little attention, Ivy was still grieving. She'd taken care of their father while he was dying from the stroke. He'd thought that Rachel was an angel. All their lives, it had been Rachel who got all the allowances, all the inherited jewelry—which Rachel pawned immediately—all the attention. Ivy was left with housework and yardwork and cooking for the three of them. It hadn't been much of a life. Her rare dates had been immediately captivated by Rachel, who took pleasure in stealing them away from her younger, plainer sister, only to drop them days later. When Rachel had opted to go to New York and break into theater, their father had actually put a lien on his small house to pay for an apartment for her. It had meant budgeting to the bone and no new dresses for Ivy. When she tried to protest the unequal treatment the sisters received, their father said that Ivy was just jealous and that Rachel needed more because she was beautiful but emotionally challenged.

Translated, that meant Rachel had no feelings for anyone except herself. But Rachel had convinced their father that she adored him, and she'd filled his ears with lies about Ivy, right up to accusing her of sneaking out at night to meet men and stealing from the garage where she worked two evenings a week keeping books. No protest was enough to convince him that Ivy was honest, and that she didn't even attract many men. She never could keep a prospective boyfriend once they saw Rachel.

"If I can learn bookkeeping, I'll have a way to support myself, Rachel," Ivy said quietly.

"You could marry a rich man one day, I guess, if you could find a blind one," Rachel conceded, and laughed at her little joke. "Although where you expect to find one in Jacobsville, Texas, is beyond me."

"I'm not looking for a husband. I'm in school at our community vocational college," Ivy reminded her.

"So you are. What a pitiful future you're heading for." Rachel paused to take an audible sip of her drink. "I've got two auditions tomorrow. One's for the lead in a new play, right on Broadway. Jerry says I'm a shoo-in. He has influence with the director."

Ivy wasn't usually sarcastic, but Rachel was getting on her nerves. "I thought Jerry didn't want you to work."

There was a frigid pause on the other end of the line. "Jerry doesn't mind it," she said coolly. "He just likes me to stay in, so that he can take care of me."

"He feeds you uppers and downers and crystal meth and charges you for the privilege, you mean," Ivy replied quietly. She didn't add that Rachel was beautiful and that Jerry probably used her as bait to catch new clients. He took her to party after party. She talked about acting, but it was only talk. She could barely remember her own name when she was on drugs, much less remember lines for a play. She drank to excess as well, just like Jerry.

"Jerry takes care of me. He knows all the best people in theater. He's promised to introduce me to one of the angels who's producing that new comedy. I'm going to make it to Broadway or die trying," Rachel said curtly.

"And if we're going to argue, we might as well not even speak!"

"I'm not arguing…"

"You're putting Jerry down, all the time!"

Ivy felt as if she were standing on a precipice, looking at the bottom of the world. "Have you really forgotten what Jerry did to me?" she asked, recalling the one visit Rachel had made home, just after their father died. It had been an overnight one, with the insufferable Jerry at her side. Rachel had signed papers to have their father cremated, placing his ashes in the grave with those of his late wife, the girls' mother. It was rushed and unpleasant, with Ivy left grieving alone for a parent who'd never loved her, who'd treated her very badly. Ivy had a big, forgiving heart. Rachel did manage a sniff into a handkerchief at the graveside service. But her eyes weren't either wet or red. It was an act, as it always was with her.

"What you said he did," came the instant, caustic reply. "Jerry said he never gave you any sort of drugs!"

"Rachel!" she exclaimed, furious now, "I wouldn't lie about something like that! I had a migraine and he switched my regular medicine with a powerful narcotic. When I saw what he was trying to give me, I threw them at him. He thought I was too sick to notice. He thought it would be funny if he could make me into an addict, just like you…!"

"Oh, grow up," Rachel shouted. "I'm no addict! Everybody uses drugs! Even people in that little hick town where you live. How do you think I used to score before I moved to New York? There was always somebody dealing, and I knew where to find what I needed. You're so naive, Ivy."

"My brain still works," she shot back.

"Watch your mouth, kid," Rachel said angrily, "or I'll see that you don't get a penny of Dad's estate."

"Don't worry, I never expected to get any of it," Ivy said quietly. "You convinced Daddy that I was no good, so that he wouldn't leave me anything."

"You've got that pittance from Aunt Hettie," Rachel repeated. "Even though I should have had it. I deserved it, having to live like white trash all those years when I was at home."

"Rachel, if you got what you really deserved," Ivy replied with a flash of bravado, "you'd be in federal prison."

There was a muffled curse. "I have to go. Jerry's back. Listen, you check with that lawyer and find out what's the holdup. I can't afford all these long-distance calls."

"You never pay for them. You usually reverse the charges when you call me," she was reminded.

"Just hurry up and get the paperwork through so you can send me my check. And don't expect me to call you back until you're ready to talk like an adult instead of a spoiled kid with a grudge!"

The receiver slammed down in her ear. She folded it back up with quiet resignation. Rachel would never believe that Jerry, her knight in shining armor, was nothing more than a sick little social climbing drug dealer with a felony record who was holding her hostage to substance abuse. Ivy had tried for the past year to make her older sibling listen, but she couldn't. The two of them had never been close, but since Rachel got mixed up with Jerry, and hooked on meth, she didn't seem capable of reason anymore. In the old days, even when Rachel was being difficult, she did seem to have some small affection for her sister. That all changed when she was a junior in high school. Something had happened, Ivy had never known what, that turned her against Ivy and made a real enemy of her. Alcohol and drug use hadn't helped Rachel's already abrasive personality. It had been an actual relief for Ivy when her sister left for New York just days after the odd blowup. But it seemed that she could cause trouble long-distance, whenever she liked.

Ivy went down the hall quickly to her next class, without any real enthusiasm. She didn't want to spend her life working for someone else, but she certainly didn't want to go to New York and end up as Rachel's maid and cook, as she had been before her sister left Jacobsville. Letting Rachel have their inheritance would be the easier solution to the problem. Anything was better than having to live with Rachel again; even having to put up with Merrie York's brother, Stuart, in order to have one true friend.

It was Friday, and when she left the campus for home, riding with her fellow boarder, Lita Dawson, who taught at the vocational college, she felt better. She'd passed her English test, she was certain of it. But typing was getting her down. She couldn't manage more than fifty words a minute to save her life. One of the male students typing with both index fingers could do it faster than Ivy could.

They pulled up in front of the boardinghouse where they both lived. Ivy felt absolutely drained. She'd had to leave her father's house because she couldn't even afford to pay the light bill. Besides, Rachel had signed papers to put the house on the market the same day she'd signed the probate papers at a local lawyer's office. Since Ivy wasn't old enough, at almost nineteen, to handle the legal affairs, Rachel had charmed the new, young attorney handling the probate and convinced him that Ivy needed looking after, preferably in a boardinghouse. Then she'd flown back to New York, leaving Ivy to dip into a great-aunt's small legacy and a part-time job as a bookkeeper at a garage on Monday and Thursday evenings to pay for her board and the small student fee that Texas residents paid at the state technical and vocational college. Rachel hadn't even asked if Ivy had enough to live on.

Merrie had tried to get Stuart to help Ivy fight Rachel's claim on the bulk of the estate, but Ivy almost had hysterics when she offered. She'd rather have lived in a cardboard box by the side of the road than have Stuart take over her life. She didn't want to tell her best friend that her brother terrified her. Merrie would have asked why. There were secrets in Ivy's past that she shared with no one.

"I'm going to see my father this weekend." Lita, dark-haired and eyed, smiled at the younger woman. "How about you?"

Ivy smiled. "If Merrie remembers, we'll probably go window-shopping." She sighed, smiling lazily. "I might see something I can daydream about owning," she chuckled.

"One day some nice man is going to come along and treat you the way you deserve to be treated," Lita said kindly. "You wait and see."

Ivy knew better, but she only smiled. She wasn't anxious to offer any man control of her life. She was through living in fear.

She went in the side door, glancing over to see if Mrs. Brown was home. The landlady must be grocery shopping, she decided. It was a Friday ritual. Ivy got to eat with Mrs. Brown and Lita Dawson, the other tenant, on the weekends. She and Lita took turns cooking and cleaning up the kitchen, to help elderly Mrs. Brown manage the extra work. It was nice, not having to drive into town to get a sandwich. The pizza place delivered, but Ivy was sick of pizza. She liked her small boardinghouse, and Lita was nice, if a little older than Ivy. Lita was newly divorced and missing her ex-husband to a terrible degree. She fell back on her degree and taught computer technology at the vocational college, and let Ivy ride back and forth with her for help with the gas money.

She'd no sooner put down her purse than the cell phone rang.

"It's the weekend!" came a jolly, laughing voice. It was Merrie York, her best friend from high school.

"I noticed," Ivy chuckled. "How'd you do on your tests?"

"I'm sure I passed something, but I'm not sure what. My biology final is approaching and lab work is killing me. I can't make the microscope work!"

"You're training to be a nurse, not a lab assistant," Ivy pointed out.

"Come up here and tell that to my biology professor," Merrie dared her. "Never mind, I'll graduate even if I have to take every course three times."

"That's the spirit."

"Come over and spend the weekend with me," Merrie invited.

Ivy's heart flipped over. "Thanks, but I have some things to do around here…"

"He's in Oklahoma, settling a new group of cattle with a sale barn," Merrie coaxed wryly.

Ivy hesitated. "Can you put that in writing and get it notarized?"

"He really likes you, deep inside."

"He's made an art of hiding his fondness for me," Ivy shot back. "I love you, Merrie, but I don't fancy being cannon fodder. It's been a long week. Rachel and I had another argument today."

"Long distance?"

"Exactly."

"And over Sir Lancelot the drug lord."

"You know me too well."

Merrie laughed. "We've been friends since middle school," she reminded Ivy.

"Yes, the debutante and the tomboy. What a pair we made."

"You're not quite the tomboy you used to be," Merrie said.

"We conform when we have to. Why do you want me there this weekend?"

"For selfish reasons," the other woman said mischievously. "I need a study partner and everybody else in my class has a social life."

"I don't want a social life," Ivy said. "I want to make good grades and graduate and get a job that pays at least minimum wage."

"Your folks left you a savings account and some stocks," Merrie pointed out.

That was true, but Rachel had walked away with most of the money and all of the stocks.

"Your folks left you Stuart," Ivy replied dryly.

"Don't remind me!"

"Actually, I suppose it was the other way around, wasn't it?" Ivy thought aloud. "Your folks left you to Stuart."

"He's a really great brother," Merrie said gently. "And he likes most women…"

"He likes all women, except me," Ivy countered. "I really couldn't handle a weekend with Stuart right now. Not on top of being harassed by Rachel and final exams."

"You're a whiz at math," her friend countered. "You hardly ever have to study."

"Translation—I work math problems every day for four hours after class so that I can appear to be smart."

Merrie laughed. "Come on over. Mrs. Rhodes is making homemade yeast rolls for supper, and we have all the pay per view channels. We can study and then watch that new adventure movie."

Ivy was weakening. On weekends, it was mostly take-out at the boardinghouse. Ivy's stomach rebelled at the thought of pizza or more sweet and sour chicken or tacos. "I could really use an edible meal that didn't come in a box, I guess."

"If I tell Mrs. Rhodes you're coming, she'll make you a cherry pie."

"That does it. I'll pack a nightgown and see you in thirty minutes, or as soon as I can get a cab."

"I could come and get you."

"No. Cabs are cheap in town. I'm not destitute," she added proudly, although she practically was. The cab fare would have to come out of her snack money for the next week. She really did have to budget to the bone. But her pride wouldn't let her accept Merrie's offer.

"All right, Miss Independence. I'll have Jack leave the gate open."

It was a subtle and not arrogant reminder that the two women lived in different social strata. Merrie's home was a sprawling brick mansion with a wrought-iron gate running up a bricked driveway. There was an armed guard, Jack, at the front gate, miles of electrified fence and two killer Dobermans who had the run of the property at night. If that didn't deter trespassers, there were the ranch hands, half of whom were ex-military. Stuart was particular about the people who worked for him, because his home contained priceless inherited antiques. He also owned four herd sires who commanded incredible stud fees; straws of their semen sold for thousands of dollars each and were shipped all over the world.

"Should I wear body armor, or will Chayce recognize me?"

Chayce McLeod was the chief of security for York Properties, which Stuart headed. He'd worked for J.B. Hammock, but Stuart had offered him a bigger salary and fringe benefits. Chayce was worth it. He had a degree in management and he was a past master at handling men. There were plenty of them to handle on a spread this size. Most people didn't know that Chayce was also an ex-federal agent. He was dishy, too, but Ivy was immune to him.

Stuart's ranch, all twenty thousand acres of it, was only a part of an empire that spanned three states and included real estate, investments, feedlots and a ranching equipment company. Stuart and Merrie were very rich. But neither of them led a frantic social life. Stuart worked on the ranch, just as he had when he was in his teens—just as his father had until he died of a heart attack when Merrie was thirteen. Now, Stuart was thirty.

Merrie, like Ivy, was only eighteen, almost nineteen. There were no other relatives. Their mother had died giving birth to Merrie.

Merrie sighed at the long pause. "Of course Chayce will recognize you. Ivy, you're not in one of your moods again, are you?"

"My dad was a mechanic, Merrie," she reminded her friend, "and my mother was a C.P.A. in a firm."

"My grandfather was a gambler who got lucky down in the Caribbean," Merrie retorted. "He was probably a closet pirate, and family legend says he was actually arrested for arms dealing when he was in his sixties. That's where our money came from. It certainly didn't come from hard work and honest living. Our parents instilled a vicious work ethic in both of us, as you may have noticed. We don't just sit around sipping mint juleps and making remarks about the working class. Now will you just shut up and start packing?"

Ivy laughed. "Okay. I'll see you shortly."

"That's my buddy."

Ivy had to admit that neither Merrie nor Stuart could ever be accused of resting on the family fortune. Stuart was always working on the ranch, when he wasn't flying to the family corporation's board meetings or meeting with legislators on agricultural bills or giving workshops on new facets of the beef industry. He had a degree from

Yale in business, and he spoke Spanish fluently. He was also the most handsome, sensuous, attractive man Ivy had ever known. It took a lot of work for her to pretend that he didn't affect her. It was self-defense. Stuart preferred tall, beautiful, independent blondes, preferably rich ones. He was vocal about marriage, which he abhorred. His women came and went. Nobody lasted more than six months.

But Ivy was plain and soft-spoken, not really an executive sort of woman even if she'd been older than she was. She lived in a world far removed from Stuart's, and his friends intimidated her. She didn't know a certificate of deposit from a treasury bond, and her background didn't include yearly trips to exotic places. She didn't read literary fiction, listen to classical music, drive a luxury car or go shopping in boutiques. She lived a quiet life, working and studying hard to provide a future for herself. Merrie was in nursing school in San Antonio, where she lived in the dorm and drove a new Mercedes. The two only saw each other when Merrie came home for the occasional weekend. Ivy missed her.

That was why she took a chance and packed her bag. Merrie wouldn't lie to her about Stuart being there, she knew. But he frequently turned up unexpectedly. It wasn't surprising that he disliked Ivy. He'd known her sister, Rachel, before she went to New York. He was scathing about her lifestyle, which had been extremely modern even when she was still in high school. He thought Ivy was going to be just like her. Which proved that he didn't know his sister's best friend in the least.

Jack, the guard on the front gate at Merrie's house, recognized Ivy in the local cab, and grinned at her. He waved the cab through without even asking for any identification. One hurdle successfully passed, she told herself.

Merrie was waiting for her at the front steps of the sprawling brick mansion. She ran down the steps and around to the back door of the cab, throwing her arms around Ivy the minute she opened the door and got out.

Ivy was medium height and slender, with long, straight, pale blond hair and green eyes. Merrie took after her brother—she was tall for a woman, and she had dark hair and light eyes. She towered over Ivy.

"I'm so glad you came," Merrie said happily. "Sometimes the walls just close in on me when I'm here alone. The house is way too big for two people and a housekeeper."

"Both of you will marry someday and fill it up with kids," Ivy teased.

"Fat chance, in Stuart's case," Merrie chuckled. "Come on in. Where's your bag?"

"In the boot..."

The Hispanic driver was already at the trunk, smiling as he lifted out Ivy's bag and carried it all the way up to the porch for her. But before Ivy could reach into her purse, Merrie pressed a big bill into the driver's hand and spoke to him in her own, elegant Spanish.

Ivy started to argue, but the cab was racing down the driveway and Merrie was halfway up the front steps.

"Don't argue," she told Ivy with a grin. "You know you can't win."

"I know," the other woman sighed. "Thanks, Merrie, but..."

"But you've got about three dollars spare a week, and you'd do without lunch one day at school to pay for the cab," came the quiet reply. "If you were in my place, you'd do it for me," she added, and Ivy couldn't argue. But it did hurt her pride.

"Listen," Merrie added, "one day when you're a fabulously rich owner of a bookkeeping firm, and driving a Rolls, you can pay me back. Okay?"

Ivy just laughed. "Listen, no C.P.A. ever got rich enough to own a Rolls," came the dry reply. "But I really will pay you back."

"Friends help friends," Merrie said simply. "Come on in."

* * *

The house was huge, really huge. The one thing that set rich people apart from poor people, Ivy pondered, was space. If you were wealthy, you could afford plenty of room in your house and a bathroom the size of a garage. You could also afford enough land to give you some privacy and a place to plant flowers and trees and have a fish pond…

"What are you brooding about now?" Merrie asked on the way up the staircase.

"Space," Ivy murmured.

"Outer?"

"No. Personal space," Ivy qualified the answer. "I was thinking that how much space you have depends on how much money you have. I'd love to have just a yard. And maybe a fish pond," she added.

"You can feed our Chinese goldfish any time you want to," the other girl offered.

Ivy didn't reply. She noticed, not for the first time, how much Merrie resembled her older brother. They were both tall and slender, with jet-black hair. Merrie wore her hair long, but Stuart's was short and conventionally cut. Her eyes, pale blue like Stuart's, could take on a steely, dangerous quality when she was angry. Not that Merrie could hold a candle to Stuart in a temper. Ivy had seen grown men hide in the barn when he passed by. Stuart's pale, deep-set eyes weren't the only indication of bad temper. His walk was just as good a measure of ill humor. He usually glided like a runner. But when he was angry, his walk slowed. The slower the walk, the worse the temper.

Ivy had learned early in her friendship with Merrie to see how fast Stuart was moving before she approached any room he was in. One memorable day when he'd lost a prize cattle dog to a coyote, she actually pleaded a migraine headache she didn't have to avoid sitting at the supper table with him.

It was a nasty habit of his to be bitingly sarcastic to anyone within range when he was mad, especially if the object of his anger was out of reach.

Merrie led Ivy into the bedroom that adjoined hers and watched as Ivy opened the small bag and brought out a clean pair of jeans and a cotton T-shirt. She frowned. "No nightgown?"

Ivy winced. "Rachel upset me. I forgot."

"No problem. You can borrow one of mine. It will drag the floor behind you like a train, of course, but it will fit most everywhere else." Her eyes narrowed. "I suppose Rachel is after the money."

Ivy nodded, looking down into her small bag. "She was good at convincing Daddy I didn't deserve anything."

"She told lies."

Ivy nodded again. "But he believed her. Rachel could be so sweet and loving when she wanted something. He drank..." She stopped at once.

Merrie sat down on the bed and folded her hands in her lap. "I know he drank, Ivy," she said gently. "Stuart had him investigated."

Her eyes widened in disbelief. "What?"

Merrie bit her lower lip. "I can't tell you why, so don't even ask. Suffice it to say that it was an eye-opening experience."

Ivy wondered how much information Stuart's private detective had ferreted out about the private lives of the Conley family.

"We just knew that he drank," Merrie said at once, when she saw her friend's tortured expression. She patted Ivy's hand. "Nobody has that perfect childhood they put in motion pictures, you know. Dad wanted Stuart to raise thoroughbreds to race in competition. It was something he'd never been able to do. He tried to force Stuart through agricultural college." She laughed hollowly. "Nobody could force my brother to do anything, not even Dad."

"Were they very much alike?" Ivy asked, because she'd only met the elder York a few times.

"No. Well, in one way they were," she corrected.

"Dad in a bad temper could cost us good hired men. Stuart cost us our best, and oldest, horse wrangler last week."

"How?"

"He made a remark Stuart didn't like when Stuart ran the Jaguar through the barn and into its back wall."

2

Ivy could hardly contain her amusement. Merrie's brother was one of the most self-contained people she'd ever known. He never lost control of himself. "Stuart ran the Jag through the barn? The new Jaguar, the XJ?"

Merrie grimaced. "I'm afraid so. He was talking on his cell phone at the time."

"About what, for heaven's sake?"

"One of the managers at the Jacobsville sales barn mixed up the lot numbers and sold Stuart's purebred cows, all of whom were pregnant by Big Blue, for the price of open heifers," she added, the term "open heifer" denoting a two-year-old female who wasn't pregnant. Big Blue was a champion Black Angus herd sire.

"That was an expensive mistake," Ivy commented.

"And not only for us," Merrie added, tongue-in-cheek. "Stuart took every cattle trailer we had and every one he could borrow, complete with drivers, went to the sale barn and brought back every single remaining bull or cow or calf he was offering for sale. Then he shipped them to another sale barn in Oklahoma by train. That's why he's in Oklahoma. He said this time, they're going to be certain which lots they're selling at which price, because he's having it written on their hides in magic marker."

Ivy just grinned. She knew Stuart would do no such thing, even if he felt like it.

"The local sale barn is never going to be the same," Merrie added. "Stuart told them they'd be having snowball fights in hell before he sent another lot of cattle to them for an auction."

"Your brother is not a forgiving person," Ivy said quietly.

The other girl nodded. "But there's a reason for the way he is, Ivy," she said. "Our father expected Stuart to follow in his footsteps and become a professional athlete. Dad never made it out of semipro football, but he was certain that Stuart would. He started making him play football before he was even in grammar school. Stuart hated it," she recalled sadly. "He deliberately missed practices, and when he did, Dad would go at him with a doubled-up belt. Stuart had bruises all over his back and legs, but it made him that much more determined to avoid sports. When he was thirteen, he dug his heels in and told Dad he was going into rodeo and that if the belt came out again, he was going to call Dallas Carson and have him arrested for beating him. Dallas," she reminded Ivy, "was Hayes Carson's father. He was our sheriff long before Hayes went into law enforcement. It was unusual for someone to be arrested for spanking a child twenty years ago, but Dallas would have done it. He loved Stuart like a son."

It took Ivy a minute to answer. She knew more about corporal punishment than she was ever going to admit, even to Merrie. "I always liked Dallas. Hayes is hard-going sometimes. What did your father say to that?" she asked.

"He didn't say anything. He got Stuart in the car and drove him to football practice. Five minutes after he left, Stuart hitched a ride to the Jacobsville rodeo arena and borrowed a horse for the junior bulldogging competition. He and his best friend, Martin, came in second place. Dad was livid. When Stuart put his trophy on the mantel, Dad smashed it with a fire poker. He never took the belt to Stuart again, but he browbeat him and demeaned him every chance he got. It wasn't until Stuart went away to college that I stopped dreading the times we were home from school."

Involuntarily, Ivy's eyes went to the painting of Merrie and Stuart's father that hung over the fireplace. Stuart resembled Jake York, but the older man had a stubborn jaw and a cruel glimmer in his pale blue eyes. Like Stuart, he'd been a tall man, lean and muscular. The children had been without a mother, who died giving birth to Merrie. Their mother's sister had stayed with the family and cared for Merrie until she was in grammar school. She and the elder York had argued about his treatment of Stuart, which had ended in her departure. After that, tenderness and unconditional love were things the York kids read about. They learned nothing of them from their taciturn, demanding father. Stuart's defiance only made him more bitter and ruthless.

"But your father built this ranch," Ivy said. "Surely he had to like cattle."

"He did. It was just that football was his whole life," Merrie replied. "You might have noticed that you don't ever see football games here. Stuart cuts off the television at the first mention of it."

"I can see why."

"Dad spent the time between football games running the ranch and his real estate company. He died of a heart attack when I was thirteen, sitting at the boardroom table. He had a violent argument with one of his directors about some proposed expansions that would have placed the company dangerously close to bankruptcy. He was a gambler. Stuart isn't. He always calculates the odds before he makes any decision. He never has arguments with the board of directors." She frowned. "Well, there was one. They insisted that he hire a pilot to fly him to business meetings."

"Why?"

Merrie chuckled. "To stop him from driving himself to them. Didn't I mention that this is his second new XJ in six months?"

Ivy lifted her eyebrows. "What happened to the first one?"

"Slow traffic."

"Come again?"

"He was in a hurry to a called meeting of the board of directors," Merrie said. "There was a little old man driving a motor home about twenty miles an hour up a hill on a blind curve. Stuart tried to pass him. He almost made it, too," she added. "Except that Hayes Carson was coming down the hill on the other side of the road in his squad car."

"What happened?" Ivy prompted when Merrie sat silently.

"Stuart really is a good driver," his sister asserted, "even if he makes insane decisions about where to pass. He spun the car around and stopped it neatly on the shoulder before Hayes got anywhere near him. But Hayes said he could have killed somebody and he wasn't getting out of a ticket. The only way he got his license back was that he promised to go to traffic school and do public service."

"That doesn't sound like your brother."

Merrie shrugged. "He did go to traffic school twice, and then he went to the sheriff's department and showed Hayes Carson how to reorganize his department so that it operated more efficiently."

"Did Hayes actually ask him to do that?"

"No. But Stuart argued that reorganizing the chaos in the sheriff's department *was* a public service. Hayes didn't agree. He went and talked to Judge Meacham himself. They gave Stuart his license back."

"You said he didn't hit anything with the car."

"He didn't. But while it was sitting on the side of the road, a cattle truck—one of his own, in fact—took the curve too fast and sideswiped it off the shoulder down a ten-foot ravine."

"I don't guess the driver works for you anymore," Ivy mused.

"He does, but not as a driver," Merrie said, laughing. "Considering how things could have gone, it was a lucky escape for everyone. It was a sturdy, well-built car, but those cattle trucks are heavy. It was a total loss."

"Even if I could afford a car, I don't think I want to learn how to drive," Ivy commented. "It seems safer not to be on the highway when Stuart's driving."

"It is."

They snacked on cheese and crackers and finger sandwiches and cookies, and sipped coffee in perfect peace for several minutes.

"Ivy, are you sure you're cut out to be a public accountant?" Merrie asked after a minute.

Ivy laughed. "What brought that on?"

"I was just thinking about when we were still in high school," she replied. "You had your heart set on singing opera."

"And chance would be a fine thing, wouldn't it?" Ivy asked with a patient smile. "The thing is, even if I had the money to study in New York, I don't want to leave Jacobsville. So that sort of limits my options. Singing in the church choir does give me a chance to do what I love most."

Merrie had to agree that this was true. "What you should really do is get married and have kids, and teach them how to sing," she replied with a grin. "You'd be a natural. Little kids flock around you everywhere we go."

"What a lovely idea," she enthused. "Tell you what, you gather up about ten or twelve eligible bachelors, and I'll pick out one I like."

That set Merrie to laughing uproariously. "If we could do it that way, I might get married myself," she confessed. "But I'd have to have a man who wasn't afraid of Stuart. Talk about limited options…!"

"Hayes Carson isn't scared of him," Ivy pointed out. "You could marry him."

"Hayes doesn't want to get married. He says he likes his life uncluttered by emotional complications."

"Lily-livered coward," Ivy enunciated. "No guts."

"Oh, he's got guts. He just doesn't think marriage works. His parents fought like tigers. His younger brother, Bobby, couldn't take it, and he turned to drugs and overdosed. It had to affect Hayes, losing his only sibling like that."

"He might fall in love one day."

"So might my brother," Merrie mused, "but if I were a betting woman, I wouldn't bet on that any time soon."

"Love is the great equalizer."

"Love is a chemical reaction," Merrie, the nursing student, said dryly. "It's nothing more than a physical response to a sensory stimulus designed to encourage us to replicate our genes."

"Oh, yuuuck!" Ivy groaned. "Merrie, that's just gross!"

"It's true—ask my anatomy professor," Merrie defended.

"No, thank you. I'll take my own warped view of it as a miracle, thanks."

Merrie laughed, then she frowned. "Ivy, what are you eating?" she asked abruptly.

"This?" She held up a cookie from the huge snack platter that contained crackers, cheese, cakes, little finger sandwiches and cookies. Mrs. Rhodes loved to make hors d'oeuvres. "It's a cookie."

Merrie looked worried. "Ivy, it's a chocolate cookie," came the reply. "You know you'll get a migraine if you eat them."

"It's only one cookie," she defended herself.

"*And* there's a low pressure weather system dumping rain on us, *and* you've had the stress of Rachel worrying you to death since your father's funeral," she replied. "Not to mention that your father's only been dead for a few weeks. There's always more than one trigger that sets off a migraine, even if you don't realize what they are. Stuart gets them, too, you know, but it's red wine or aged cheese that causes his."

Ivy recalled one terrible attack that Stuart had after he'd closed a tricky big business deal. It had been the day after he'd attended a band concert at Ivy and Merrie's school soon after the girls had become friends. They were both in band. It had been Ivy who'd suggested strong coffee and then a doctor for Stuart. He'd never realized that his terrible sick headaches were, in fact, migraines, much less that there were prescriptions for them that actually worked. Ivy had suffered from them all her life. Her mother and her mother's father had also had migraine headaches. They tended to run in families. They ran in Stuart's, too. Even though Merrie hadn't had one, her father had suffered with them. So had an uncle.

"The doctor gave Stuart the preventative, after diagnosing the headache," Merrie commented.

"I can't take the preventative," Ivy replied. "I have a heart defect, and the medication causes abnormal heart rhythms in me. I have to treat the symptoms instead of the disease."

"I hope you brought your medicine."

Ivy looked at the chocolate cookie and ruefully put the remainder down on her plate. "I forgot to get it refilled." Translated, that meant that she couldn't afford it anymore. There was one remedy that was sold over the counter. She took it in desperation, although it wasn't as effective as the prescription medicines were.

"Stuart has pain medicine as well as the preventative," Merrie said solemnly. "If you wake up in the night screaming in pain because of that cookie, we can handle it. Maybe when your father's estate is settled, Rachel will leave you alone."

Ivy shook her head. "Rachel won't rest until she gets

every penny. She convinced Dad that I was wilder than a white-tailed deer. He cut me out of his will."

"He knew better," Merrie said indignantly.

She laughed. "No, he didn't." Nor had he tried to find out. He drank to excess. Rachel encouraged him to do it. When he was drunk, she fed him lies about Ivy. The lies had terrible repercussions. That amused Rachel, who hated her prim younger sister. It made Ivy afraid every day of her life.

She pulled her mind from the past and forced a smile. "If having the estate will keep Rachel in New York, and out of my life, it will be worth it. I still have Aunt Hettie's little dab of money. That, and my part-time job, will see me through school."

"It's so unfair," her friend lamented. "It's never been like that here. Stuart split everything right down the middle between us. He said we were both Dad's kids and one shouldn't be favored over the other."

Ivy frowned. "That sounds as if one was."

She nodded. "In Dad's will, Stuart got seventy-five percent. He couldn't break the will, because Dad was always in his right mind. So he did the split himself, after the will was probated." She smiled. "I know you don't like him, but he's a great brother."

It wasn't dislike. It was fear. Stuart in a temper was frightening to a woman whose whole young life had been spent trying to escape male violence. Well, it was a little more than fear, she had to admit. Stuart made her feel funny when she was around him. He made her nervous.

"He's good to you," Ivy conceded.

"He likes you," she replied. "No, really, he does. He admires the way you work for your education. He was furious when Rachel jerked the house out from under you and left you homeless. He talked to the attorney. It was no use, of course. It takes a lot to break a will."

It was surprising that Stuart would do anything for her. He always seemed to resent her presence in his house. He tolerated her because she was Merrie's best friend, but he was never friendly. In fact, he stayed away from home when he knew Ivy was visiting.

"He's probably afraid of my fatal charm," Ivy murmured absently. "You know, fearful that he might succumb to my wiles." She frowned. "What, exactly, are wiles anyway?"

"If I knew that, I'd probably have a boyfriend," Merrie chuckled. "So it's just as well I don't. I'm going to get my nursing certificate before I get involved with any one man. Meanwhile, I'm playing the field like crazy. There's a resident in our hospital that I adore. He takes me out once in a while, but it's all very low-key." She eyed Ivy curiously. "Any secret suitors in your life?"

Ivy shook her head. "I don't ever want to get married," she said quietly.

Merrie frowned. "Why not?"

"Nobody could live with me," she said. "I snore."

Merrie laughed. "You do not."

"Anyway, I'm like you. I just want to graduate and get a real job." She considered that. "I've dreamed of having my own money, of supporting myself. In a lot of ways, I led a sheltered life. Dad didn't want to lose me, so he discouraged boys from coming around. I was valuable, free hired help. After all, Rachel couldn't cook and she'd never have washed clothes or mopped floors."

Merrie didn't smile. She knew that was the truth. Ivy had been used her whole young life by the people who should have cherished her. She'd never pried, but she noticed that Ivy hardly ever talked about her father, except in a general way.

"You really do keep secrets, don't you?" Merrie asked gently. She held up a hand when Ivy protested. "I won't pry. But if you ever need to talk, I'm right here."

"I know that." She smiled back. "Thanks."

"Now. How about a good movie on the pay channels? I was thinking about that fantasy film everyone's raving about." She named it.

Ivy beamed. "I really wanted to see that one, but it's no fun going to the movies alone."

"I'll ask Mrs. Rhodes for some popcorn to go with it. In fact, she might like to watch it with us. She doesn't have a social life."

"She's married, isn't she?" Ivy probed gently.

"She was," came the reply. "He was an engineer in the Army and he went overseas with his unit. He didn't come back. They had no kids; it was just the two of them for almost twenty years." She grimaced. "She came to us just after it happened, looking for a live-in job. She'd lost everything. He got a good salary and was career Army, so she hadn't worked except as a temporary secretary all that time. When he was gone, she had to go through channels to apply for widow's benefits, and the job market locally was flat. She came to work for us as a temporary thing, and just stayed. We all suited each other."

"She's very sweet."

"She's a nurturing person," Merrie agreed. "She even gets away with nurturing Stuart. Nobody else would dare even try."

Ivy wouldn't have touched that line with a pole. She just nodded.

She was looking through the program guide on the wide-screen television when Merrie came in with a small, plump, smiling woman with short silver hair.

"Hi, Mrs. Rhodes," Ivy said with a smile.

"Good to see you, Ivy. I'm making popcorn. What's the movie?"

"We wanted to see the fantasy one," Merrie explained.

"It's wonderful," came the surprising reply. "Yes, I went to the theater to see it, all by myself," Mrs. Rhodes chuckled. "But I'd love to see it again, if you wouldn't mind the company."

"We'd love it," Ivy said, and meant it.

"Then I'll just run and get the popcorn out of the microwave," the older woman told them.

"I'll buy the movie," Merrie replied, taking the remote from Ivy. "This is the one mechanical thing I'm really good at—pushing buttons!"

The movie was wonderful, but long before it was over, Ivy was seeing dancing colored lights before her eyes. Soon afterward, she lost the vision in one eye; in the center of it was only a ragged gray static like when a television channel went off the air temporarily. It was the unmistakable aura that came before the sick headaches.

She didn't say a word about it to Merrie. She'd just go to bed and tough it out. She'd done that before. If she could get to sleep before the pain got bad, she could sleep it off most of the time.

She toughed it out until the movie ended, then she

yawned and stood up. "Sorry, I've got to get to bed. I'm so sleepy!"

Merrie got up, too. "I could do with an early night myself. Mrs. Rhodes, will you close up?"

"Certainly, dear. Need anything else from the kitchen?"

"Could I have a bottle of water?" Ivy asked. "I always keep one by my bed at home."

"I'll bring it up to you," Mrs. Rhodes promised. "Merrie?"

Merrie shook her head. "No, thanks, I keep diet sodas in my little fridge. I drink enough bottled water at school to float a boat!"

"You said you could lend me a nightgown?" Ivy asked when they were at the top of the staircase.

"Can and will. Come on."

Merrie pulled a beautiful nightgown and robe out of her closet and presented it to Ivy. It was sheer, lacy, palest lemon and absolutely the most beautiful thing Ivy had ever seen. Her nightgowns were cheap cotton ones in whichever colors were on sale. She caught her breath just looking at it.

"It's too expensive," she protested.

"It isn't. It was a gift and I hate it," Merrie said honestly. "You know I never wear yellow. One of my roommates drew my name at Christmas and bought it for me. I didn't have the heart to tell her it wasn't my color, I hugged her and said thank you. Then I hung it in the closet."

"I would have done the same," Ivy had to admit. "Well, it's beautiful."

"It will look beautiful on you. Go on to bed. Sleep late. We won't need to get up before noon if we don't want to."

"I never sleep past seven, even when I try," Ivy said, smiling. "I always got up to make breakfast for Dad and Rachel, and then just for Dad after she left home."

"Mrs. Rhodes will make you breakfast, whenever you want it," Merrie said. "Sleep well."

"You, too."

Ivy went into the bedroom that adjoined Merrie's. There was a bathroom between the guest room and Stuart's room, but Ivy wasn't worried about that. Stuart was out of town and she'd have the bathroom all to herself if she needed it. She probably would, if she couldn't sleep off the headache. They made her violently ill.

She put on the nightgown and looked at herself in the full-length mirror. She was surprised at how she looked in it. Her breasts were small, but high and firm, and the gown emphasized their perfection. It flowed down her narrow waist to her full hips and long, elegant legs. She'd never worn anything so flattering.

With her long blond hair and dark green eyes and

silky, soft complexion, she looked like a fairy. She wasn't pretty, but she wasn't plain, either. She was slender and medium height, with a nice mouth and big eyes. Only one of the big eyes was seeing right now, though, and she needed sleep.

There was a soft knock at the door. She opened it, and there was Mrs. Rhodes with the water. "Dear, you're very pale," the older woman said, concerned. "Are you all right?"

Ivy sighed. "It was the chocolate. I've got a headache. I don't want Merrie to know. She worries. I'll just go to sleep, and I'll be fine."

Mrs. Rhodes wasn't convinced. She'd seen Ivy have these headaches, and she'd seen Stuart suffer through them. "Have you got something to take?"

"In my purse," Ivy lied. "I've got aspirin."

"Well, if you need something stronger, you come wake me up, okay?" she asked gently. "Stuart keeps medicine for them. I know where to look."

She smiled. "Thanks, Mrs. Rhodes. I really mean it."

"You just get some sleep. Call if you need me. I'm just across the hall from Merrie."

"I will. Thanks again."

She dropped down on the queen-size bed and pulled the silken covers up over her. The room was a palace compared to her one-room apartment. Even the bathroom was larger than the room she lived in. Merrie took such wealth and luxury for granted, but Ivy didn't. It was fascinating to her.

The pain was vicious. The headaches always settled in one eye, and they felt as if a knife were being pushed right through the pupil. Some people called them "headbangers" because sufferers had been known to knock their heads against walls in an effort to cope with the pain. Ivy groaned quietly and pushed her fist against the eye that had gone blind. The sight had returned to it, and the pain came with it.

Volumes had been written on the vicious attacks. Comparing them to mild tension headaches was like comparing a hurricane to a spring breeze. Some people lost days of work every year to them. Others didn't realize what sort of headaches they were and never consulted a doctor about them. Still others wound up in emergency rooms pleading for something to ease the pain. Hardly anything sold over the counter would even faze them. It usually took a prescription medicine to make them bearable. Ivy had never found anything that would stop the pain, regardless of its strength. The best she could hope for was that the pain would ease enough that she could endure it until it finally stopped.

Around midnight, the pain spawned nausea and she

was violently sick. By that time, the pain was a throbbing, stabbing wave of agony.

She dabbed her mouth and eyes with a wet cloth and laid back down, trying again to sleep. But even though the nausea eased a little, the pain increased.

She would have to go and find Mrs. Rhodes. On the way, she'd stop in the bathroom long enough to wet the cloth again.

She opened the door, half out of her mind with pain, and walked right into a tall, muscular man wearing nothing except a pair of black silk pajama bottoms. Blue eyes bit into her green ones as she looked up, a long way up, into them.

"What the hell are you doing here?" Stuart York demanded with a scowl.

3

Ivy hadn't seen him in months. They didn't travel in the same circles, and he was never at home when she was visiting Merrie. The sight of him so unexpectedly caused an odd breathlessness, an ache in the pit of her stomach.

He was watching her intently, and there was an odd glint in his pale blue eyes, as if she'd disappointed him. He rarely smiled. He certainly wasn't doing it now. His wide, sexy mouth was thin with impatience. She couldn't take her eyes off him. His chest was broad and muscular and thick with black, curling hair that narrowed on its way down his belly. The silk pajama bottoms clung lovingly to the hard muscles of his thighs. He was as sexy as any television hero. Even with his thick, straight black hair slightly tousled and his eyes red from lack of sleep, he was every woman's dream.

"I was…looking for something," she faltered.

"Me?" he drawled sarcastically, and he reached for her. "Rachel told me all about you before she left town. I didn't believe her at first." His eyes slid down her exquisite body in the revealing gown. "But it looks as though she was right about you all along."

The feel of all that warm strength so close made her legs wobbly. There was the faint scent of soap and cologne that clung to his skin, and the way he was looking at her made it even worse. Over the years, she'd tried very hard not to notice Stuart. But close like this, her heart ran away with her. She felt sensations that made her uneasy, alien sensations that made her want things she didn't understand. She couldn't take her eyes off him, but he was misty in her vision. Her head was throbbing so madly that she couldn't think. Which was unfortunate, because he misinterpreted her lack of protest.

A split second later, she was standing with her back against the cold wall with Stuart's hard body pressing down against hers. His hands propped against the wall, pinning her, while his eyes took in the visible slope of her breasts in the wispy gown. He couldn't seem to stop looking at her.

"I need…" she began weakly, trying to focus enough to ask for some aspirin, for anything that might make the headache ease.

"…me?" he taunted. His voice was deep and velvety soft, husky with emotion as his head bent. His pale eyes went to her parted lips. "Show me, honey."

While she was working out that odd comment, his mouth was suddenly hard and insistent on her own. She stiffened with apprehension. She'd never been so close, so intimately close, to a man before. His mouth was demanding, twisting on hers as though he wanted more than he was getting.

She really should protest the way he was holding her, so that she felt every inch of muscle that pressed against her. But his mouth was erotic, masterful. She'd only been kissed a few times, mostly at parties, and never by a boy who knew much about intimacy. It had been her good fortune that she'd never felt violent attraction to a man who wouldn't accept limits. But her luck had just run out, with Stuart. He knew what he was doing. His mouth eased and became coaxing, caressing. His teeth nipped tenderly at her lower lip, teasing it to move down so that he had access to the whole of her soft, warm mouth.

She shivered a little as passion grew inside her. She felt his bare chest under her hands, and she loved the warmth and strength of him so close. Her fingers burrowed through the thick hair that covered the hard muscle, making them tingle even as she felt the urgent response of his body to the soft caress. She let her lips part as he pressed harder against them and she moved, involuntarily, closer to the source of the sudden pleasure she was feeling.

It was like an invitation, and he took it. His hips ground into hers and she felt the sudden hardness of him against her with real fear. He groaned harshly. His body became even more insistent. He didn't seem capable, at that moment, of stopping.

The throbbing delight she felt turned quickly to fear as his hands dropped to her hips and dragged them against the changing contours of his body with intent enough that even a virgin could feel his rising desire. Frightened by his headlong ardor, she pushed at his chest frantically, trying to drag her lips away from the hard, slow drugging pressure of his mouth.

He was reluctant to stop. He could feel his own body betraying his hunger for her. He couldn't help it. She was exquisite to touch, and she tasted like sweet heaven. He couldn't think past her body under him in the bed behind them. But finally the violence of her resistance got through to his foggy brain. He managed to lift his head just long enough to meet her eyes.

When he saw the fear, he began to doubt for the first time what Rachel had said about her little sister. If this was the permissive behavior that had been described to him, it was unlikely that she'd had many boyfriends. On the contrary, she looked as if she was scared to death of what came next.

"No," she choked huskily, her eyes bright with feeling, pleading with his. "Please don't."

For just an instant, his hands tightened on her waist. But her gasp and stiffening posture told its own story. Promiscuous? This little icicle? Just on the strength of her response, he would have bet his life on her innocence.

As his head began to clear, anger began to smolder in his chest. He'd lost his self-control. He'd betrayed his hunger for her. He couldn't pretend that he hadn't felt desire while he was kissing her. She'd felt his momentary weakness. His own raging desire had betrayed him, with this innocent child-woman who was only eighteen years old. Eighteen!

Anger and shame and guilt overwhelmed him. He pushed her away from him roughly, his eyes blazing as he looked down at her body in the revealing nightgown. Despite everything, he still wanted her, desperately.

"What did you expect, when you go looking for a man, in the middle of the night, dressed like that!?" He emphasized her attire with one big hand.

Shivering, her arms crossed over her breasts. She swayed, putting a hand up to her eye. She'd forgotten the headache for a few seconds while he'd been kissing her, but it came back now with a fury. She leaned back against the wall for support. Stronger than shame, than anger, was pain, stabbing into her right eye like a heated poker.

Her face was white and contorted. It began to occur to him that she was unwell. "What's the matter with you?" he asked belatedly.

"Migraine," she whispered huskily. "I was looking for aspirin."

He made a rough sound in his throat. "Aspirin, for a migraine," he scoffed. He bent suddenly, swung her up into his arms and strode back into his bedroom with her. The feel of her softness in his arms was intoxicating. She was as light as a feather. He noticed that she wasn't protesting the contact. In fact, her cheek was against his bare chest and he could hear her breathing change, despite the pain he knew she was feeling. "You'll get something stronger than aspirin to stop the pain, but not before I've checked with your doctor. Sit." He put her down on the bed and went to the dresser to pick up his cell phone.

"It's Dr. Lou Coltrain," she began.

He ignored her. He knew who her doctor was. "Lou? Sorry to bother you so late. Ivy Conley's spending the weekend with Merrie, and she's got a migraine. Can she take what you give me for it?"

There was a pause, during which he stared at Ivy, trying not to look at her the way he felt like looking. She was beautifully formed. But her age tortured him. She was too young for him. He was thirty, to her eighteen. He didn't dare touch her again. In order to keep his distance, he was going to have to hurt her. He didn't want to, but she was looking at him in a different way already. The kiss had been very much a shared pleasure until he'd turned up the heat and frightened her.

A minute later he shifted, listened, nodded. "Okay. Yes, I'll send her in to the clinic tomorrow if she isn't better by morning. Thanks."

He hung up. "She said that you can have half the dose I take," he said, pulling a prescription bottle from his top drawer and shaking out one pill. He poured water from a carafe into a crystal glass and handed her the pill and the glass. "Take it. If you're not better in the morning, you'll need to go to her clinic and be seen."

"Could you stop glaring at me?" she asked through the pain.

"You aren't the only one who's got a pain," he said bluntly. "Take it!"

She flushed, but she put the pill in her mouth and swallowed it down with two big sips of water.

He took the glass from her, helped her up from the bed and marched her back through the bathroom to her own room. He guided her down onto the bed.

"I didn't know you'd be home," she defended herself. "Merrie promised you wouldn't. I didn't expect to walk into the bathroom and run into you."

"That goes double for me. I didn't know you were on the place," he added curtly. "My sister has a convenient memory."

In other words, she hadn't told him Ivy was here. Ivy wondered if her friend knew he was due back home. It would have been a dirty trick to play, and Merrie was bigger than that. So maybe she hadn't known.

"Thank you for the pill," she said tautly.

He let out a harsh breath. "You're welcome. Go to bed."

She slid the covers back and eased under them, wincing as the movement bumped the pain up another notch.

"And don't read anything romantic into what just happened," he added bluntly. "Most men are vulnerable at night, when temptation walks in the door scantily clad."

"I didn't know…!"

He held up a hand. "All right. I'll take your word for it." His eyes narrowed. "Your sister fed me a pack of lies about you. Why?"

"Why were you even talking to her about me?" she countered. "You always said you couldn't stand her, even when you were in the same class in high school."

"She phoned me when your father died."

"Ah, yes," she said, closing her eyes. "She didn't want to take any chances that you might come down on my side of the fence during the probate of the will." She laughed coldly. "I could have told her that would never happen."

"She thought you might ask Merrie for help."

She opened her eyes. The pain was throbbing. She could see her heartbeat in her own eyes. "She would have. Not me. I can stand on my own two feet."

"Yes," he said slowly, studying her pale face. "You've done remarkably well."

That was high praise, coming from him. She looked up into his lean face and wondered how it would have felt if she hadn't pulled back. Warm color surged into her cheeks.

"Stop that," he muttered. "I won't be an object of desire to some daydreaming teenager."

His tone wasn't hostile. It was more amused than angry. Her eyebrows arched. "Are you sure?" she asked, returning the banter. "Because I have to have somebody to cut my teeth on. Just think, I could fall into bad company and become a lost sheep, and it would all be your fault, because you wouldn't let me obsess over you."

At first he thought she was being sarcastic. Then he saw the twinkle in those pretty green eyes.

"You're too young to be obsessing over a mature man. Go pick on a boy your own age."

"That's the problem," she pointed out, pushing her hand against her throbbing eye. "Boys my own age are *just* boys."

"All men started out that way."

"I guess so." She groaned. "Could you please hit me in the head with a hammer? Maybe it would take my mind off the pain."

"It takes pills a long time to work, doesn't it?" he asked. He moved to sit beside her on the coverlet. "Want a cold wet cloth?"

"I'd die before I'd ask you to go and get one."

He laughed shortly. But he got up, went into the bathroom and was back a minute later with a damp washcloth. He pressed it over her eyes. "Does it help?"

She held it there and sighed. "Yes. Thank you."

"I have to have heat," he replied conversationally. "I can't bear cold when my head's throbbing."

"I remember."

"Where did you get the chocolate, Ivy?" he asked after a minute.

She grimaced. He really did know too much about her. "There was a cookie this afternoon. I didn't realize it was chocolate until I'd eaten half of it. Merrie warned me."

"I can eat ten chocolate bars and they don't faze me."

"That's because chocolate isn't one of your triggers. But Merrie says you won't drink red wine."

"Wine is no substitute for a good Scotch whiskey. I gave it up years ago."

"Aged cheese probably has the same effect."

He grimaced. "It does. I love Stilton and I can't eat it."

She smiled. "A weakness! I thought you were beyond them."

"You'd be surprised," he replied, and he was looking at her with an expression he was glad she couldn't see.

The door opened suddenly and Merrie stopped, frozen, in the doorway. "Are you having a pajama party?" she asked the occupants of the room.

"Yes, but you're not invited. It's exclusive to migraine sufferers, and you don't have migraines," he added with a faint smile.

She closed the door and came in, to stand by the bed. "I was afraid of this," she told Ivy. "I should have noticed there was chocolate on the tray."

"She's the one who should have noticed," Stuart said harshly.

"Well, talk about intolerance," Ivy muttered from under the washcloth. "I'll bet nobody fusses at you for what you ate when you've got one of these. I'll bet you'd throw them out the window if they did."

"You're welcome to try throwing me out the window," he offered.

"Don't be silly. I'd never be able to lift you."

"Do you need some aspirin, Ivy?" Merrie asked, sending a glare at her brother.

"I've already given her something."

Merrie was outraged. "We're taught that you never give anything to another person without consulting their physician…!"

"I'm glad you know procedure, but so do I," Stuart replied. "I phoned Lou before I gave it to her." He glanced toward the clock on the bedside table. "It should be taking effect very soon."

It was. Ivy could hardly keep her eyes open. "I'm very sleepy," she murmured, amazed at the sudden easing of the pain that had been so horrific at first.

"Good. When you wake up, your head will feel normal again," Stuart told her.

"Thanks, Stuart," she said, the words slurring as the powerful medication did its job.

"You're welcome," he replied. "I know a thing or two about migraines."

"And she taught you a thing or two about seeing the doctor for medicine that actually helped them," Merrie couldn't resist saying.

He didn't reply. His eyes were on Ivy's face as she went

to sleep. He lifted the washcloth and took it away. Her eyes were closed. Her breathing regulated. He was glad that the cover was up to her chin, so that he didn't have to see that perfect body again and lie awake all night remembering it.

He got up from the bed, gently so as not to awaken her, the washcloth still clutched in his hand.

"That was nice of you, to get her something to take," Merrie said as they left Ivy's room.

He shrugged. "I know how it feels."

"How did you come out in Oklahoma?" she asked.

"Everything's ready for the auction," he replied. "I still can't believe they let me down like that at the Jacobsville sales barn."

"They don't have a history of messing up the different lots of cattle they sell," she said in their defense.

"One mistake that big can be expensive," he reminded her. "In this economic climate, even we have to be careful. Losing the Japanese franchise hurt us."

"It hurt the Harts and the Dunns worse," she replied. "They'd invested a lot in organic beef to send over there. They were sitting in clover when the ban hit."

"But they recovered quickly, and so did we, by opening up domestic markets for our organic beef. This organic route is very profitable, and it's going to be even more profitable when people realize how much it contributes to good health."

"Our signature brand sells out quickly enough in local markets," she agreed.

"And even better in big city markets," he replied. "How's school?"

She grinned. "I'm passing everything. In two years, I'll be working in a ward."

"You could come home and go to morning coffees and do volunteer work," he reminded her with a smile.

She shook her head, returning the smile. "I'm not cut out for an easy, cushy life. Neither are you. We come from hardworking stock."

"We do." He bent and brushed his mouth over her cheek. "Sleep tight."

"Are you home for the weekend?"

He glanced at her. "Are you wearing body armor?"

"You and Ivy could get along for two days," she pointed out.

"Only if you blindfold me and gag her."

She blinked. "Excuse me?"

"It's an in-joke," he said. "I have to fly to Denver tomorrow to give a speech at the agriculture seminar on the subject of genetically engineered grain," he added.

She grimaced. "Don't come home with a bloody nose this time, will you?"

He shrugged. "I'm only playing devil's advocate," he told her. "We can't make it too easy on people who want to combine animal cells and vegetable cells and call it progress." His pale eyes began to glitter. "One day, down the road, we'll pay for this noble meddling."

She reached up and touched his face. "Okay, go slug it out with the progressives, if you must. I'll treat Ivy to the new *Imax* movie about Mars."

"Mars?"

"She loves Mars," Merrie told him.

"I'd love to send her there," he replied thoughtfully. "We could strap her to a rocket..."

"Stop that. She's my best friend."

He shook his head. "The things I do for you," he protested. "Okay, I'll settle for sending her to the moon."

"She's only just lost her father, her house and she'll soon lose her inheritance as well," she said solemnly. "I could strangle Rachel for what she's done."

He could have strangled Rachel himself, for the lies she'd fed him about Ivy. He should have known better. She'd never been forward with men, to his knowledge. He was certain now that she wasn't. But he wondered why Rachel would make a point of downgrading her to him. Perhaps it was as Ivy said—her sister wanted him to stay out of the probate of her father's will. Poor Ivy. She'd never get a penny if Rachel had her way.

"You look very somber," Merrie observed.

"Ivy should have had the house, at least," he said, betraying the line of his thoughts.

"She couldn't have lived there, even if she'd inherited it," she told him. "There's no money for utilities or upkeep. She can barely keep herself in school and pay her rent."

His eyes narrowed. "We could pay it for her."

"I tried," Merrie replied. "Ivy's proud. She won't accept what she thinks of as charity."

"So she works nights and weekends to supplement that pitiful amount of money her aunt left her," he grumbled. "At least one of those mechanics she keeps books for is married and loves to run around with young women."

"He did ask Ivy out," Merrie replied.

He looked even angrier. "And?"

"She accidentally dropped a hammer on his foot," Merrie chuckled. "He limped for a week, but he never asked Ivy out again. The other men had a lot of fun at his expense."

He felt a reluctant admiration for their houseguest. If she'd been older, his interest might have taken a different form. But he had to remember her age.

"Rachel called her today harping about the probate," she said slowly. "I expect that's why she had the migraine. Rachel worries her to death."

"She needs to learn to stand up to her sister."

"Ivy isn't like that. She loves Rachel, in spite of the way she's been treated by her. She doesn't have any other relatives left. It must be lonely for her."

"She'll toughen up. She'll have to." He stretched. "I'm going to bed. I probably won't see you before I leave. I'll be back sometime Monday. You can reach me on my cell phone if anything important comes up."

"Chayce handles the ranch very well. I expect we'll cope," she said, smiling. "Have fun."

"In between fistfights, I might," he teased. "See you."

"See you."

He went back to his room and closed the door. He had to put Ivy out of his mind and never let history repeat itself. Maybe it wouldn't hurt to have himself photographed with some pretty socialite. He didn't like publicity, but he couldn't take the chance that Ivy might warm up to him.

He recalled reluctantly the dossier a private detective had assembled on Ivy's father. The man had been a closet alcoholic and abusive to his late wife as well as Ivy, although he'd never touched Rachel. He'd wanted to know why Ivy had backed away from him once when he'd been yelling at one of the cowboys. He was never going to tell her what he'd learned. But he was careful not to yell when she was nearby. Still, he told himself, he had to discourage her from seeing him as her future. It would be a kindness to kill this attraction before it had a chance to bloom. She was years too young for him.

The rest of the weekend passed without incident. The two women worked on Merrie's anatomy exam. They watched movies and shared their dreams of the future. On Monday morning, Merrie dropped Ivy off at the local college on her way to San Antonio.

"I'll phone you the next time I have a free weekend," Merrie promised as they parted. "Don't let Rachel make you crazy, okay?"

"I'll try," Ivy said, smiling. "It was a lovely weekend. Thanks."

"I had fun, too. We'll do it again. See you!"

"See you!"

Ivy spent the week daydreaming about what had happened in the guest room at Merrie's house. The more she relived the torrid interlude with Stuart, the more she realized how big a part of her life he was. Over the years she'd been friends with Merrie, Stuart had always been close, but in the background. Because of the age difference, he didn't really hang out in the places that Merrie and Ivy frequented. He was already a mature man while they were getting through high school.

But now, with those hard, insistent kisses, everything

between them had changed. Ivy had dreams about him now; embarrassing, feverishly hot dreams of a future that refused to go away. Surely he had to feel something for her, even if it was only desire. He'd wanted her. And she'd wanted him just as much. It was a milestone in her young life.

But toward the end of the week, as she waited in line at the grocery store to pay for her meager purchases, she happened to look at one of the more lurid tabloids. And there was Stuart, with a beautiful, poised young woman plastered against his side, looking up at him adoringly. The caption read, Millionaire Texas Cattleman Donates Land to Historical Trust. Apparently the woman in the photo was the daughter of a prominent businessman who was head of the trust in question. She was a graduate of an equally prominent college back east. The article went on to say that there was talk of a merger between the millionaire and the socialite, but both said the rumors were premature.

Ivy's heart shattered like ice. Apparently Stuart hadn't been as overwhelmed by her as she had been by him, and he was making it known publicly. She had no illusions that the story was an accident. Stuart knew people in every walk of life, and he numbered publishers among his circle of friends. He wanted Ivy to know that he hadn't taken her seriously. He'd chosen a public and humiliating way to do it, to make sure she got the point. And she did.

Merrie called her to ask if she'd seen the story.

"Oh, yes," Ivy replied, her tone subdued.

"I don't understand why he'd let himself be used like that," Merrie muttered irritably. It was obvious that she knew nothing of what had happened between her brother and her best friend, or she'd have said so. She never pulled her punches.

"Even the most reclusive person can fall victim to a determined reporter," Ivy said in his defense. "Maybe the photographer caught him at a weak moment."

"Maybe he's giving a public cold shoulder to some woman who's pursuing him, too," Merrie said innocently. "It would be like him. But there hasn't been anybody in his life lately. Nobody regular, I mean. I'm sure he takes women out. He just doesn't get serious about any of them."

"How did you do on your exam?" Ivy asked, deliberately changing the subject.

"Actually, I passed with flying colors, thanks to you."

"You're welcome," came the pert reply. "You can do the same for me when I have my finals."

"That won't be for a while yet. Coming over next weekend?"

Ivy thought quickly. "Merrie, I promised my roommate that I'd drive up to Dallas with her to see her mother. She doesn't like to make that drive alone." It wasn't the whole truth. Lita had asked her to go, and Ivy had promised to think about it. Now, she was sure that she'd agree.

"Well, it's nice of you to do it." There was a pause. "I'm not going to be able to come home much, once I take the job I've been offered at the hospital here. I'll be working twelve-hour shifts four days a week, and a lot of them will be on weekends."

"I understand," Ivy said quickly, thankful that she wouldn't have to come up with so many excuses to escape seeing Stuart again. "When I graduate, I'll be doing some weekend work myself, I'm sure. But when I can afford a car, I can drive up to see you and we can go to a movie or out to eat or something."

"Of course we can." There was a pause. "Ivy, is anything wrong?"

"No," she said at once. "The lawyer is ready to hand over Dad's estate to Rachel. I'm to get a small lump sum. Maybe Rachel will leave me alone now."

"I hope so. Please keep in touch," Merrie added.

"I will," Ivy agreed. But she crossed her fingers. It was suddenly imperative that she find a way to avoid Stuart from now on. She couldn't afford to let her heart settle on him again, especially now that he'd made his own feelings brutally clear. She'd miss Merrie, but the risk was too great. Broken hearts, she assured herself, were best avoided.

4

Two years later...

"Ivy, would you like a cup of coffee while you work?" her latest client asked from the doorway of the office where she was writing checks and balancing bank statements.

She looked up from her work, smiling, her long blond hair neatly pinned on top of her head. Her green eyes twinkled. "I'd love one, if it isn't too much trouble," she said.

Marcella smiled back. "I just made a pot. I'll bring it in."

"Thanks."

"It's no trouble at all, really. You've saved me from bankruptcy!"

"Not really. I just discovered that you had more money than you thought you did," she replied.

The older woman chuckled. "You say it your way, I'll say it mine. I'll bring the coffee."

Ivy contemplated the nice office she was using and the amazing progress she'd made in the past two years since her disastrous weekend at Merrie's house. She'd been able to give up the part-time job at the garage when Dorie Hart offered her a bookkeeping service, complete with clients. Dorie had enjoyed the work very much, and she'd kept handling the books for her clients long after her marriage to Corrigan Hart. But her growing family kept her too busy to continue with it. Ivy had been a gift from heaven, Dorie told her laughingly. Now she could leave her clients in good hands and retire with a clear conscience.

Dorie had some wonderful accounts. There was a boutique owner, a budding architect, the owner of a custom beef retail shop, an exercise gym and about a dozen other small businesses in Jacobsville. Ivy had met the businesspeople while she was in her last semester of college, when Dorie had approached her with the proposal. Dorie and Lita, who carpooled with Ivy, were friends. Lita had mentioned Ivy's goals and Dorie had gone to see her at the boardinghouse. It had been an incredible stroke of good luck. Ivy had resigned herself to working in a C.P.A. firm. Now she was a businesswoman in her own right.

And as if her blessings hadn't multiplied enough, she'd also volunteered to do the occasional article for the Jacobs County Cattlemen's Association in what little free time she had. She would have done it as a favor to the Harts, since Corrigan was this year's president, but they wouldn't hear of it. She got a check for anything she produced. Like her math skills, her English skills were very good.

Merrie was nursing at a big hospital in San Antonio. The two spoke on the phone at least twice a month, but they stayed too busy for socializing. Ivy had never told her friend what had happened that last night she spent under Stuart's roof. She never asked about Stuart, either. Merrie seemed to sense that something had gone wrong, but she didn't pry. She didn't talk about her brother, either.

Autumn turned the leaves on the poplars and maples beautiful shades of gold and scarlet. Ivy felt restless, as if something was about to change in her life. She did her job and tried not to think about Stuart York, but always in the back of her mind was the fear of something unseen and unheard. A premonition.

There was a party to benefit a local animal shelter, which Shelby Jacobs had organized. Ivy wouldn't have gone, but Sheriff Hayes Carson was on the committee that had planned the party, and he was showing an increasing interest in Ivy.

She didn't know if she liked it or not. She was fond of Hayes, but her heart didn't do cartwheels when he was around. Maybe that was a good thing.

When he showed up at her boardinghouse late one Friday afternoon, she sat on the porch swing with him. Her room contained little more than a bed and a vanity, and she was uncomfortable taking a man there. Hayes seemed to know that, because he sat down in the swing with no hesitation at all.

"We're having the benefit dance next Friday night," he told her. "Go with me."

She laughed nervously. "Hayes, I haven't danced in years. I'm not sure I even remember how."

His dark eyes twinkled. "I'll teach you."

She studied him with pursed lips. He really was a dish. He had thick blond hair that the sun had streaked, and a lean, serious face. His dark eyes were deep-set, heavy browed. His uniform emphasized his muscular physique. He was built like a rodeo rider, tall, with wide shoulders, narrow hips and long, powerful legs. Plenty of single women around Jacobsville had tried to land him. None had succeeded. He was the consummate bachelor. He seemed immune to women. Most of the time, he looked as if he had no sense of humor at all. He rarely smiled. But he could be charming when he wanted to, and he was turning on the charm now.

Ivy hadn't been asked out in months, and the man who'd asked had a reputation that even Merrie knew about, and Merrie didn't live at home anymore.

Having turned down the potential risk, Ivy kept to herself. Now Hayes was asking her to a dance. She walked around in jeans. She looked and acted like a tomboy. She frowned.

"Come on," he coaxed. "All work and no play will run you crazy."

"You ought to know," she tossed back. "Didn't you take your last vacation day four years ago?"

He chuckled deeply. "I guess so. I love my job."

"We all noticed," she said. "Between you and Cash Grier, drug dealers have left trails of fire behind them running for the border."

"We've got a good conviction rate," he had to admit. "What's holding you back? Nursing a secret passion for someone hereabouts?"

She laughed. It was half true, but she wasn't admitting it. "Not really," she said. "But I'm not used to socializing. I didn't even do it in college."

He frowned. "I know why you don't date, Ivy," he

said unexpectedly. "You can't live in the past. And not every man is like your father."

Her face closed up. Her hands clenched in her lap. She stared out at the horizon, trying not to let the memories eat at her consciousness. "My mother used to say that she thought he was a perfect gentleman before they married. They went together for a year before she married him. And then she discovered how brutal a man he really was. She was pregnant, and she had no place to go."

He caught one of her small hands in his big one. "He was an outsider," he reminded her. "He moved here from Nevada. Nobody knew much about him. But you know people in Jacobsville." He pursed his lips. "I daresay you know all about me."

That droll tone surprised her into laughing. "Well, yes, I do. Everybody does. The only brutal thing about you is your temper, and you don't hit people unless they hit you first."

"That's right. So you'd be perfectly safe with me for one evening."

She sighed. "You're hard to refuse."

"You'll have fun. So will I. Come on," he coaxed. "We'll help add some kennel space to the animal shelter and give people something to gossip about."

"It would be fun," she came back. "You don't date anybody locally."

He shrugged. "I like my own company too much. Besides," he said ruefully, "there's Andy. He stunts my social life."

She shivered. "I'm not going home with you," she pointed out.

"I know. I haven't found a single woman who will." He sighed resignedly. "He's really very tame. He's a vegetarian. He won't even eat a mouse."

"It won't work. Your scaly roommate is going to keep you single, just like Cag Hart's did."

"I've had him for six years," he said. "He's my only pet."

"Good thing. He'd eat any other pet you brought home."

He scowled. "He's a vegetarian."

"Are you sure? Have any dogs or cats disappeared on your place since you got him?" she teased.

He made a face at her. "It's silly to be afraid of a vegetarian. It's like being afraid of a cow!"

Her eyebrows arched. "Andy doesn't look like any cow I ever saw," she retorted. "His picture was on the front page of the paper when you took him to that third grade class to teach them about herpetology. I believe there was some talk about barring you from classrooms…?"

He glowered. "He wasn't trying to attack that girl.

She was the tallest kid in the room, and he tried to climb her, that's all."

She had to fight laughter. "I'll bet you won't take him out of the cage at a grammar school ever again," she said.

"You can bet on that," he agreed. He frowned thoughtfully. "I expect he'll have a terror of little girls for the rest of his life, poor old thing."

She shook her head. "Well, I'm not going into the room with him unless he's confined."

"He hates cages. He's too big for most of them, anyway. Besides, he sits on top of the fridge and eats bugs."

"You need to get out more," she pointed out.

"I'm trying to, if you'll just agree," he shot back.

She sighed. "All right, I'll go. But people will gossip about us for weeks."

"I don't care. I'm immune to gossip. So are you," he added when she started to protest.

"I guess I am. Okay. I'll go. Is it jeans and boots?"

"No," he replied. "It's nice dresses and high heels."

"I hate dressing up," she muttered.

"So do I. But I can stand it if you can. And it's for a good cause," he added.

"Yes, it is."

"So, I'll pick you up here at six next Friday night."

She smiled. "I'll buy a dress."

"That's the spirit!"

★ ★ ★

Word got around town that she was going to the dance with Hayes. Nobody ever knew exactly how gossip traveled so fast, but it was as predictable as traffic flow in rush hour.

Even Merrie heard about it, although Ivy had no idea how. She phoned her best friend two days before the dance.

"Hayes actually asked you out?" Merrie exclaimed. "But he doesn't date anybody! At least, he hasn't dated anybody since that Jones girl who dumped him for the visiting Aussie millionaire."

"That was two years ago," Ivy agreed, "and I still don't think he's really over her. We're only going to a dance, Merrie. He hasn't asked me to marry him."

"You never know, though, do you?" the other girl wondered aloud. "He might be feeling lonely. He loves kids."

"Slow down!" Ivy exclaimed. "I don't want to get married any more than Hayes does!"

"Why not?"

"I like living by myself," she said evasively. "Anyway, I expect Hayes doesn't know that many single women."

"There are plenty of divorced ones around," came the droll reply.

"The dance will benefit our animal shelter," Ivy told

her. "It will add new kennels. We've got so many strays. It's just pitiful."

"I like animals, too, but Hayes isn't asking you to any dance because of stray dogs, you mark my word. Maybe he's going to flash you to deter some woman who's chasing him. That's the sort of thing my brother does."

"Your brother is better at it than Hayes is," Ivy said, not wanting to think of Stuart. She hadn't seen him in a long time.

"Well, of course he is. He gets plenty of practice." There was a sigh. "Except he doesn't seem to be dating anybody lately. I asked him why and he said it wasn't fun anymore. If I didn't know him better, I'd think he'd found someone he wanted to get serious about."

"That's unlikely," Ivy said, but she wondered if Merrie was right. It made her sad.

"Unlikely, but not impossible. I think I might come to the dance, too," she said out of the blue. "I can get someone to work my shift. Everybody owes me favors."

"Who will you come with?"

"I'll come by myself," Merrie returned. "I don't need a date. Tell Hayes to save me a dance, though."

Ivy laughed. "He can take both of us. That will really shake people up locally. They'll think he's putting around a new sort of double-dating."

Merrie laughed, too. "I had a flaming crush on Hayes

when we were in high school, but he couldn't see me for dust. That was about the time he fell in with the she-tiger who ditched him for the Aussie. Served him right. Anybody could see that she was only a gold digger."

"Hayes owns his own ranch," she began.

"And he inherited a trust from his grandfather," Merrie agreed. "But Hayes isn't the sort to live on an income he didn't earn. He's like Stuart. They're both independent."

"Same as you," Ivy accused.

She laughed. "I guess so."

"How do you like being a nurse?"

"I love it," Merrie said honestly. "I've never enjoyed anything so much. I love knowing that I helped keep someone alive. It's the best job in the whole world."

"Merrie, you work all day with sick people," Ivy pointed out.

"Sick people? Me? Are you sure?"

"You work in a hospital," Ivy returned.

"No kidding? No wonder there are sick people everywhere!"

Ivy laughed. "Okay, you made your point. You're in the right place. I'm glad you like your job. You might not believe it, but I like mine just as much. I'm working with some really interesting people."

"So I've heard," Merrie replied. "I'm glad you're

happy. But speaking of pleasant things, have you heard from Rachel?"

Ivy's happy face fell. She drew in a long breath. "As a matter of fact, I haven't. Not in over two months. The last I heard, she was trying to get away from Jerry the drug dealer so that she could shack up with a richer man. She wouldn't tell me his name. She did mention that he was married."

"Married. Why doesn't that surprise me?"

"I could barely make sense of what she said," Ivy replied. "She slurred her words so badly that she was incoherent. I can't imagine what a rich man would see in a woman who stays stoned all the time. How she can still act in that condition is beyond me."

"As long as she's leaving you alone, that has to be a bonus."

"I suppose. I just worry about her. She's the only living relative I have," she added. "Maybe the rich guy will wean her off drugs and get her away from Jerry for good. Unless his wife finds out." She groaned. "That's just what it would take to send Rachel over the edge. I'm sure she's convinced herself that he'll divorce his wife to stay with her. I don't think he will."

"Most of them don't," Merrie agreed. "Did she argue with the drug dealer?"

"I have no idea. But from what I understood, she

thinks she's landed in a field of clover. The rich guy buys her diamonds."

"I won't ask what he gets in return."

Ivy grimaced. "Neither would I."

"Well, I'll see you at the dance. Where is it, and when?"

Ivy gave her the particulars, but she was morose when she hung up. What if Rachel was involved with someone well-known and the wife found out and went after her in the press? Rachel was brassy and demanding and totally lacking in compassion. But she was weak in every other way. A scandal would drive her over the edge. There was no telling what she might do.

There had been something unusual in their last conversation as well. Rachel had asked her to pass a message along to the owner of the only bakery in town, the Bun Shop. It hadn't made sense to Ivy; something about a shipment of flour that hadn't arrived on schedule. She wanted to know why Rachel was concerned with a bake shop. Rachel said it was a friend who needed the message passed along.

That conversation had been more volatile than she felt comfortable divulging to Merrie. Rachel had mentioned the ultimatum she'd given her rich lover, that either he divorce his wife or she'd go public with the truth of their relationship. Ivy had pleaded with her to do no such thing, that if the man was that rich, his wife could hire someone to hurt her. Rachel had only laughed, saying that the wife was a cold fish who was half out of her mind, and that she posed no threat at all. But in case that fell through, she said, she'd discovered another good way to get a lot of money. She taunted Ivy with her newfound sources of wealth, intimating that Ivy couldn't get a man even if she had millions. Ivy didn't care. She was tired of Rachel's sarcasm.

They'd parted on not good terms. Rachel had accused her of being jealous. She'd never gotten the attention Rachel had, not even from their father. Ivy was just a loser, Rachel said, and she'd never be more than a clerk. Ivy had agreed that Rachel had gotten more attention at home, by lying about Ivy to their father and letting her take the punishment their father had deemed appropriate for her supposed sins.

Rachel had sounded shocked at the description of their father's idea of punishment. Ivy was lying, she'd accused. The old man hadn't had a violent bone in his body. He loved Rachel, Ivy reminded her sister bitterly. Ivy was just the servant, and the more Rachel denounced her, the more critical and angry he became.

For a few seconds, Rachel actually sounded regretful. But it passed, as those rare bouts of sympathy always did. Rachel hung up abruptly, mumbling that her lover was at the door.

Ivy put down the phone and realized that she was shaking. Reliving those last days Rachel was at home made her miserable. Her memories were terrible.

She did go shopping for a dress, but the boutique owner she kept books for insisted on letting her borrow one of her own designs for the affair.

"It's my display model," Marcella Black insisted, "and just your size. Besides, it's the exact shade of green that your eyes are. You come by here at five, and I'll help you into it and I'll do your hair and makeup as well. No arguments. You're going to be a fairy princess Friday night."

"I'll turn into the frog at midnight," Ivy teased.

"Fat chance."

"All right. I'll come by at five on Friday. And thanks, Marcella. Really."

The older woman wrinkled her nose affectionately. "You just tell everybody who made that dress for you, and we're even."

"You bet I will!"

Hayes wasn't wearing his uniform. He had on a dark suit with a white cotton shirt and a blue patterned tie.

His shoes were so shiny that they reflected the porch light at Mrs. Brown's rooming house.

Ivy had just returned in the little used VW she'd bought and learned to drive two years earlier from Marcella's boutique, where she'd been dressed and her long blond hair had been put up in a curly coiffure. She had on just enough makeup to make her look sensational. She was shocked at the results. She'd never really tried to look good. Her mirror told her that she did.

Hayes gave her a long, appreciative stare. "You look lovely," he said quietly. He produced a plastic container with a cymbidium orchid inside. He offered it with a little shrug. "She said that women wear them on their wrists these days."

"Yes," she said, "so they don't get crushed when we dance. You didn't have to do this, Hayes," she said, taking the orchid out of the box. "But thank you. It's just beautiful."

"I thought you might like it. Ready to go?"

She nodded, pulling the door closed behind her. She had a small evening bag that Marcella had loaned her to go with the dress. She really did feel like Cinderella.

The community center was full to the brim with local citizens supporting the animal shelter. Two of the veterinarians who volunteered at the animal clinic were there with their spouses, and most of the leading lights of Jacobsville turned up as well. Justin and Shelby Ballenger came with their three sons. The eldest was working at the feedlot with Justin during the summer and working on his graduate degree in animal husbandry the rest of the year. The other two boys were still in high school, but ready to graduate. The three of them looked like their father, although the youngest had Shelby's blue-gray eyes. The Tremayne brothers and the Hart boys came with their wives. Micah Steele and his Callie came, and so did the Doctors Coltrain, Lou and her husband "Copper." J. D. Langley and Fay, and Matt Caldwell and his wife Leslie, and Cash Grier with his Tippy were also milling around in the crowd. Ivy spotted Judd Dunn and his wife, Christabel, in a corner, looking as much in love as when they'd first married.

"Amazing, isn't it, that the hall could hold all these people?" Hayes remarked as he led Ivy up the steps into the huge log structure.

"It really is. I'll bet they'll be able to add a whole new kennel with what they make tonight."

He smiled down at her. "I wouldn't doubt it."

They bumped into another couple, one of whom was Willie Carr, who owned the bakery. Then she remembered Rachel's odd message that she was supposed to give him.

"Willie, Rachel asked me to tell you something," she said, frowning as she struggled to remember exactly what it was.

Willie, tall and dark, looked uncomfortable. He laughed. "Now why would Rachel be sending me messages?" he asked, glancing at his wife. "I'm not cheating on you, baby, honest!"

"Oh, no, it wasn't that sort of message," Ivy said quickly. "It was something about a shipment of flour you were expecting that didn't arrive."

Willie cleared his throat. "I don't know anything about any shipment of flour that would go to New York City, Ivy," he assured her. "Rachel must have been talking about somebody else."

"Yes, I guess she must have. Sorry," she said with a sheepish smile. "She's incoherent most of the time lately."

"I'd say she is, if she's sending me messages about flour!" Willie agreed. He nodded at her and then at Hayes, and drew his wife back out onto the dance floor.

Hayes caught her hand and pulled her aside. "What shipment of flour was Rachel talking about?" he asked suddenly, and he wasn't smiling.

"I really don't know. She just said to tell Willie one was missing. She doesn't even eat sweets…"

"How long ago did she tell you to give Willie that message?" he persisted.

"About two days ago," she said. She frowned. "Why?"

Hayes took her by the hand and drew her along the dance floor to where Cash Grier was standing at the punch bowl with his gorgeous redheaded wife, Tippy.

"How's it going?" Cash greeted them, shaking hands with Hayes.

Hayes stepped closer. "Rachel sent Willie over there—" he jerked his head toward Willie, who was oblivious to the attention he was getting "—a message."

Cash was all business at once. "What message?"

Hayes prompted Ivy to repeat it.

"Code?" Cash asked Hayes.

The other man nodded. "It was two days ago that Ivy got the message."

Cash's dark eyes twinkled. "What a coincidence."

"Yes."

"Which proves that connection we were discussing earlier." He turned to Ivy. "If your sister sends any more messages to Willie, or anyone else, by you, tell Hayes, would you?"

She was all at sea. "Rachel's mixed up in something, isn't she?"

"Not necessarily," Hayes said at once. "But she knows someone who is, we think. Don't advertise this, either."

Ivy shook her head. "I'm no gossip." She grimaced. "Rachel's getting mixed up with some rich man, and she's trying to get away from her boyfriend, who deals drugs. The rich man is married. I'm afraid it's all going to end badly."

"People who get involved with drugs usually do end badly," Hayes said somberly.

"Yes, they do," Ivy had to agree. She smiled at Tippy, who was wearing a green and white dress made of silk and chiffon. "You look lovely."

"Thanks," Tippy replied, smiling. "So do you, Ivy. Marcella made my dress, you know. She made yours, too, didn't she?"

Ivy nodded, grinning. "She's amazing."

"I think so, too," Tippy agreed. "I've sent photos of her work to some friends of mine in New York. Don't tell her. It's a surprise."

"If anything comes of it, she'll be so thrilled. That was sweet of you."

Tippy waved away the compliment. "She's so talented, she deserves a break."

"Well, I came here to dance," Hayes informed them, taking Ivy's hand.

Cash pursed his lips. "Really?"

"I know I'm not in your league, Grier," Hayes said dourly, "but I can do the Macarena, if we can get somebody to play it."

"You can?" Cash chuckled. "By a strange coincidence, so can I. And I taught her." He indicated Tippy.

"In that case," Hayes replied, grinning, "may the best sheriff win."

And he went off to talk to the bandleader.

The band stopped suddenly, talked among the members and they all started grinning when Hayes came back to wrap his arm around Ivy.

"One, two, three, *four,*" the bandleader counted off, and the band broke into the Macarena.

Ivy knew the steps, having watched a number of important people dance it on television some years before. She wasn't the only one who remembered. The dance floor filled up with laughing people.

Hayes performed the quick hand motions with expertise, laughing as hard as Ivy was. They got through the second chorus and Ivy almost collapsed into Hayes's strong arms, resting her cheek against his chest.

"I'm out of shape!" she exclaimed breathlessly. "I need to get out more!"

"Just what I was thinking," he replied, smiling down at her.

Ivy happened to glance toward the doorway at that moment. Her gaze met a pair of pale blue eyes that were glittering like a diamondback rattlesnake coiling. Ivy's heart ran away as Stuart York gave her a look that could have fried bread.

5

Ivy had never seen that particular expression in Stuart's pale eyes, and she was amazed that he seemed so furious. Beside him, Merrie was also watching her with Hayes, and even though she smiled, she seemed a little shocked.

The two Yorks moved through the crowd, pausing now and again to exchange greetings as they came to stand beside Ivy and Hayes, who had broken apart by then. Ivy stared helplessly at Stuart. It had been a long time since she'd seen him. She knew that he'd been avoiding her ever since the unexpected and explosive interlude that last night she'd spent at Merrie's house, over two years ago.

If she was self-conscious, he wasn't. His pale eyes were narrow, glittering, dangerous as they met hers.

"I thought you didn't dance, Hayes," Merrie said. She was smiling, but she seemed ill at ease.

"I don't, as a rule," he agreed, smiling back. "But I can manage it once in a while."

"We're all here to support the local animal shelter," Ivy told Merrie. "From the looks of this crowd, they're going to end up with plenty of donations."

"I send them a check every year," Stuart said curtly.

"Did you two come together?" Hayes asked curiously.

"We were both at a loose end tonight," Merrie replied. "I got someone to cover for me at the hospital. I really came because I knew Ivy would be here. I haven't seen her in so long!"

Ivy was bemused. She wondered why Merrie seemed so unlike herself.

"I never believed you'd make a nurse," Hayes told Merrie with a grin. "I still remember you fainting when we had to sew up a wound on that old horse you used to trot around on."

"I wish I could forget." Merrie groaned. "It wouldn't have been so bad, except for where I landed."

"It was the only fresh manure on the place," Stuart inserted with a chuckle. "I swear she took three baths that day before she got rid of the smell."

The band started up again, this time playing a dreamy

slow tune. Hayes looked down at Merrie. "Want to dance?"

She hesitated.

"Go on," Ivy coaxed, smiling.

Merrie relaxed a little and let Hayes take her hand. He led her onto the dance floor and into a lazy box step. Was it Ivy's imagination, or did Merrie look as if she'd landed in paradise, wrapped up in Hayes Carson's strong arms?

"Do you dance, Mr. York?" Tippy asked.

He shook his head, sliding his big hands into his pockets. "Afraid not."

She smiled. "Neither do I. At least, not very well. I'm learning, though."

Cash drew her to his side. "Yes, you are, baby," he said affectionately. "Come on. We can always do with a little practice. See you both later," he added.

Which left Ivy alone with Stuart for the first time in over two years. She was ill at ease and it showed.

He turned and looked down at her deliberately, his pale eyes narrow and searching. "I like the dress," he said, his voice deep and slow.

"Thanks," she said, a little self-conscious because of the way he was looking at her. "I keep books for a boutique owner. It's a model she's hoping to sell."

"So what are you, walking advertising?" he asked.

She smiled. "I suppose so."

He glanced at his sister dancing with Hayes. "She used to have a horrific crush on him," he said out of the blue. "I was glad when she outgrew it. Hayes takes chances. He's been in two serious gun battles since he became sheriff. He barely walked away from the last one. She'd never make a lawman's wife."

"She made a nurse," she pointed out.

"Yes, well, patients go home when they've healed. But a lawman's wife waits up all hours, hoping he'll come home at all." He looked down at her. "There's a difference."

She felt guilty when she remembered the way Merrie had looked when Hayes asked her to dance, as if she'd trespassed on someone else's property. Considering Stuart's attitude, it wasn't out of the realm of possibility that Merrie might be hiding her interest in Hayes. Stuart liked him, but he'd always said that Hayes was too old for his sister, not to mention being in one of the more dangerous professions. Merrie idolized her brother. She wouldn't deliberately cross him.

"Why are you here with Hayes?" he asked abruptly.

She blinked at the boldness of the question. She should have told him it was none of his business. But she couldn't. He had that air of authority that had always opened doors for him.

"He didn't want to come alone and neither did I," she said.

"He's well off, and he's a bachelor," he replied.

"Are you making a point?" she asked.

His eyes narrowed on her face. "You'll be twenty-one soon."

She was surprised that he kept up with her age. "Yes, I suppose so."

He didn't blink. "Merrie said you wanted to study opera."

"Then she must have also said that I don't want to leave Jacobsville," she replied. "It would be a waste of time to train for a career I don't want."

"Do you want to keep books for other people for the rest of your life?"

"I like keeping books. You might remember that I also do the occasional article for the local cattlemen's association."

He didn't reply to that. His eyes went back to his sister, moving lazily around the dance floor with Hayes. After a minute, his big hand reached down and caught Ivy's. He tugged her gently onto the dance floor and slid his hand around her waist.

"You said you didn't dance," she murmured breathlessly.

He shrugged. "I lied." He curled her into his body

and moved gracefully to the music, coaxing her cheek onto his chest. His arm tightened around her, bringing her even closer.

She could barely breathe. The proximity was intoxicating. It brought back that one sweet interlude between them, so long ago. It was probably a dream and she'd wake up clutching a pillow in her own bed. So why not enjoy it, she thought? She closed her eyes, gave him her weight, and sighed. For an instant, she could almost have sworn that a shudder passed through his tall body.

She felt his lips against her forehead. It was the closest to heaven she'd ever come.

But all too soon it was over. The music ended and Stuart stepped away from her.

She felt cold and empty. She wrapped her arms around herself and forced a smile that she didn't really feel.

Stuart was watching her intently. "That shade of green suits you," he said quietly. "It matches your eyes."

She didn't know how to handle a compliment like that from him. She laughed nervously. "Does it?"

He smiled slowly. It wasn't like any smile she'd ever had from him. It made his pale eyes glitter like sun-touched diamonds, made him look younger and less care-worn. She smiled back.

Merrie joined them, an odd little smile touching her lips. "Having fun?" she asked Ivy.

"It's a very nice dance," Ivy replied, dragging her eyes away from Stuart.

"It is," Merrie agreed.

Hayes had been stopped on the way off the dance floor by a somber Harley Fowler, who motioned Cash Grier to join them. Hayes made a face before he rejoined them, disappointment in his whole look.

"We've had word of a drug shipment coming through," he said under his breath. "Harley was watching for it. He says they've got a semi full to the brim with cocaine. I have to go. We've been setting this sting up for months, and this is the first real break we've had." He stared at Ivy. "I can get one of my deputies to swing by and take you home," he began.

"She can ride with us," Stuart said easily. "No problem."

"Thanks," Hayes said. He grinned at Ivy. "Our first date and I blew it. I'll make it up to you. I promise."

"I'm not upset, Hayes," she replied. "You go do your job. There will be other dances."

"You're a good sport. Thanks. See you, Merrie," he added with a wink, nodding to Stuart as he headed for the front door.

Merrie was biting her lower lip, her eyes on Hayes's back as he left. Ivy noticed and didn't say a word.

"How about some of this punch?" Ivy asked her best friend. "It looks very good."

Merrie was diverted. "Yes. I'll bet it tastes good, too. But I want a word with Shelby Ballenger before I indulge. I'll be right back." She went toward Shelby. Ivy filled two glass cups with punch and handed one to Stuart.

He made a face. "It's tropical punch, isn't it? I hate tropical punch."

"They have coffee, too, if you'd rather," Ivy told him, putting the punch down on the table.

He met her searching eyes. "I would. Cream. No sugar."

She poured coffee into a cup, adding just a touch of cream. She handed it to him, but her hands shook. He had to put his around them, to steady them.

"It's all right," he said softly. "There's nothing to be afraid of."

She didn't understand what was happening to her. The feel of his big, warm hands around hers made her heart race. The look in his pale eyes delighted, thrilled, terrified. She'd never had such a headlong physical reaction to any other man, and especially not since that incredible night when he'd held her and kissed her as if he couldn't bear to let her go. It had haunted her dreams for more than two years, and ruined her for a relationship with any other man.

She let go of the cup with a nervous little laugh. "Is that enough cream?" she asked.

He nodded. He sipped it in silence while she sipped at her punch. The music was playing again, this time a slow, bluesy two-step.

Merrie came back to them, grinning. "I asked Shelby if she'd save me one of those border collies she and Justin are breeding. They're great cattle dogs."

Stuart scowled at her. "What the hell do you need with a cattle dog?"

"It's not for me," she replied. "There's a sweet little girl on my ward who has to have a tumor removed from her brain. She's scared to death. I asked her parents what might help her attitude, and they said she'd always wanted a border collie. It might be just what she needs to come through the surgery. You see," she added sadly, "they don't know if it's malignant yet."

"How old is she?" Ivy asked.

"Ten."

Ivy winced. "What a terrible age to have something so deadly."

"At least she'll have something to look forward to," Stuart added. "You really are a jewel, Merrie."

She made an affectionate face at him. "So are you.

Now let's dance or eat or something so we don't burst into tears and embarrass Ivy."

He cocked an eyebrow and gave Ivy a mischievous look. "God forbid that we should embarrass her." He put down his coffee cup. "Dancing seems more sensible."

He took Ivy's glass of punch and put it down, only to draw her back onto the dance floor.

It was the sweetest evening of Ivy's life. She danced almost exclusively with Stuart, and he didn't seem to mind that people were watching them with fond amusement. It was well-known that Stuart played the field, and that Ivy didn't date anyone. The attention Stuart was showing her raised eyebrows.

Merrie didn't lack for partners, either, but she seemed subdued since Hayes had left. Ivy wondered if there wasn't something smoldering under Merrie's passive expression that led back to that old crush she'd had on Hayes.

When it came time to leave, Merrie informed Stuart that she was going to ride home with one of the Bates twins, who passed right by their house. She didn't give a reason, but Stuart didn't ask for one, either. He linked his fingers into Ivy's and drew her outside to his big, sleek Jaguar.

"I can't remember when I've enjoyed a party more," he remarked.

"It was fun," she agreed, smiling. "I don't get out much at night. Usually I'm trying to keep up with the accounts, including doing estimated taxes for all my clients four times a year. It keeps me close to home."

"You and Merrie have lost touch since she went to work in San Antonio."

"A little, maybe," she replied. "But Merrie is still the best friend I have. That doesn't go away, even when we don't see each other for months at a time."

He was quiet for a minute. "Have you heard from Rachel?" he asked.

She drew in a painful breath. "Yes. Last week."

"How was she?"

She wondered why he was asking her questions about her sister, whom he hated. "Pretty much the same, I guess." Except that she was steadily higher than a kite when she called Ivy, and she was running around with someone else's rich husband, she added silently.

He shot a glance at her. "That isn't what I hear."

Her heart welled up in her throat. She'd forgotten that he moved in the same circles as other rich, successful men. Rachel's garden slug of a boyfriend knew such people in New York. Stuart might even know Rachel's latest lover. "What do you hear?" she asked.

"That she's about to create a media sensation," he said flatly. "Which is why I brought Merrie to the dance. Hayes mentioned that he was bringing you, and I wanted to talk to you without the whole town knowing. Your boardinghouse isn't private enough, and my Mrs. Rhodes is a terrible gossip. That left me looking for a neutral spot. Here it is."

Her heart was hammering. Rachel again. It was always something, her whole life. Would she ever be free of her sister's messy problems?

"Don't look like that," he said curtly. "I know you don't have any influence on her. I just don't want you to be surprised by some enthusiastic journalist out of the blue, asking you personal questions about your sister for print. Scandals pay well, especially if the victim's relatives can be shocked into a printable reaction."

She put her face in her hands. "How bad is it?" she asked.

"Bad enough." He pulled the car off the main road onto a dirt road and cut off the engine. When she looked around, disturbed, he added, "This is on my land. I don't want to sit in front of Mrs. Brown's boardinghouse and have curtains fluttering the whole time we're talking." He freed his seat belt and turned to her, one arm curved around the back of her bucket seat. "You need to know what you're up against before the story hits the tabloids."

She grimaced. Tippy Moore had gone through the tabloid mills before her marriage to Cash Grier. So had Leslie, Matt Caldwell's wife. She knew the devastating effect they could have on people's lives. But she never dreamed that she could become a victim of them. Surely Rachel's sister wouldn't be interesting news to anyone? On the other hand, Rachel had actually landed a few roles on Broadway, despite her drug habit, and one review had called her talent "promising." After years of auditions, it seemed that Rachel might actually make it as an actress. But Stuart looked uncomfortable.

"Tell me," she prodded gently.

"She's been supplying drugs to an elderly recluse who fancies himself in love with her," he replied curtly. "The problem is that he's recently married to a former beauty queen who doesn't want to share him and his fortune with anyone, least of all a minor actress with a drug dealer for a boyfriend. A mutual friend says she's about to go public with the story. If she does, it will ruin Rachel's chances of any more roles on Broadway, and it may put her drug-dealing boyfriend in prison. It might even put her there, if the wife decides to go public with what her very expensive private detective dug up on Rachel. She found a connection to some very big drug lords across the border; some of the same ones Hayes and Cash and Cobb of the DEA are trying to catch."

By now, Ivy was noticeably pale despite the semidarkness of the front seats. That message Rachel had given her for the baker had been code, after all. Her sister was a drug dealer. Her heart ran away with fear. She pulled at a curl beside her ear. "I wonder if I could get lost in the Amazon jungle before Rachel gets it in the neck?"

"You'd have to come home one day. Running away never solved a problem."

She leaned back against the seat, sick to her soul. In a small town like Jacobsville, a tabloid story would be a gossip fest. There wouldn't be a place she could go where people wouldn't be talking about her.

She wrapped her arms around herself, feeling a sudden chill.

"Rachel told a lot of lies about you around town, when you were in high school," he said after a minute, his eyes narrow and thoughtful. "She fed me a dose of them, too. I actually believed her, until two years ago. But just the same, I made sure that she left town."

She felt her cheeks go hot, and she hoped he couldn't see. So that was why Rachel had gone away so suddenly, why her attitude toward Ivy had changed. She thought Stuart was protecting her little sister, and she was jealous!

"Copper Coltrain says that you were in his office frequently with injuries from 'falls' when you were in school," he persisted.

Her heart jumped. "I was clumsy," she said quickly.

"Bull! Your father drank to excess and Rachel fed him the same lies she fed other people about you," he countered. "She bragged about getting you in trouble with your father. It suited her to have you constantly out of favor, so that she'd inherit everything. Which she did."

The news that he knew all her problems, although she'd secretly suspected as much, made her sick. "Dad thought she was wonderful."

"Yes, and he was fairly certain that you weren't his child."

She gasped aloud, her eyes as wide as saucers. "What?!"

"I didn't think you knew that," he murmured, watching her. "Rachel said that your mother told her, before she died, that she'd had an affair and you were the result."

Of all the things Rachel had done to her, that was the absolute worst. She couldn't even find words to express how horrified she was. "Is it…is it true?" she asked unsteadily.

He was hesitant. "I don't know. There's an easy way to find out, if you want to know for sure. If you can get a hair from your father's brush, or if Coltrain has a blood sample from him on file, we can have a DNA profile done. If there isn't a sample, but if Coltrain has his blood type on file, we can have your blood typed. Paternity can be determined by blood groups. It won't prove anything for sure, unless we could get a DNA sample from your father, but it would at least show if you could have been your father's child."

"You'd do that, for me?" she asked, surprised at his indulgence.

"Of course," he said matter-of-factly.

It was a lot to swallow at once. No wonder her father had been so brutal to her! He thought she wasn't his child. And Rachel had used that knowledge—if it wasn't a lie—to cheat Ivy out of anything that belonged to her family. Rachel had inherited it all, and sold it all.

"She must hate me," Ivy said aloud.

"She was jealous of you," he corrected flatly.

"Oh, sure, I'm such a peach of a beauty, why wouldn't she be?" she asked sarcastically.

He reached out and tugged a lock of her hair. "Stop that. You're no ugly duckling, except in your own mind. But I wasn't talking about looks. Rachel was jealous because of the way you are with people. You're always looking for the best in people, making them feel good about themselves, making them feel important. You never gossip or tell lies, and you're always around if anyone's in trouble or grieving. Rachel has never given a damn for anyone except herself. You made her feel inferior, and she hated you for it."

"She was beautiful," she said. "All the boys loved her."

"Even boys you tried to date," he added, as if he knew. He nodded. "Yes, I heard about that, too. Rachel delighted in stealing away any boy you brought home. She turned your girlfriends against you, everyone except Merrie. She told Merrie some whoppers about your social life." He looked away, his body stiffening. It didn't take a mind reader to know that Merrie had repeated the lies to him.

"I'm amazed you didn't forbid Merrie to have anything to do with me."

"I did," he said surprisingly, glancing at her. "She wouldn't listen, of course. And I stopped pressuring her about it when I realized how badly Rachel had lied about your character."

She knew what he was talking about, and it made her uneasy. He was remembering what a novice she was in a man's arms.

"Copper doesn't usually talk about patients," he continued. "But we're second cousins as well as good friends, and I've felt responsible for you since your father's death. He thought I should know about your home life. Just in case Rachel ever came down here and tried to start trouble. He didn't know I'd already gotten the news from a private detective I hired."

She couldn't look at him. It felt as if all the bruises and lacerations were plainly visible to anyone looking.

"You've never talked about it, have you?"

She shook her head. "Not even to Merrie."

"Merrie is more perceptive than you realize. She knew why you covered your legs when you went to school. You didn't want anyone to see the bruises he left on you with that doubled-up belt."

She bit her lower lip and looked up at him. She was remembering what Merrie had said about his own childhood, and how his father had punished him for refusing to give his life to football.

"You got your share, too, didn't you?" she asked quietly.

He hesitated for a moment. His dark brows drew together. "Yes," he replied finally. "I've never talked about it to anyone outside my family. The memories sting, even now."

"They would have locked my father up and thrown away the key if he'd done it today."

"Mine, too," he agreed. He smiled faintly. "Our fathers would probably be occupying adjoining jail cells." He sighed and traced a pattern at her throat, making her heartbeat throb. "Nobody's using a belt on my kids."

"Mine, either," she replied at once.

He smiled down at her. "We're all products of our upbringing. Pity we don't get to choose our relatives."

"You can say that again." She searched his eyes. "Rachel isn't afraid of anything except losing her chance to act in a starring role on Broadway. But if she gets caught up in a public scandal, it will kill her career stone dead. And she might go to prison for drug dealing. I don't know what she'd do if she had all that to contend with. She's not very strong emotionally."

"Only when she's on the receiving end," he agreed. "But she chose her own path, Ivy. We all do. Then we take the consequences of those choices."

She cocked her head. "What path did you choose that had consequences?"

"It was one I didn't choose," he said enigmatically. His hand slid under the silken fist of hair at her nape, warm and strong. "But we've done enough talking for one night."

As he spoke, he tugged her face gently under his. "Don't panic," he whispered against her mouth as his lips teased at it. "There are some things you just can't do in bucket seats..."

She went under in a daze of throbbing pleasure. It was like the first time he'd held her and kissed her, but much more explosive. The long years between kisses made her bold, made her hungry. She slid her arms around his neck and opened her mouth under his. He groaned. A shudder went through him. He hesitated, but only for a split second. Then he gathered her up whole and dragged her over the console and into his lap, and the kisses grew harder and more insistent.

She felt his big hand under the neckline of her gown, gently tracing patterns down into the soft flesh under her bra. She gasped.

He lifted his head and looked into her wide, shocked eyes, with affectionate amusement. "Think of it as exploration into new territory," he teased gently. "You've got a lot of catching up to do."

"And you're offering to guide me through the undergrowth?" she gasped.

"Frilly undergrowth," he murmured, looking down at the quick beat of her heart that was echoed in the trembling of her bodice as her pulse increased madly.

"I'm not sure," she began breathlessly.

"Neither am I," he agreed as he bent again to her mouth. "But it's been a long, dry spell and I've waited as long as I can and stay sane."

While she was trying to figure that out, his mouth opened on her parted lips and his hand trespassed right under her bra onto her soft flesh with a sureness and mastery that chased any thought of protest right out of her head. She clung to him and gave in to the sweetness of the moment.

6

Just as Ivy was seeing stars, there was the purr of a big cat somewhere in the jungle of pleasure she was exploring.

Stuart must have heard it, too, because he raised his head and frowned as he looked into the rearview mirror. "I don't believe it!" he burst out.

She followed his gaze and saw flashing blue lights coming at breakneck speed right down the dirt road behind them.

"Hayes!" he muttered, and let out a word that made her blush.

The all-white Jacobs County Sheriff's car pulled up past them, whipped around, and came back again, so that Hayes and Stuart were facing each other through open drivers' windows. In the time it had taken Hayes to turn around, Ivy had slid discreetly back into her own seat, straightened her clothing and smoothed her hair. She was grateful that it was dark, so that Hayes wouldn't be able to see the lingering traces of Stuart's demanding passion on her lips and hair.

"Aren't you a little far out of your territory?" Stuart drawled. "This is my land."

Hayes just stared at him. "We flushed a drug transport with three armed men inside," he said at once. "We got two of them, but one escaped not far from here. He's carrying an automatic weapon."

"Good God," Stuart exclaimed.

"I didn't think he'd be driving a Jag," he continued dryly, "but you can't rule out a carjacking. And this car was all alone in a field." He scowled. "What the hell are the two of you doing out here?"

"Talking about DNA profiles," Stuart shot back.

Hayes pursed his lips. "Oooookay," he said, but clearly not believing it. "Just the same, I'd take her home, if I were you. These guys don't play nice. One of my deputies is in the emergency room with a bullet in his hip."

"I hope you get them," Stuart said.

"Me, too. See you."

He roared away, sirens still going.

Stuart glanced wryly at Ivy. "I suppose we've talked enough for one night. I don't fancy fighting off drug dealers at this hour."

"Neither do I," she agreed, but there was disappointment about having to come down from the clouds. It had been a sweet few minutes.

"I'm not anxious to leave, either, Ivy," he said as he started the car. "But there's a time and place, and this isn't it."

With that enigmatic statement, he pulled the car back into the highway, and sped toward her boardinghouse. They arrived there too soon.

He got out of the car, opened her door and walked her to her front door. He noted the quick flutter of a curtain with an amused smile, and then positioned them where no windows intruded. He took her by the waist and looked down into her sad eyes in the porch light. "I shouldn't have told you about your father like that," he said apologetically. "I'm sorry."

"The tabloids wouldn't have been very kind about it, if I'd had to hear it from them," she said philosophically. "Thanks for the heads-up."

His big hands tightened on her small waist. "Go see Copper," he coaxed. "He'll do what he can to help you find out, one way or another. I'll take care of the bill. I'll tell him that, too," he added.

"All right."

"And don't worry yourself to death about your sister,"

he said firmly. "If the situation was reversed, I promise she wouldn't waste a night's sleep about you."

"I know that. But she's still the only family I have left in the world."

He drew in an audible breath. "That doesn't help, I'm sure." He bent and brushed his mouth gently over her soft, sensitized lips. She stood on her tiptoes to increase the pressure, shivering a little when he accepted the silent invitation and gathered her in close, so that they were riveted together, hip to hip.

She'd never known such pleasure. It felt as sweet as it had in his car, but much more intense. Her nails dug into the hard muscles of his shoulders as she gave in to the sheer delight of being close to him.

When she moaned, he drew back. His hands were briefly cruel as he fought the need to back her into the wall and devour her. He had to force himself to let her go.

She saw that, and was fascinated by the sudden change in him. It was so sweet to kiss him, beyond her wildest dreams of delight.

"We can't do much more of that," he whispered. "Not in public."

"Are we in public?" she whispered back, dazed.

He drew in a long breath. "If I don't stop kissing

you, we're going to be. It's sweet, Ivy. Sweeter than my dreams."

"Sweeter than mine, too," she confessed, aching to have his mouth on hers again.

He knew that, but he had to be strong for both of them. It wasn't the place. He held her gently by the waist. "I have to fly to Denver for a conservation workshop. I'll call you when I get there."

She stared up at him with her heart flipping around. Her surprise was noticeable.

He searched her wide eyes. "Times change. So do people. You're twenty-one next month, aren't you?"

She nodded, spellbound.

He looked very somber for a minute. "Still years too young," he murmured as he bent his head. "But what the hell..."

He lifted her up against him and kissed her until her mouth felt bruised. She didn't complain. She held on for dear life, her arms tight around his neck, her feet just barely touching the floor at all. If this was a dream, she never wanted to wake up.

When she moaned softly, he put her back on her feet and let her go abruptly. His breathing was noticeably faster. "Stay out of trouble," he told her.

"I don't ever get into trouble," she replied dimly, her eyes on his hard mouth.

He smiled slowly. "Yes, but that was before."

"Before what?" she asked.

He bent and kissed her quickly. "Before me. Lock the door behind you."

He was walking away before she realized what he'd said. He was hinting at a new relationship between them. It made her breath catch in her throat. Her eyes followed him hungrily all the way to his car. He started it and turned on the lights, but he didn't budge. Finally she realized that he wasn't going until she was inside. She smiled at that protectiveness, which was so alien to their relationship. She waved, went inside and closed the door. Only when she turned off the porch light did she hear the car driving away.

Next morning at breakfast, Mrs. Brown and Lita were beaming at her, both affectionately amused.

"Have fun last night, dear?" Mrs. Brown asked. "I noticed that Sheriff Hayes didn't bring you home. Wasn't that Stuart York's car?"

"Yes, it was," Ivy confessed, and hated the warm color that blushed her cheeks. "Hayes had a call and had to leave."

"We heard on the radio that there was a shootout," Lita said. "Deputy Clark was admitted to the hospital with a gunshot wound."

“So was one of the suspects,” Mrs. Brown said shortly. “They said Hayes got him.”

“We saw him on the way home,” Ivy confessed, but not how they’d seen him, or where. “He said the deputy was shot in the hip. He didn’t mention the drug dealers getting shot, too.”

“It was the one who went missing when they stopped the truck,” Mrs. Brown said. “My daughter works as a dispatcher,” she reminded the other women. “She said he was hiding in a chicken coop just off the highway. Hayes saw chickens flying out of the coop and went to investigate.” She chuckled. “People shut their chickens up at sunset to keep them from getting eaten by foxes or raccoons. Nobody turns them out at night. Sure enough, there was this miserable little drug dealer, hiding there. He shot at Hayes and missed. Hayes didn’t.”

Ivy shook her head. “He takes so many chances,” she said. “It will take a brave woman to marry him.”

“Probably why no woman ever has,” Lita remarked. “He was always a hothead, even when he was in high school. Always taking risks. He joined the police force when he was just seventeen. I guess his father influenced him.”

“His father was a lovely man,” Ivy remarked with a smile. “He loved flowers, did you know? He always had the most beautiful garden of them, and everybody thought it was his wife who did all the planting. But it wasn't."

"I'll bet Hayes doesn't raise flowers," Mrs. Brown remarked.

"He had a younger brother," Lita continued, frowning, "who died of a drug overdose. You know, they never found the person who bought him that bad batch of cocaine that did him in. They say that Hayes is out to get his brother's killer, that he'll never quit until the drug dealer goes to prison." She sighed. "He still thinks that Minette Raynor gave that drug to Bobby Carson, but I don't. Minette isn't the sort."

Ivy nodded. "I know, but he won't see it that way. He never stops once he's got a suspect in view. That's sort of scary, in a way."

"Makes me feel safe," Mrs. Brown chuckled. "I like knowing he doesn't let criminals get away."

"Me, too," Ivy had to admit. But she was thinking about Stuart and their changed relationship, going through the motions of eating and behaving normally. Inside, she was blazing with new hungers, new hope.

She went out to see her clients that day, but she was missing Stuart and waiting, hoping, for a phone call. She knew that he could have been joking. Maybe he'd just said it to tease. But the look in his eyes on the porch had been possessive, acquisitive. Her heart jumped every time she remembered how that last, desperate kiss had felt. Surely something so powerful had to be shared. After all, she hadn't been the only one breathing hard after the hungry kisses they'd shared. It was just that Stuart was older and more experienced. Maybe to him it was just a pleasant few minutes. To her, it was a taste of heaven.

Merrie called her at lunchtime, just to talk. Ivy was having a sandwich at Barbara's Café, but she didn't taste it. When the phone rang, she jumped to pull it out of her purse and answer it. It had to be Stuart. It had to be!

"Hi," Merrie said cheerfully.

"Oh. Hi," Ivy replied, trying to compose herself and not let her disappointment show. "How are you?"

"Lonely. You need to come spend a weekend with me," Merrie said. "I'm coming home next weekend. How about it?"

Once, Ivy would have jumped at the chance. Now, she was keeping secrets from her best friend. She didn't know whether she should agree. What she felt for Stuart might show, if she was under his roof. She didn't want Merrie to see it. Not yet. It was too new, too private, too precious to share. And what if he didn't want her around there at all? What if he'd just been playing some sophisticated game to which she didn't know the rules? Her insecurities floated to the top like cream in a churn.

"Ivy, you don't have to worry about me," Merrie said before Ivy could speak. Her tone was subdued, quiet. "I won't interfere."

"Excuse me?"

Merrie drew in a breath. "Hayes is a great catch."

Ivy was speechless. "Hayes?"

"He seems to like you a lot. He was really happy last night."

Now here was a problem she didn't know how to resolve. She couldn't admit that she was crazy about Merrie's brother, for fear that her friend might tease Stuart or do something to make him draw back from Ivy. On the other hand, she wasn't involved with Hayes and wasn't ever likely to be.

"Hayes is very nice," she compromised. "But he doesn't want to get serious about anyone, and neither do I. I don't want to get married for years yet. I want to enjoy being out on my own, and being single."

There was another sigh, but this one sounded strange. "Then, you're not involved with Hayes?"

"We're friends, Merrie. That's all."

"I'm glad," she said. "By the way, have you heard anything, about how he is?" Merrie added after a minute. "I heard that there was a shootout and someone got shot apprehending a drug dealer. Was it Hayes?"

"No!" Ivy said. "It was one of his deputies. One of the suspects got shot, too. Hayes is fine."

"Thank God."

"You've known Hayes a long time," Ivy recalled.

"Yes, since he used to stay with us when his father and mother had to go out of town to see about her parents in Georgia. Even though he was Stuart's friend, I always felt as if he were part of my family. He's a lot older than me, of course. Like someone I know in San Antonio," she added enigmatically.

The age difference between Merrie and Hayes was about the same as that between Stuart and Ivy. Stuart didn't seem to have a problem with it anymore, if his new attitude toward Ivy was any indication. So maybe there was hope for Merrie.

"He's not that much older, Merrie," Ivy said gently.

"Stuart thinks he is."

There was an edge in that usually calm tone. "He's your brother. He loves you. He just thinks…" She stopped at once.

"He thinks what?" Merrie prompted.

"He thinks that Hayes's profession puts him out of the running for you," she said reluctantly. "Hayes does take chances, Merrie. He can be a lot of fun, but under it all is a man who takes risks, who walks right into gun battles. Stuart's just thinking about what's best for you."

"So that's what's been eating him lately," Merrie said dryly. "Old worrywart. But no relative, no matter how caring, can decide your life for you, you know."

"I know that. Merrie, Stuart loves you. He'd want you to marry someone you love."

There was a husky laugh. "Think so?"

"Yes."

"Well. That's something."

"You're very depressed. Why don't you come to the boardinghouse and have supper with us tonight? You know Mrs. Brown wouldn't mind. I could phone her."

"No. Thanks, anyway, but we've got a flu epidemic. I can't be spared, with so many health care workers out sick."

"Maybe when it's all over..." She let her voice trail off.

"Yes. I'd love it."

"Take care of yourself," Ivy said. "And stop worrying about everything. Life evens out. Wishes come true."

"Sure they do," Merrie said cynically.

"I mean it. They do!"

Merrie sighed. "You always did believe in fairies."

"Angels, too, don't forget."

"If I have a guardian angel, he's asleep at the wheel."

"Stop that. Come and see me when you can."

"How about that invitation to spend the weekend?"

Merrie persisted. "You and Stuart weren't fighting, for a change, at the dance. You might enjoy it."

"I'll let you know," Ivy said, stalling. "I've got a new client."

"You and your blessed clients. Okay, then. Call me?"

"I'll call you. Take care, Merrie."

"You, too."

Ivy hung up. Poor Merrie.

She waited and waited, but there was no other phone call. She even checked to make sure the phone was working. By late evening, she was certain she'd misunderstood what Stuart had said. He was probably just joking. But he wasn't a man who usually cracked jokes.

She got ready for bed, climbed under the covers and was just about to turn out the light when the phone began to ring noisily.

Heart pounding, she leaped out of bed and upended her purse to find the small flip phone. She opened it with trembling hands and put it to her ear. "Hello?"

There was a deep, soft chuckle. "Dived for the phone, did you?"

She laughed breathlessly. "Yes," she confessed.

"I would have waited. I told you I'd call."

"Yes, but I thought maybe you got busy," she began.

"So you gave up on me."

She fidgeted on the bed. “Not really. Well, maybe. I wasn’t sure that you weren’t teasing.”

There was a brief pause. “It’s early days, isn’t it, Ivy?” he asked quietly. “We’re only beginning to learn each other.”

She wasn’t sure what he meant. Her hand tightened on the phone. “Merrie invited me to spend the weekend.”

“What did you tell her?”

“I said I’d let her know,” she hesitated.

There was a short pause.

She felt insecure. “I didn’t know if you’d approve.”

The pause grew.

She felt her spirits hit the floor. She drew in a slow, shivery breath. “Stuart?”

There was a clink, like that of ice in a glass. “You don’t know me at all.”

“Of course I don’t,” she replied. “You’ve avoided me for two whole years.”

“I had to,” he said harshly.

She didn’t understand what he meant. She was shy with him. It wasn’t helping things.

He drew in another harsh breath. “Oh, hell.” Ice sloshed in liquid again.

“I should go,” she said sadly.

“Is it Hayes?” he asked harshly.

“What?”

"Are you in love with Hayes Carson?"

"I most certainly am not!" she exclaimed before she stopped to think.

There was a sigh. "Well, that's something, I guess." Another pause. "When I come back, we'll go for a drive and talk."

"That would be…nice."

"Nice."

She was lost for words. She loved the sound of his deep, slow voice. She didn't want him to hang up. But she didn't know what to say, to keep him talking.

"What are you doing?"

"Sitting on the bed in my nightgown, talking to a madman."

He burst out laughing. "Is that how I sound?"

"I feel like apologizing, but I don't know what for."

"I've had a long day," he told her. "We always get at least one tree hugger who comes to these conferences and demands that we set up special homes for our cattle where they can be properly housed and clothed and educated. This guy thinks we should learn to communicate with them."

She burst out laughing. "If you could, they'd say, 'don't eat me.'"

"You stop that," he muttered. "You know I don't raise beef cattle."

That was true. He had purebred Black Angus cattle. He knew the names and pedigrees of all his bulls, and they were as tame as dogs. The pedigree cows were treated almost as gently as the bulls. He was dangerous to cowboys who thought they could mistreat his livestock.

"I know that," she said gently. "What did you say to the tree hugger?"

"Oh, I didn't say anything to him."

There was an odd inflection in his voice. "But somebody else did?"

"One of the delegates from the national association invited him outside. The guy thought they were going to share a nice discussion. The delegate picked him up and put him down in the ornamental fountain."

She gasped. "But it's freezing in Colorado! There's snow!"

He chuckled. "I know."

"The poor man!"

"They gave him a blanket and a bus ticket," he said. "Last I saw of him, he was shivering his way back west into the sunset."

"That wasn't kind."

"Last year, it was a global warming advocate who said that we needed to find ways to stop cattle from belching and destroying the ozone layer. But I won't mention what happened to him."

"Why not?"

He only laughed. "You'll read all about it in the book he's writing. Last I heard, he was still looking for a publisher."

"Poor man."

"Poor man, hell. Humans belch as much as cattle do."

"I have never belched."

"Baloney," he shot back.

She sighed. "Well, I've burped quietly. But I never considered that it was doing damage to the planet."

He laughed. "I'm kidding. They actually let him present his program. One cattleman even bought him a drink."

"That was nice."

"It wasn't. The drink he bought him was a 'Wallbanger.'"

"What's that?"

"You wake up eventually with a hell of a hangover."

"You guys are terrible."

"I don't buy drinks for advocacy groups."

"You might influence them if you did."

"Not a chance." There was another pause. "I've got to go. There's someone at the door."

"An advocacy group?" she teased.

He laughed again. "No. A buddy of mine from Alaska."

"Does he raise cattle up there?"

"He's stationed at a military base there. Active military."

"Oh."

"I'll talk to you when I get back. Take care."

"You, too," she said, her voice softening.

"Good night, sugar."

He hung up before she was sure she'd really heard that. He'd never called her a pet name in all the time they'd known each other. It sounded as if they were actually going to be friends. Maybe even more. She slept finally in a welter of delightful, impossible dreams.

The next morning, her whole world fell apart. She answered her phone, thinking drowsily that it might be Stuart again, when a stranger addressed her.

"Miss Conley?" the voice inquired. And when she said yes, he continued, "I had this number from your police chief. I'm Sergeant Ed Ames, of the New York Police Department, Brooklyn Precinct. It's about your sister."

Her heart fell. "Is she all right?" she asked at once. "Has she been arrested?"

There was a loaded pause. "I'm sorry to tell you that she was found dead in her apartment this morning… Miss Conley? Miss Conley!"

She could barely breathe. She'd known this was coming, deep in her heart. But she wasn't ready to face it.

"Yes," she said heavily. "I'm still here. Sorry. It's… it's a shock…"

"I can imagine," he replied.

"You said she was found dead. Did she commit suicide?" she asked. "Or did someone else…"

"We don't know. There's going to have to be an autopsy, I'm afraid, to decide that. We'll need you to identify the body, to make sure it is your sister. Then someone has to arrange for disposition of her personal effects and her burial, or cremation."

"Yes. Of course. I'll have to come up there and deal with it." She hesitated, her mind spinning. "I'll come today. As soon as I can get a flight."

He gave her his telephone number and contact information. She wrote it all down and said goodbye.

She sat back down on her bed, rocking quietly with her arms wrapped around herself. Rachel was dead. Rachel was dead. She hadn't even gotten to say goodbye. And now she had to go and deal with the funeral arrangements. Worse, she didn't even know if her sister had killed herself, or if someone had murdered her.

She thought of Jerry, her sister's drug-dealing boyfriend. Had he tired of her habit and killed her with an overdose? Had the millionaire's wife sent someone to kill her? Her head buzzed with all sorts of horrible images.

Then came the thought that she was all alone. Rachel had been the last living member of her family. The anguish of her sister's machinations and lies was over, but so was the last bond of kinship she had.

She thought of their father and wondered if he'd been there to meet Rachel when she crossed over. He'd loved the other sister so much. He hadn't loved Ivy. He didn't think Ivy was his. Was she? Had Rachel lied about that, too, as she'd lied about so many other things?

Maybe Rachel had left a note, a letter, something, to explain her hatred of Ivy. If she went to New York, maybe she could find it. Maybe she could understand the other woman, at long last.

She started packing.

7

Luckily, Ivy had enough in her savings account to cover a reduced fare round-trip airline ticket to New York. But once there, she would have expenses. She'd have to find somewhere to stay—she couldn't bear to stay at Rachel's apartment with the drug-dealing boyfriend lurking nearby—and there would be cab fare and then the cost of bringing Rachel home. It was a nightmare. If Stuart had been at home, she might have been bold enough to call him and ask for help. But it was too soon in their changing relationship for that.

On the other hand, she could call Merrie. But Ivy was too proud. It would sound as if she needed charity. No, she had to stand on her own two feet and do what was necessary. She was a grown woman, not a child. She could do this.

She'd never been on an airplane in her life. It was an adventure, from going through security to takeoff, which she compared in her mind to blasting off in a spaceship. She was sitting next to a nice elderly couple in tourist class. They were friendly, and seemed amused at her fascination with air travel.

Once at La Guardia, she took a cab to a modestly priced hotel that Lita had told her about, which was in Brooklyn, not too far from Rachel's apartment. She also had the number of the police sergeant who'd told her about her sister's death.

She checked in at the hotel and took time to go upstairs with her single suitcase. The room was small, but neat and clean, and there was a lovely view of the city skyline. She wondered how she was going to bear the loneliness of it, though, after she went to the morgue to identify her sister's body. The ordeal was one she dreaded.

Sergeant Ames wasn't in his office when she got there, so she took a seat in the waiting room. The police precinct seemed in a constant case of chaos. People came and went. Lawyers came to see clients. Reporters came to talk to detectives. Uniformed officers came and went. It was a colorful mix of people, especially to Ivy, who was used to living in a town of only two thousand people.

A few minutes later, a tall, dark-haired, good-looking man in a suit approached her.

"Miss Conley?" he asked, smiling.

She stood up. "Yes. Are you Sergeant Ames?"

"I am." They shook hands. "Sorry I was late," he added, leading her to his cubicle and offering her a seat. "I had to testify in a murder trial. Court just let out."

"Have you learned anything else about my sister's death?" she asked.

"Just that her boyfriend has a record as long as my desk," he replied curtly. "He has clients in high places around town. Apparently your sister was involved with one of them, a married man, and the client's wife was none too happy about the affair. She made threats against your sister's life. Then there's the boyfriend. A neighbor of theirs told one of our investigators that your sister and her boyfriend had frequent violent arguments. During their latest one, he told her to leave his client alone and she threatened to go to the police with information she said could convict him of drug smuggling." He folded his hands on the cluttered desk. "As you can tell, there's no shortage of suspects if it does turn out to be a case of murder." He frowned. "Is someone with you? Family? A boyfriend, perhaps?"

She shook her head. "I don't have any relatives, except Rachel," she replied. She thought about Stuart, but kisses didn't make relationships. "And no boyfriend," she added reluctantly. "There was no one I could ask to come with me."

He grimaced. "You're not going to try to stay in your sister's apartment?" he asked quickly.

"No," she told him. "I couldn't bear to stay there. I have a room in a small hotel for the night."

"Have you ever had to deal with a death in your family before?"

"My father died two years ago," she said. "But Rachel made all the arrangements. I just paid the bills. I don't know exactly what to do," she confessed.

"I'll walk you through the procedure," he said in a gentler tone. "What can you tell me about your sister's private life?"

"Probably no more than you know already," she said apologetically. "Rachel was older than me, and she didn't like me. She only got in touch with me when I could do something for her."

He studied her quietly. "You weren't close?"

She shook her head. "Rachel didn't want to live in a small town. She wanted to be an actress on Broadway." She felt a terrible emptiness in the pit of her stomach. "I knew that she used drugs. She's done that for a long time, ever since high school. But I never thought she'd die so young." Tears ran down her cheeks. "It's just been so sudden."

"May I make a suggestion?"

She wiped her eyes. "Of course."

"You said that you have a hotel room?"

"Yes," she replied.

"Go to it and rest for a couple of hours. Call me when you're ready and I'll take you to the morgue to identify her. How about that?"

She almost argued. But he was a kind man, she could see it in his dark eyes. She smiled. "I would like to do that. Thank you."

He stood up. "I'll have one of the guys drop you off at your hotel," he added, as if he knew how limited her funds were.

"Thank you," she said gently.

He smiled. "No problem. I'll see you later."

It wasn't even lunchtime yet. She wasn't hungry. The flight had taken away her appetite. She lay down on the bed covers and closed her eyes. The ordeal was still in front of her. But the sergeant had been right, a few minutes' rest might help her face the morgue.

She must have drifted off, because a persistent knocking sound brought her back to the present. She climbed off the bed, wiping at her sleepy eyes, and went to the door. She looked through the peephole and couldn't believe her eyes.

She threw open the door and ran into Stuart's warm, strong arms. She held on for dear life, sobbing, so happy to see him that she couldn't even pretend.

"It's all right, honey," he said softly, drawing her into the room. He closed and locked the door and then lifted her, carrying her to the bed. He sat down on it and cradled her across his knees. "I know it's hard. Whatever else she was, she was still your sister."

"How did you know?" she sobbed into his shoulder.

"The cabdriver who took you to the airport is Mrs. Rhodes's second cousin. He phoned her and she phoned me." His arms tightened. "Why didn't you call me?" he asked. "I would have been there like a shot."

She didn't have that much self-confidence, especially where he was concerned. But miraculously, here he was. She'd never needed someone this much in her life. She wasn't alone anymore.

She cuddled up against him, shivering a little with relief. "I have to call Sergeant Ames and he'll take me to identify…identify the body."

"I'll do that for you," he said softly.

She looked up into his pale blue eyes. "I can do it," she said. "If you'll go with me."

He smiled. "Of course I will." The smile faded. "How did she die?"

"I don't know. The police aren't sure, either. He said they'll have to do an autopsy to find the cause of death." She laid her cheek against his broad chest. "Her apartment will have to be gone through and her things removed. Then I have to decide whether to have her cremated or bring her home to Jacobsville and bury her there, near our parents."

"Rachel wouldn't have cared what you did with her," he said coldly.

"I'd really rather have her cremated," she told him sadly. She didn't want to mention that the expense of transporting a coffin to Jacobsville was too overwhelming for her. She was sure that Rachel had no health insurance, or life insurance. And even if she had, there was no doubt that Jerry would have had himself put on the policy as beneficiary. But that still left Ivy with the funeral expense.

"Then, we'll see about doing that," Stuart said after a minute. "But first things first. We'll go to the morgue, then we'll find a funeral home. After we've made the arrangements, we'll go back to her apartment and see what needs doing there."

"You make everything sound so simple," she remarked.

"Most things are. It's just a matter of organization."

She sat up on his lap, dabbing at her eyes. "Sorry. I just lost it when I saw you. I thought I'd have to do all this alone."

He pulled out a white handkerchief and put it in her hands. "Dry your eyes. Then we'll call your sergeant and get the process started. Okay?"

She smiled. "Okay."

Stuart tried to keep her from looking at Rachel, but she insisted. She wanted to see how her sister looked.

It was bad. Rachel was gray. There was no expression on her face, although it was pockmarked and very thin. She looked gruesome, but it was definitely Rachel.

Stuart and Sergeant Ames escorted her back to Ames's office, where they sat around his desk drinking cups of black coffee until Ivy was fortified enough to talk.

"We're going to have an autopsy done," Ames told them, "but the medical examiner says it's pretty conclusive that she died of a massive overdose of cocaine."

"Is that why she looks the way she does?" Ivy asked, dabbing at her eyes with Stuart's handkerchief. "I mean, her face looks pockmarked."

"That's the crystal meth she'd been using," he replied. "It's the most deadly drug we deal with these days. It ravages the user. A few months on it and they look like zombies."

"Why?" she asked suddenly. "Why would anyone use something like that in the first place?"

"People have been asking that question for years, and we still don't have an answer. It's one of the most addictive drugs," the detective told her gently. "Once it gets into their systems, people will literally kill to get it."

"How horrible," she said, and meant it.

"How long had she been using?" he asked Ivy.

"Since she was in high school," she told him dully. "I told my father, but he didn't believe me. He said Rachel would never do drugs." She laughed hollowly. "She'd come to see us when she was high as a kite, and my father never even noticed."

"Her father drank," Stuart interrupted solemnly. "I don't think he noticed much."

Ivy grimaced. "I never imagined she'd end up like this."

"What about her boyfriend?" Stuart wanted to know.

Ames shrugged. "We've managed to get a couple of convictions against him, but even so, he gets out of jail in no time, and goes right back to his old tricks. A couple of his clients are powerful figures in the city."

"On all the best television shows, the drug dealers go away for life," Ivy pointed out.

Ames chuckled. "I wish it was that way. It's not. For hundreds of reasons, drug dealers never get the sentences they deserve."

"When will they do the autopsy?" Ivy asked.

"Probably tonight," Ames said. "They don't have a backlog, for the first time in months. Once we have a cause of death, we can decide where to go from there."

"What about her apartment?" Ivy asked. "Is it all right for us to go there?"

"Yes," he replied and, reaching into his middle desk drawer, produced a key. "This is a copy of the key to her apartment, which we have in the property room. I thought you'd need access, so I had this one made. We've already processed her apartment."

"I'll need to clean it out and pack up whatever little family memorabilia she kept, so I can take it home with me," Ivy said dully.

"How well do you know Jerry Smith?" the detective asked her.

"I've seen him a few times," she replied. "I never liked him. I have migraine headaches," she added. "He came home with Rachel when our father died. I had the headache and he switched my medicine for some powerful narcotics. I realized he'd substituted something for my prescription pills, and I refused to take what he gave me. He thought it was funny."

Stuart looked murderous. "You never told me that," he accused.

"I knew what you'd do if you found out," she replied. "That man looks to me like he has some really dangerous connections."

"I have a few of my own," Stuart replied curtly. "Including two Texas Rangers, an FBI agent and our local sheriff. You should have told me."

She grimaced. "I was glad when Rachel and Jerry went back to New York."

"I'm not surprised," the sergeant said. "I have your sister's effects in the property room. If you'll come with me, I'll get them for you. You'll have to sign them out."

"All right." She stood up, feeling numb. "Thank you for being so kind."

"It goes with the job description," he assured her.

Stuart had hired a limousine. Ivy found it fascinating. She wished she wasn't so transparent to him. He seemed amused that she wanted to know everything about the expensive transportation.

He had the driver wait for them at Rachel's apartment building. He escorted Ivy up the stairs to the second floor apartment and opened the door. It was just the way Rachel had left it, except for the white outline that showed where her body had been.

Ivy was taken aback at the graphic evidence of her sister's death. She stood there for a moment until she could get her emotions under control. "I don't know where to begin," she said.

"Try the bedroom," Stuart suggested. "I'll go through the drawers in the living room."

"Okay."

She wandered into Rachel's bedroom, her eyes on the ratty pink coverlet, the scattered old shoes, the faded curtains. Rachel had always told everybody back home that she was getting good parts in Broadway plays and making gobs of money. Ivy had even believed it.

But she should have realized that Rachel wouldn't have been so persistent about their father's money unless she was hurting for it. A rich woman would have less need for a parent's savings.

Ivy opened the bedside table, feeling like a thief as she looked inside. There was a small book with an embroidered cover. A diary. Absently, Ivy stuck it in the pocket of her jacket and moved to the dresser.

There was hardly anything in the dresser except for some faded silk lingerie and underwear. The closet, however, was a surprise. Inside were ten exquisite and expensive evening gowns and two coats. Ivy touched them. Fur. Real fur. There were expensive high heeled shoes in every color of the rainbow on the floor of the closet.

She opened the jewelry box on the dresser and gasped. It could be costume jewelry, of course, but it didn't look cheap. There were emeralds and diamonds and rubies in rings and necklaces and earrings. It looked like a king's ransom of jewelry. What in the world had Rachel done to get all this, she wondered?

Stuart came in, his hands deep in his pockets, frowning. "She's got a big plasma television, a top-of-the-line DVD player and some furniture that came from exclusive antique shops. How did she manage all that without visible means of support?"

"That's a good question," Ivy replied. "Look at this."

Stuart looked over her shoulder at the jewels. He picked up a ring and looked at the inscription inside the band. "Eighteen karat gold," he murmured. "The stones are real, too."

"Do you think she stole them?" Ivy asked worriedly.

"I don't think it's likely that she owned them," he replied. "There's about a hundred thousand dollars worth, right here in this tray."

Her gasp was audible. "I thought it might be costume jewelry."

He tilted her chin up to his eyes. "You don't know a lot about luxury, do you, honey?" he asked softly. He bent and touched his mouth gently to hers. "I like you that way."

The touch of his mouth was almost her undoing, but she couldn't forget the task at hand. "Where do you think she got all this?" she persisted.

"If she was hanging out with a millionaire, I imagine he gave it to her."

"His wife will want it all back."

He nodded. "If she knows it's here." He frowned. "I'm surprised that Ames didn't take it and put it in the property room."

"Maybe he thought it was fake, too."

He chuckled. "No. That guy knows his business. He may have some sort of surveillance camera in here, waiting to see if anyone carries off the jewels."

"That's not a bad idea," she mused.

He closed the lid of the jewelry box. "No, it isn't." He checked his watch. "It's going on lunchtime. We can go back to my hotel and have room service send something up to us."

"I have my own room," she reminded him.

"We'll cancel it and pick up your suitcase," he replied. "I'm not letting you out of my sight," he added somberly. "Especially while we don't know exactly why your sister died."

She started to argue. He held up a hand. "I won't give up or give in. Just come along and don't fight it."

"You're very domineering," she accused.

"Years of working cattle has ruined me for polite society," he said with a twinkle in his pale eyes.

She laughed, as she was meant to. "All right," she said after a minute. She didn't mind being guided at the moment. She was worn. He picked up the jewelry box and put it in her hands.

"Her boyfriend will say these belong to him," he said. "But he's not getting them without a fight. We'll put them in a safe-deposit box for the time being."

"That's a good idea," she agreed. "He may not have killed her, but he helped her get where she is now. He shouldn't profit from her death."

"I agree."

On the way to the hotel, he stopped at a bank where he obviously had an account and asked for access to his own safe-deposit box. They deposited the jewelry box in it. He asked to speak to one of the vice presidents of the bank, who came out of his office, smiling, to motion Stuart and Ivy into it. Stuart asked him about funeral parlors in the city and was referred to a reputable one. The bank officer gave Stuart the number.

When they were back in the limousine, Stuart dialed the number and spoke to one of the funeral directors. He made an appointment for them later that afternoon to speak about the arrangements. The funeral home would arrange for transport of Rachel's body when the medical examiner released it. Then they went by Ivy's hotel and picked up her suitcase. Stuart, despite her protests, paid for the room.

"We can argue about it when we're back home," he told her.

His hotel room made hers look like a closet. It was a penthouse suite, one of those that figured in presidential visits, she guessed. Stuart took it for granted. He phoned room service and ordered food.

"You should have asked for more than that," he said when she was through a bowl of freshly made potato soup.

"It was all I thought I could eat," she said simply. "It hasn't been the best day of my life." She put down the spoon. "I don't think it's hit me yet," she added solemnly. "I feel numb."

"So did I, when my father died," he said, putting down his fork. He poured second cups of coffee for them both before he spoke again. "I was sure that I hated him. He'd spent his life trying to force me to become what he couldn't. But when it happened, I was devastated. You never realize how important a parent, any parent, is in your life until they're not there anymore."

"Yes," she agreed. "Nobody else shares your memories like a parent. My father was bad to me. He always preferred Rachel, and he never tried to hide it." She sighed. "Maybe it's a good thing that I know he didn't believe I was his child. It makes the past a little easier to bear. I wish I knew for sure, though."

"We'll find out. I promise you we will."

She stared at him across the table. "You must be letting deals get by while you're up here with me," she said.

He shrugged. "There's nothing any of my managers can't handle. That's why I hire qualified people, so that I can delegate authority when I need to."

She smiled. "I'm very glad. I could have done this by myself. But I'm glad that I didn't have to."

He finished his coffee and put his napkin on the table. His pale eyes caught hers from the other side of the table. "I'd never have let you go through this alone," he said quietly.

The words were mundane, but his eyes were saying things that made her heart jump up into her throat. A faint wave of color stained her cheeks.

He smiled slowly, wickedly. "Not now," he said in a deep, slow drawl. "We've got too much to do. Business now. Diversions later."

The blush went nuclear. She got up from the table, fumbling a little with her coffee cup in the process.

He laughed. She was as transparent as glass to a man with his experience. It made him feel taller to see that helpless delight in her face. He was glad he'd come to New York. And not just because Ivy needed help.

They sat in the funeral director's office, going over final arrangements for Rachel. Ivy decided on cremation. It was inexpensive, and Stuart had already mentioned that he was flying his own twin-engine plane home. There wouldn't be any problem with getting the urn containing Rachel's ashes through security.

She picked out an ornate black and gold brass urn. "I can have our local funeral director bury it in the space next to Daddy," she told Stuart.

"Some people keep the ashes at home," the director remarked.

"No, I don't think I could live in the house if Rachel was sitting on the mantel," Ivy said quietly. "My sister and I didn't get along, you see."

The director smiled. "I have a brother I couldn't get along with. I know how you feel."

They went back into his office and Ivy signed the necessary papers and wrote a check for the cost of the expenses, despite Stuart's protests.

Later, in the limousine, he voiced his disapproval. "You've got enough to do supporting yourself," he said curtly. "Rachel's funeral cost is pocket change to me."

"I know that," she replied. "But you have to understand how I feel, Stuart. It's my sister and my responsibility."

He caught her hand in his and held it tight. "You always were an independent little cuss," he mused, smiling at her.

She smiled back. "I like the feeling that I can stand on my own two feet and support myself," she replied. "I never had a life of my own as long as Rachel was alive. She was even worse than Dad about trying to manage me."

He pursed his lip. "Do I detect a double meaning?"

She laughed. "No. Well, yes. You do try to manage me." She stared at him curiously. "And I don't know why. You were just going around with some beautiful debutante. There was a photograph of you in a tabloid two weeks ago," she added and then flushed because that sounded like jealousy.

But he only smiled. "That photo was taken four years ago. God knows where they dug it up."

She blinked. "Excuse me?"

"The photograph was taken years ago. See this?" He indicated a tie tack that she'd given him for his birthday three years ago. "I always wear it with my suits. Look in the photo and see if you see it."

In fact, she hadn't seen it in that photo. It amazed her that he prized such an inexpensive present. And that he wore it constantly. "You like it that much?" she asked, diverted.

Instead of a direct answer, his hand slipped to her collar and dipped under it to produce a filigree gold cross that he'd given her for Christmas three years past. "You never take it off," he said, his voice deep and slow. "It's in every photo of you that my sister takes."

"I…it's very pretty," she stammered. The feel of his knuckles against her soft skin was delightful.

"Yes, it is. But that isn't why you wear it, any more than I wear the tie tack because it's trendy."

He was insinuating something very intimate. She stared into his pale eyes as they narrowed, and darkened, and her breath began to catch in her throat.

"We're both keeping secrets, Ivy," he said in a deep, soft tone. "But not for much longer."

She searched his pale eyes, looking for a depth of feeling that matched her own. He was familiar, dear. When she and Merrie were in high school, she'd felt breathless when he walked into a room. She hadn't realized, then, that the feelings she got when he was around were the beginnings of aching desire.

He traced the outline of her soft lips with his forefinger, making her tingle all over. He smiled, so tenderly that she felt she could fly. Any idea she'd had that he was playing a game with her was gone now. No man looked at a woman like this unless he cared, even if only a little.

8

Ivy felt as if the ground had been pulled out from under her as she stared into Stuart's pale eyes. His gaze dropped to her soft, full mouth and lingered there until she thought her heart would burst out of her chest. She stared at his hard mouth and remembered, oh, so well, the feel of it against her own. The need was like a desperate thirst that nothing could quench. She started to lean toward him. His hand contracted. His face hardened. She could see the intent in his eyes even before he reached for her.

And just then, the car lurched forward as the traffic light changed, separating them before they'd managed to get close.

Ivy laughed breathlessly, nervous and shy and on fire with kindling desire.

He cocked an eyebrow. "You're safe," he murmured, although he still had her hand tight in his. "But don't get too comfortable."

She only smiled. His eyes were promising heaven. It seemed impossible that they'd been enemies for so long. This familiar, handsome, compelling, sexy man beside her had become someone she didn't know at all. The prospect of the future became exciting. But even as she felt the impact of her own feelings for him, she remembered why she was in New York City. Dreams would have to wait for a while.

They went back to Rachel's apartment to arrange things. Stuart went down to talk to the apartment manager. Ivy stayed in the apartment and began going through drawers again.

She found a photo album. She sat down with it on the couch and opened it. As she expected, the photos were all of Rachel. There was one of their father, sitting on the porch swing at his house. There were a few of their mother. There wasn't one single picture of Ivy anywhere in the album. It stung. But it wasn't unexpected.

She put the album aside and picked up a letter, addressed to Rachel and marked Private. It was trespassing. She felt guilty. But she had to know what was in the letter, especially when she read the return address. It was an expensive stationery, and the return address was that of a law firm in Texas.

Just as she started to open it, she heard footsteps. They weren't Stuart's. She stood up and slipped the letter into her slacks' pocket just as the door flew open.

Jerry Smith walked into the apartment as if he owned it. He was somber and angry. His narrow eyes focused on Ivy with something like hatred.

"What are you doing here?" Ivy asked coldly.

He shut the door behind him and smiled. The smile was sleazy, demeaning. He looked at Ivy as if she were a streetwalker awaiting his pleasure.

"So, it's the little sister, come looking for buried treasure, is it? Don't get too comfortable here, sweetheart. Everything in this apartment is mine. I paid for all this." He swept his arm around the room. "Mustn't steal things that don't belong to you," he added in a sarcastic undertone.

She would have backed down even a year ago. But she'd spent too much time around Stuart to cave in, especially when she knew he was nearby and likely to return any minute. This sleazy drug dealer didn't know that, and it was her ace in the hole.

"Any photographs and quilts and paintings in here are mine," she returned icily. "You don't get to keep my family heirlooms."

"Quilts." He made the word sound disgusting. "Rachel thought they were worth a fortune, because they were handmade. She took them to an antique dealer. He said they were junk. She tried to give them away, but nobody wanted them. She used them to pack her crystal in, for when she planned to move next month." He shrugged. "I guess she won't be moving anywhere."

Her relief at knowing the quilts weren't trashed disappeared when he made that odd statement. "Rachel never said anything about moving. Where was she moving to?"

"Back to your little hick town, apparently," he said. "She owned a house there."

"She didn't," Ivy returned, and felt guilty as relief flooded her. Rachel had planned to come home and let Ivy be her personal slave. "She sold the house two years ago."

"Whatever. She didn't remember much. I warned her about that damned meth. I don't even sell it, because it's so dangerous, but she got hooked on it and wouldn't quit."

"Did you kill her?" Ivy asked curtly.

"I didn't have to," he muttered. "She stayed comatose half the time, ever since she lost that big part she'd just landed in a play that's starting on Broadway in a couple of months. Her lover's wife knew the producer. She had him drop Rachel, then she called and told her all about it. She promised Rachel that she'd never get a starring role ever again. That was when she hit bottom."

"They're doing an autopsy."

He shrugged. "They usually do, when people die suddenly. I didn't kill her," he repeated. "She killed herself." He looked around, his eyes narrowing. "Don't take anything out of here until I have time to go through her things."

"I've already taken her jewelry to a bank for safekeeping," Ivy returned.

"You've what?" He moved toward her, his hands clenched at his sides. "That jewelry is worth a king's ransom! She wheedled it out of that old man she was sucking up to!"

"Which means it belongs to him," Ivy replied.

"You'd really give it back to him, wouldn't you?" he taunted. "God, what an idiot you are! Tell you what, you give me half of it and I'll forget where it went."

"You can only bribe dishonest people," she said quietly. "I don't care that much about money. I only want to make a living."

"Rachel would have kept the lot!"

"Yes, she would have. She took and took and took, all her life. The only human being she ever cared about was herself."

"Well, you're not blind, are you?" He moved into the

bedroom and opened drawers while Ivy hoped that Stuart would come back soon. Seconds later, Jerry barreled out of the bedroom. "Where is it?"

She blinked. "Where is what?"

"The account book!"

She frowned. "What account book? There wasn't any account book here!"

He went white in the face. "It's got to be here," he muttered to himself. He started going through drawers in the spacious living room, taking things out, scattering them. "It's got to be here!"

She couldn't understand what he was so upset about. Obviously there would be some sort of record of rent and other expenditures, but who kept a journal in this day and time?

"Wouldn't it be on the computer?" she asked, indicating the laptop on the dining room table.

"What? The computer?" He turned on the computer and pulled up the files, one by one, cursing harshly as he went along. "No, it's not here!" He stared at her over the computer. "You took it, when you took the jewelry, didn't you?" he demanded. "Did you get my stash, too?"

He strode into the bathroom. Loud noises came from the room. He appeared again with some small bags of white powder. "At least only one is missing," he said, almost to himself. He stuffed the bags into his pants pockets. He glared at Ivy. "I don't know what your game is, but you'd better find that journal, and quick, if you know what's good for you."

"What journal?" she demanded. "For heaven's sake, my sister just died! I'm not interested in your household accounts!"

He glared back.

"Did she have any life insurance?" she asked, forcing herself to calm down. "A burial policy?"

"She didn't expect to die this young," he returned. "No, there's no life insurance." He smiled coolly. "You can leave the apartment and its contents to me. Now take whatever you want of her 'heirlooms,' and then get the hell out of this apartment."

She wanted to argue, but Stuart would be here soon, and after Jerry got his comeuppance, he wasn't likely to let her back in again. She retrieved the quilts out of the closet, leaving the crystal stacked neatly on the floor. She took the photo album, although the photos were mostly of Rachel. She took none of the dresses or gowns or shoes or furs. Rachel's whole life boiled down to frivolous things. There wasn't a single book in the entire apartment.

Clutching the quilts and the photo albums, she moved back into the living room, where Jerry was still pulling open drawers, looking for the mysterious journal.

He seemed surprised when he saw what she had. "There were evening gowns in the closet. Weren't you interested in them? You and Rachel were almost the same size."

"I can buy my own clothes," she replied. It was a sore spot. Just once, when she was sixteen, she'd asked to borrow one of Rachel's gowns to wear to the prom. Rachel had asked why, and Ivy had confessed that a nice boy from the grocery store had invited her to the prom. So when he came to the house, Rachel had flirted with him and before he left, Rachel had teased him into driving her to Houston to see some friends on the same night as the prom. Then Rachel had mocked Ivy about borrowing the gown, adding that she hardly needed one since she no longer had a date.

"Did Rachel send you anything to keep for her?" Jerry persisted.

"Rachel only phoned me when she wanted me to send her something," she replied. "She wouldn't have trusted me with anything. She never did."

"Yeah, she said you stole her stuff when she was living at home."

Ivy's face went red with bad temper. "I never took anything of hers. It was the other way around. She could tell a lie to anyone and be believed. It was her greatest talent."

"I guess you were jealous of her, because she was so beautiful," he replied.

"I'm not jealous of people who don't have hearts."

He laughed coldly. "Beauty makes up for character."

"Not in my book."

He moved toward her, noting her quick backward movement. He smiled tauntingly. "Maybe you and me could get together some time. You're not pretty, but you've got spirit."

"I'd rather get together with a snake."

He lifted an eyebrow. "Suit yourself. I guess you'll grow old and die all alone in that hick town you come from." He touched her long, blond hair. "You could have some sweet times if you stayed here with me."

The door flew open and Jerry's face went rigid as the tall, dangerous man saw what Jerry was doing, stalked right up to him, took his hand from Ivy's hair and literally pushed him away.

"Touch her again and I'll break your neck," Stuart said, his whole demeanor threatening.

"Hey, man, I'm cool!" he said, backing even further away with both hands raised, palms out.

The flippant, cocksure young man of seconds before was flushed with nerves. Ivy didn't blame him. Stuart in a temper was formidable. He never lost control of himself, but he never flinched when confronted. The meanest of his cowboys walked wide around him on the ranch.

Ivy felt relief surge up inside her. Instinctively she moved closer to Stuart—so close that she could feel his strength and the warmth of his body. His arm slid around her shoulders, holding her near. She felt safe.

"I was just telling Ivy that this stuff is mine," Jerry said, but not in a forceful tone. "My money paid for it."

"And I told him," Ivy replied, "that all I wanted was whatever heirlooms from my family that Rachel kept here. I've got them…three quilts and a photo album." She was holding them.

"Ready to go?" Stuart asked her calmly, but his cold eyes were pinning Jerry to the wall.

"Yes," she said.

"All right, then."

She grabbed her purse from the table and went through the doorway. Stuart gave Jerry one last, contemptuous look before he closed the door behind them.

"The drug dealer, I take it?" he asked, relieving Ivy of the quilts.

"Yes. He was being very nasty until you showed up. Thanks for saving me."

He chuckled. "You were doing pretty well on your own, from what I saw." He led the way into the elevator and pressed the button for the lobby. "At least you won't have to dispose of the apartment and its contents."

"Yes, that's one worry gone." She looked up at him. "He was desperate to find some sort of account book he said Rachel had. He was frantic when he couldn't locate it."

"Did you find it?" he asked.

She shook her head. "There weren't any account books that I could see. He was furious about the jewelry, too," she added.

"He can try to get them back, if he likes. I have some great attorneys."

"I told him they were going back to the millionaire who gave them to her," she replied.

He laughed. "That must have given him hives."

"He was upset. I meant it, though." She grimaced. "But how am I going to find out who he is?"

"I'll take care of that," he said, so easily that Ivy relaxed. "All you have to worry about is the funeral. And I'll help with that."

"You've been so kind," she began.

He held up a hand. "Don't start."

She smiled. "Okay. But thanks, anyway."

"I couldn't leave you to do it alone." He led her out of the elevator when it stopped and out to the limousine, which was waiting for them just beyond the entrance.

Stuart motioned to the driver and he pulled out of his parking space and around to the front of the apartment building.

The quilts were placed in the trunk and Stuart helped Ivy into the limousine.

They went back to the hotel. Ivy felt drained. She hadn't done much at all, but the stress of the situation was wearing on her nerves.

"You can have the master bedroom," he offered. "I'll have the one across the living room..."

"But I don't need all that room," she protested. "Please. I'd really rather have the smaller of the two."

He shrugged. "Suit yourself." He put her suitcase onto the bed in the smaller room and left her to unpack. "Why don't you lie down and rest for a while? I've got some phone calls to make. Then we'll see about supper."

"I haven't got anything fancy with me," she said as she opened the suitcase. "Oh, no," she muttered, grimacing as she realized that she'd only packed another pair of slacks and two blouses and an extra pair of shoes. She'd forgotten that she was going to spend the night.

"What's wrong?" he asked.

"I didn't pack a nightgown..."

"Is that all?" He pursed his lips, letting his eyes slide down her body. "I can take care of that. You get some rest. I'll be back in a little while. Don't answer the door," he added firmly. He didn't add why. He was sure the tabloids would pick up the story, and some enterprising reporter could easily find out that Ivy was in town to see to her sister's burial arrangements. He didn't want Ivy bothered.

"I won't answer the door." She wanted to offer to give him some money to get her a nightgown, but she didn't have it. The airfare and taxis had almost bankrupted her.

He was gone before she could even make the offer. She kicked off her shoes and put the open suitcase on the folding rack. Then she sank down onto the comfortable bed, in her clothes. She didn't mean to doze off, but she did. The long day had finally caught up with her.

She woke to the smell of freshly brewed coffee. She started sitting up even before she opened her eyes, and a deep, masculine chuckle broke the silence.

"That's exactly how I react to fresh coffee when I've been asleep," he murmured, standing over her with a cup and saucer. The cup was steaming. He handed it to her. "Careful, it's hot."

She smiled drowsily as she took it. The color told her that he'd poured cream in it. He'd remembered that she only liked cream in her coffee. It was flattering. It was exciting. So was the way he was looking at her.

"Hungry?"

"I could eat," she replied.

"I had room service send up a platter of cold cuts," he told her. "Come on in when you're ready."

She took a minute to bathe her face and put her hair back up neatly before she joined him in the suite's living room. The table held a platter of raw vegetables with several dips, as well as cold meats, breads and condiments.

"Have a plate." He offered her one. "I like a steak and salad, but it's too late in the day for a heavy meal. Especially for you," he added, studying her. "You need sleep."

She grimaced. "I haven't really slept since this happened," she confessed. "I always knew Rachel could overdose. But she'd been using drugs for years without any drastic consequences."

"Anyone can take too many pills," he said, "and die without meaning to."

"Yes, like Hayes Carson's brother did," she remarked. "Hayes still isn't over that, and it's been years since his brother died."

He didn't like the reference to Hayes, and it showed. He didn't answer her. He loaded a plate and sat down with his own cup of coffee.

She sat at the table alone, nibbling on food she didn't taste. He was more taciturn than usual. She wondered why the mention of Hayes set him off like that. Perhaps they'd been rivals for a woman's affection. Or maybe it was just because he didn't want to see his sister get serious about Hayes.

"He's not a bad person," she ventured.

He glowered at her. "Did I say that he was?"

"You can't tell Merrie who to date," she pointed out.

He looked totally surprised. "Merrie?"

"She and Carson are friends," she persisted. "That doesn't mean that she wants to marry him."

He didn't answer. He frowned thoughtfully and sipped coffee.

She didn't understand his odd behavior. She finished her food and her coffee. She was worn-out, and the ordeal wasn't over. She still had the cremation ahead of her. There was something else, too. She would be truly alone in the world now. The thought depressed her.

"Are you going to call that man about the jewelry Rachel had?" she asked.

He nodded. "Tomorrow. We'll get everything else arranged then as well." His eyes narrowed. "I'm curious about that ledger Rachel's boyfriend mentioned."

"Me, too," she said wearily. "If he wants it that bad, it must have something to do with his clients."

He didn't say anything immediately. He looked thoughtful, and concerned. "I've heard it mentioned that Rachel knew where to buy drugs in Jacobsville. We both know that it's been a hub for illicit drug trafficking in the past. It still is." He frowned. "That ledger might have some incriminating evidence in it, and not just about Rachel's boyfriend." He stared at her. "You don't have any idea what it looks like?"

She shook her head. "I didn't ask. He was being obnoxious." She smoothed back her hair. "I wish I could feel something," she said dully. "I'm sorry she died that way, but we were never close. She did everything she could to ruin my reputation. I used to think we might grow closer as we aged, but she only got more insulting."

"Rachel liked living high," he said. "She didn't care how she achieved status."

There was something in his tone that made her curious. "She was in your class in high school, wasn't she?"

"Yes." His dark eyes narrowed. "She made a play for me. I put her down. She was vengeful, and you and Merrie were best friends."

That explained why Rachel had suddenly turned against Ivy; she thought Ivy's friendship with Merrie gave her access to Stuart. If Rachel had wanted Stuart, it must have galled her that Ivy was welcome in his house. Rachel might even have guessed how Ivy felt about him, which would have given her a motive to try to convince Stuart that Ivy was promiscuous.

"So she set out to make you think I was running wild," she guessed.

He grimaced. "Yes, she did. I'm sorry to say she might have succeeded, except that Merrie knew you and defended you."

She smiled. "Merrie was always more like a sister to me than Rachel ever was."

"She likes you, too." He got up. "Bed. You need rest."

She hesitated.

He guessed why and chuckled. "I didn't forget." He produced a bag from Macy's and handed it to her. "Sleep well."

"I'll pay you back," she said with determination.

He shrugged. "Suit yourself. Good night."

"Good night." She hesitated at the door to her room. "Stuart…thanks. For everything."

"You'd do the same for anyone who needed help," he replied easily.

She smiled. "I guess so."

She went into her room and closed the door. When she opened the bag, she caught her breath. He'd purchased a gown and peignoir set for her. The gown was pale lemon silk with white lace trim, ankle-length, with a dipping bodice and spaghetti straps. The peignoir had long sleeves and repeated the pattern of the gown. She'd sighed over similar styles in Macy's herself and dreamed of owning something so beautiful. It was even prettier than the set Merrie had loaned her that long-ago night.

She'd never have been able to afford something like this on her budget. She didn't know how she was going to repay Stuart for it, but she had to. She couldn't let him buy something so intimate for her.

She put on the ensemble and brushed out her blond hair so that it haloed around her shoulders and down her back. When she looked in the mirror, she was surprised at how sensual she looked. That was a laugh. What she knew about men would fit on the back of an envelope.

She climbed into bed and turned out the light. She wished she had something to read. She wasn't even sleepy. Her mind went back to the sight of Rachel in the morgue. She forced the memory out and replaced it with lines from a book she'd read about meteorites. That amused her and she laughed to herself. Stuart probably didn't know how fascinated she was about the space rocks, or that she was constantly borrowing books from the library about their structure. She loved rocks. She had boxes of them at her apartment. Everyone teased her about their number and variety. She was forever looking for anything unusual. Once she walked right out into a plowed field to search for meteorites and came away with projectile points instead. Merrie said she should be studying archaeology, and Ivy had replied that chance would be a fine thing.

Even if she didn't study it formally, she knew quite

a lot about the subject. Everyone should have a hobby, after all.

She closed her eyes and thought about the projectile points. She'd taken them to a professor of anthropology at the community college, who'd surprised her by dating them at somewhere around six thousand years old. It had never occurred to her that they were more than a hundred years old. That prompted her to get more books from the library about projectile points. She was surprised to learn that you could date them by their shape and the material from which they were made.

She thought back to the summer she was eighteen. Stuart had been out on the ranch with his cowboys rounding up the bulls, to move them to greener pastures. She'd watched him stand up in the saddle and ride like the wind. The picture had stayed with her when he'd come in for lunch. He had seen her rapt attention as he'd swung down out of the saddle with lazy grace.

He'd looked at her in a curious way, his pale eyes glittering. "Staring at me like that will get you in trouble," he'd said in a deep, slow tone.

She'd laughed nervously. "Sorry. I love to watch you ride," she'd added. "I've never seen anybody look so much at home in the saddle."

He'd given her a strange look. "I did rodeo for several years when I was in my teens," he'd said.

"No wonder you make it look so easy."

He'd reached out and touched her soft hair. His eyes had been intent on her face, and he hadn't smiled. Some odd magnetism had linked them at that moment, so that she could hardly breathe. Even now, almost three years later, she could still feel the pure intensity of that look he gave her. It was when she'd realized how she was starting to feel about him.

For just a few seconds, his pale eyes had dropped to her soft mouth and lingered until she flushed. She waited, breathless, for his head to bend. And it had started to. Then one of the cowboys had called to him. He'd walked away as if nothing at all had happened. After that, he'd avoided Ivy. Right up until that fateful night she'd spent with Merrie in a borrowed lemon-colored gown…

Somewhere music was playing softly. Perhaps Stuart had the radio on in the adjoining part of the suite. It was sweet music, sultry and slow. As she listened to it, she began to drift away.

She was a little girl again, running out through the fields around the house where she'd grown up. She was wearing jeans and an old white shirt and, as usual, she searched for unusual rocks.

Behind her, Rachel was dancing around in a full white gown and high heeled shoes, singing off-key and stumbling around.

Ivy turned and called to her, cautioning her about the sudden deep crevasses in the field. Rachel made a face and replied that she knew what she was doing. Just then, she tripped and fell into one of the deep trenches.

Ivy ran toward her. Rachel was hanging on to a small bush at the edge of the crevasse, screaming at the top of her lungs.

"If I fall, I'll tell everyone that you pushed me!" she threatened.

"I'll save you, Rachel!" Ivy shouted. "Here. Grab my hand!"

"Your hands are dirty," Rachel shouted back. "Dirty, dirty, dirty! You're dirty. You aren't my sister! I hate you! Go away! Go away!"

"Rachel, please…" she pleaded.

But Rachel jerked her hand back. She made a rude gesture with her hand and leaned back, falling deliberately into the darkness below.

"You killed me, Ivy. You killed me!" she yelled as she fell faster. Then there was a scream, piercing and terrifying. It went on and on and on…

9

"Ivy. Ivy! Wake up!"

Strong hands held her by the wrists. She was being lifted, higher and higher. Rachel had fallen to her death, but this determined voice wouldn't let Ivy follow her. She took a deep breath and slowly opened her eyes.

Stuart's eyes were there, filling the world. She blinked sleepily.

"Wake up, sweetheart," he said gently. "You were having a nightmare."

She searched his face. "Rachel wouldn't let me help her. She fell into a crevasse. I couldn't save her."

His hands became caressing on her wrists. "It was only a dream. You're safe."

"Safe."

His gaze dropped to her bodice and his face seemed to clench. "You're sort of safe," he amended.

She was awake now, and she realized suddenly why Stuart was staring at her like that. Her bodice had dropped so that one of her pretty, firm breasts was on open display. Stuart had a ruddy color across his high cheekbones and his teeth were clenched, as if he were exerting maximum self-control.

"You…you shouldn't look at me, like that," she stammered as color shot into her own cheeks.

"I can't help it," he said huskily. "You have the most beautiful breasts I've ever seen, Ivy."

She couldn't have uttered a word to save her life. He knew it, too. His big hands let go of her wrists and took her by the shoulders instead. His thumbs eased the tiny straps over her shoulders and down her arms. The bodice fell to her waist.

He was only wearing silk pajama bottoms. His broad, hair-covered chest was almost touching her bare breasts.

"As I recall," he whispered, "this is about where we left off, two years ago. I even got the color of the gown right."

He had, but she couldn't answer him. She couldn't breathe. The clean, sexy scent of his body wafted up into her nostrils. She felt his breath against her lips as his hands became lightly caressing on her upper arms. The tension between them twisted like cord. Ivy trembled all over as the slow, exquisite pleasure began to grow.

"What the hell," he whispered at her mouth. "It's this or go crazy…"

His mouth opened on her soft lips in a hard, insistent pressure that held traces of desperation. His arms swallowed her, grinding her bare breasts against the warm muscles of his chest.

She moaned jerkily at the rush of sensation.

He hesitated. "Did I hurt you?" he whispered.

"Oh, no," she whispered back, shyly lifting her arms around his neck. "I didn't know…it would feel like this."

He smiled slowly. "Didn't you?" He bent again, but this time his mouth was less desperate. It was tender, teasing. He nibbled her lower lip and smiled again as she parted her lips to lure him closer. His thumb probed gently, coaxing her mouth to open. When it did, his tongue slowly trespassed inside. "No, don't fight it," he whispered against her lips. "It's as natural as breathing…"

She felt him lift and turn her, so that she was lying on her back. His powerful body eased down over hers, one long leg insinuating itself between both of hers over the gown.

She stiffened, wanting more and afraid of it, all at once.

He lifted his head and searched her wide, apprehensive

eyes. He brushed the hair back from her temples. His body was half over her and half beside her on the wide bed. But he didn't seem to be in a hurry. He bent and brushed his mouth over her eyelids, closing them. She felt her breasts go tight, pressed so hard up against him. She was aching for something she didn't understand.

He seemed to know it. "Ivy?"

"What?" she managed shakily.

"Lie back and think of England," he murmured wickedly.

A laugh jerked out of her tight throat.

He lifted his head, grinning down at her. He propped on an elbow while his other hand began to trace lightly, boldly, around a distended nipple. "Or, in our case, lie back and think of Texas." He bent again, brushing his open mouth along her collarbone. He felt her body shudder. He smiled against her soft skin as his mouth slowly trespassed down, close to but never touching the nipple. She began to twist helplessly as the sensations overwhelmed her. She was new to this kind of physical pleasure. Her reactions were unexpected, even to herself.

Her short nails bit into his shoulders as his mouth teased at her breast.

"You haven't done this before," he murmured, savoring her response.

"No," she agreed. She shivered as his mouth grew

slowly insistent. "Stuart…!" she ground out as his lips traced very lightly closer and closer to the nipple.

"What do you want?" he whispered against her breast. "Tell me."

"I…can't," she moaned.

His hand slid under her, lifting her hips up against the slowly changing contour of his powerful body. "Tell me," he coaxed. "You can have anything you want."

She moaned aloud. "You…know!"

"Stubborn," he pronounced. He lifted his head to look down into her misty, fascinated eyes staring blindly up at him. Her whole body was trembling with passion. "You can't imagine how badly I've wanted your breasts under my mouth, Ivy," he told her as his gaze fell to her bodice. "But even in dreams, it was never this good." He moved closer. "I like feeling you tremble when I do this," he whispered as his mouth began to open on the soft flesh. "But it's going to be like a jolt of lightning when I do what you really want me to do…"

As he spoke, his warm mouth moved right onto the nipple and pressed down, hard.

She arched off the bed, crying out. Her whole body shuddered as the pleasure bit into her. She clutched him helplessly, whimpering as his mouth became demanding.

He rolled onto her, nudging her long legs out of the

way so that she could feel him from hip to breast in an intimacy that burst like sensual fireworks in her body.

"Yes," she groaned. "Please, Stuart, please…!" Her voice rose as he pressed her down into the mattress. "Oh, please, don't stop!"

His mouth slid up to cover hers, devouring it, possessing it, as his body moved sensuously over hers. She hung on for dear life. She was losing it. She wanted him. She wanted him so badly that it was almost painful when he suddenly rolled away from her and got to his feet.

She lay there, bare to the waist, shivering in the aftermath, too weakened by her own surrender to even manage to cover herself. She stared at his long back, watching him fight to regain control.

After a minute, he took a long, shuddering breath, and then another, before he turned. He stared at her hungrily, his eyes making a meal of her as she lay there, bare-breasted, her hands by her head on the pillow. He stood over her with eyes that burned like dark fires.

She moved helplessly on the bed.

"No," he said quietly. "There's a time and place. This isn't it."

"You want to," she said with new knowledge of him.

"Good God, of course I do!" he ground out. "I hurt like a teenager after his first petting session. Just for the record, I don't seduce virgins. Ever."

She drew in a short, jerky breath. "How do you know…?"

"Don't be absurd," he interrupted.

Which meant that she was as transparent as glass to him, with his greater experience. Oddly she didn't feel embarrassed or self-conscious. He was looking at her boldly, and she loved his eyes on her body.

"I ache all over," she whispered.

"So do I." He sat down beside her and blatantly traced her breasts with the tips of his fingers. "I could do anything I wanted to you. But in the morning, you'd hate both of us."

It was the truth. She wished it wasn't. "Everybody else does it. They had a poll…"

"Polls can be manipulated." He bent and put his mouth tenderly against her breasts. "Virginity is sexy," he whispered. "I lie awake nights thinking about how I'd take yours."

She flushed.

He laughed. "Tell me you've never thought about doing it with me," he dared.

The flush got worse.

He drew in a long breath. "One of us has to be sensible, and I'm giving up on you," he mused, watching her body move on the sheets. "Come here."

He slid under the covers and tucked her close against

his side. He turned out the light and cuddled her closer. "You can take my word for the fact that I'm violently aroused and desperate for relief. So just lie still, recite multiplication tables and try to sleep."

"You're staying?" she whispered, fascinated.

"Yes. And you won't have any more nightmares. Now go to sleep."

She closed her eyes. She was sure that she couldn't sleep with his warm, powerful body so close to her. But she drifted off almost at once and slept until morning.

When she woke, it was to a throbbing pain in her right eye and nausea that made her lie very still. The headache wasn't unexpected. Stress often combined with other factors to cause them.

Stuart came in with a cup of coffee, but he stopped smiling when he saw Ivy holding her head and pushing against her right eye. "Migraine," he murmured.

She nodded, swallowing hard to keep the nausea down. "I'm so sorry."

"Don't be ridiculous, you don't plan to have headaches. Lie back down."

When he came back, scant minutes later, he had a doctor with him. The doctor smiled pleasantly, asked her a few questions, listened to her heart and lungs and popped a shot into her arm. She closed her eyes, unable even to thank him, the pain was so severe. She eventually dozed off.

The second time she awoke, the pain had reduced itself to a dull echo of its former self. She sat up, drowsy, and smiled at Stuart.

"Thanks," she said huskily.

"I know how those headaches feel," he reminded her. "Can you eat some scrambled eggs and drink some coffee?"

"I think so." She got out of bed and staggered a little from the drugs. "It was just all the pressure," she added. "I always get headaches when I'm under stress."

"I know. Come on." Instead of letting her walk to the table, he swung her up in his arms, in the pale gown, and carried her there. He sat down with Ivy in his lap, within reach of the late breakfast he'd ordered, and began to spoon-feed her eggs and bacon.

She was amazed at the transformation of their relationship, as well as his sudden tenderness. She reacted to it hungrily, never having had anyone treat her so gently in all her life.

He smiled down at her, his dark eyes soft and full of strange lights. When he finished, he cuddled her close and shared a cup of coffee with her. Neither of them spoke. Words weren't even necessary. She felt safe. She felt...loved.

Later, the limousine took them to the funeral home where Rachel's cremated remains were already interred in an ornate bronze urn. The limousine took them from there to the airport, where Stuart's pilot was waiting to fly them home in the Learjet.

It was like a beginning. He held hands with her on the jet. When they loaded her few possessions into his car, which had been left parked at the airport, he held her hand as he drove toward her boardinghouse.

She didn't question it. The feeling was too new, too precious. She was afraid that words might shatter it.

He pulled up in front of Mrs. Brown's house and cut the engine. He helped her out first, then he carried her suitcase and her bags of quilts and photo albums up onto the porch for her. He sat Rachel's urn carefully beside the suitcase.

It was dark. Mrs. Brown hadn't left on the porch light.

"Are you going to be all right?" he asked gently, holding her by the shoulders.

"Yes. My head's fine, now. Stuart," she added slowly, "thank you, for all you've done."

"It was nothing," he replied. "If you hear from that drug-dealing boyfriend of Rachel's, you call me. Okay?"

She nodded. "I will."

"And if you remember anything about where that journal might be, call me."

"I'll do that."

He lifted his hand to her face and traced her soft cheek. "We didn't get to do anything about those jewels, but I promise you I'll get in touch with the man in a day or so and arrange to get them back to him. If you're sure that's what you want."

"It's what's right," she countered quietly. "Rachel had no scruples. I do."

He smiled. "Yes, I know."

She didn't want him to leave. She'd gotten used to being with him, almost intimately, in the past couple of days. Tonight she'd sleep alone. If her headache came back, she'd have to take aspirin and pray for sleep, because he wouldn't be there.

"Don't look like that, or I won't be able to leave you," he said suddenly, his jaw tautening. "I don't want to go home alone, either."

Her soft expulsion of breath was audible.

"Blind little woman," he whispered tenderly, and bent his head. He lifted her completely against his hard body while he kissed her. It took a long time, and when he finally let her down, she shivered with the overwhelming desire he'd kindled in her.

A sudden flash of lightning lit up the sky, followed by a crash of thunder. She jumped. "You be careful going home," she said firmly.

He smiled. "Wear a raincoat if it's still raining in the morning when you go to work," he countered.

She smiled back. Rain was blowing onto the porch, getting them both wet. Neither was wearing a raincoat.

"Go inside," he said, giving her a gentle push toward the door. "I'll phone you tomorrow."

"Okay. Good night."

"Sleep tight," he replied, and winked at her.

She watched him from the open door, after she'd put all her things inside, including the urn with Rachel's ashes. It was as if her life was just now beginning.

Mrs. Brown had gone to bed. Apparently, so had Lita. Ivy moved all her things into her room and placed Rachel's ashes on the mantel. The next day, she was going to see about having them interred in the cemetery next to their father.

She lay awake for a long time, thinking about her new relationship with Stuart. She hoped his attitude meant that they had a shared future ahead. She wished for it with all her heart.

The next day, she remembered that she'd put Rachel's diary in her purse. So before she started her rounds of clients, she took it out and read it. What she'd thought was an ordinary recitation of events turned out to be something quite different. There were names, phone numbers and other numbers that seemed more like map coordinates than anything else.

She read them over and over, and grew even more puzzled. Then she pulled out the letter Rachel had received from a San Antonio law firm. It was dynamite. The letter referenced certain materials she'd put in a safe-deposit box in Jacobsville, to be opened if anything unexpected happened to her. The attorneys wrote to remind her that she hadn't forwarded them the key.

She sat back with a harsh sigh. Rachel was involved in something illegal, she just knew it. And she was clearly blackmailing someone else. Was it the millionaire whose jewels she'd kept? Or was it her boyfriend? Or one of his clients?

She knew immediately that this was too big for her to handle. She phoned Sheriff Hayes Carson and had him come to the boardinghouse. She met him on the porch, smiling as she invited him into the house and into the kitchen, where she had coffee brewing.

"Thanks for coming so quickly," she said, sitting down after she'd poured coffee for them both. "I'm in over my head on this stuff. Here. See what you make of it."

She handed him the journal and the letter from the attorneys in San Antonio that she'd found in Rachel's apartment. He read them, frowning. "These are GPS coordinates," he remarked, running his finger along the columns in the diary. "I recognize two of the names, too," he added. His dark eyes met hers. "They're deep in the Mexican drug cartel that Cara Dominguez was running until her arrest. One of the Culebra drug cartel named here," he added, "is Julie Merrill. The other is Willie Carr, the baker you gave the message about flour to."

She grimaced. "Oh, boy."

"This information is worth its weight in gold, all by itself. But the key she mentioned is missing," he continued. "That key is dynamite. Your life could be in danger if any of her associates even think you might have it. We're talking multimillion dollar drug shipments here."

"But I don't know where the key is," she said miserably. "I looked through all the stuff I got from her apartment. I even checked the quilts to make sure she hadn't slipped it into the backing." She shook her head. "I can't imagine where she might have left it."

"Was there anything else that you took from the apartment?" he asked.

"Just the jewelry she was hoarding," she said miserably. "From that elderly millionaire she was involved with. Stuart and I put them in a safe-deposit box in New York City, under his name. He's arranging to get them back to the man."

He frowned. "Was there a locket, or any sort of thing a key could be hidden in?"

"No," she assured him.

He sipped coffee, frowning. "I don't want to spook you, but isn't there someone you could move in with until we find that key?"

She would have said Stuart and Merrie only a day before. But Stuart hadn't called her, as he'd promised he would. She hadn't heard from Merrie, either. She couldn't just invite herself to be a houseguest under the circumstances.

"No," she said sadly.

"Okay," he said with resolution. "I want to know where you are day and night for the next few days. I'm going to get in touch with Alexander Cobb at DEA and talk to our police chief, Cash Grier, as well. We'll arrange to keep you under surveillance." He picked up the padded diary. "Will you trust me with this?" he asked.

"Of course."

His thumb smoothed over the back of it. Suddenly he went still. His eyes went to the diary. He put it on the table and pulled out his pocketknife. Before she could ask what he was doing, he opened the diary with the pages down on the table and slit the fabric of the back. Seconds later, he pulled out a safe-deposit box key.

"Good heavens!" she exclaimed. "How did you...?"

"Sheer luck," he said. "I felt it under my thumb. I'll have to contact those attorneys in San Antonio and see what the key fits. I may need you, as next of kin, to authorize me to access it."

"Before I can do that, I'll need to meet with Blake Kemp," she replied, "and see about the paperwork to get Rachel's estate—such as it is—into probate."

"If you're not busy right now, I'll drive you over there," he said. "I'd like to talk to him as well."

She grinned. "That would be terrific. Thanks."

Hayes went out onto the porch while she phoned Blake Kemp's office and found him free if they could make it there within the half hour. She assured his new secretary—he'd only recently married his old secretary Violet and they were expecting a child—that she and Hayes would be right over.

She climbed into the unmarked sheriff's car with Hayes, cradling the diary and the attorney's letter with her purse on her lap.

As they pulled out of the driveway, a car that had been sitting parked by the side of the road was quickly started. It pulled onto the road, following slowly behind Hayes Carson's car.

Hayes sat in the waiting room while Ivy spoke to Blake Kemp about Rachel's estate. She didn't have bank statements or any documentation about her possessions, but the attorney's letter intimated that they did. He read the letter, frowning.

Blake shook his head. "She was nothing like you," he said quietly.

"She told Dad that I wasn't his," she replied. "Is there a way to find out…?"

"Not his?" he exclaimed. His blue eyes darkened. "For God's sake, your mother would never have cheated on your father! She worshipped him, despite his bad temper and the way he knocked her around. Besides all that, he'd have killed any man who touched her!"

"Are you sure?" she asked, relieved.

"Yes, I am," he said flatly. "Rachel got exactly what she deserved, Ivy. She was a horror of a human being. Why in God's name would she tell a lie like that?"

"Can't you guess? I can. She wanted everything Dad had when he died. If he thought I wasn't his blood daughter, why would he want to leave me anything?" she asked sadly.

"How many lives did that woman shatter?" he wondered aloud.

"Quite a few, I expect. Her boyfriend was trying to find the journal she kept. He was frantic about it," she recalled, "but it turned out to be her diary. I gave it to

Hayes," she added. "He says it has some vital information about drug smuggling, of all things."

"There's one more thing about Rachel I don't imagine you know," he began, his face solemn. "She didn't just use drugs, Ivy. She sold them, beginning when she was a senior in high school. She always had a direct pipeline to the local drug trade. If she has the documentation mentioned in this letter, it probably names names. That would give Cash Grier a heads-up while he's trying to shut down the newest drug cartel members locally."

"That's what Hayes said," she replied with a smile. "He thinks it may show the position of some drug caches."

"I hope it does," he said. "This little community has gone through some hard times because of drug smuggling. I'd love to see the suppliers shut down."

"So would I."

"Don't worry about the rest of this," he told her. "I'll handle it. But I should talk to Stuart York about that jewelry."

"Yes," she said, concerned that he hadn't phoned her yet. She had her cell phone turned on and she'd been checking it all morning to make sure it was working. It was.

"Let's call Hayes in." He touched the intercom button and had the receptionist send Hayes down the hall to his office.

Hayes showed him the journal. It really was dynamite. It would be wonderful, Ivy thought, if they could really use it to shut down the drug dealers.

"Rachel's boyfriend knows this journal exists," Hayes said somberly. "I wouldn't put it past him to come down here if he thinks Ivy might have it. If Rachel gave her attorneys something damaging about him, and he knows it, he won't have a lot to lose. No evidence, no case."

Both men looked at Ivy.

"I can buy a gun," she began.

"No, you can't," Hayes said firmly. "I have an idea, about where you could stay."

"I can get a motel room…"

"You aren't thinking of Minette and her brood?" Blake asked hesitantly.

Hayes's face went taut. "She lives out of town, where anybody coming to the house would be immediately visible, and her ranch manager was a Secret Service agent some years ago."

"But Merrie York is your best friend," Blake interrupted, eyeing Ivy. "Surely you could stay with her. Stuart has an ex-fed working for him, too."

Her face colored. "Merrie lives in San Antonio," she said. "And I don't think Stuart's home…"

"Sure he's home," Hayes returned. "I saw him driving by this morning with that debutante from Houston he's been seeing."

Ivy felt the life drain out of her. The words kept repeating in her head. Stuart had held her and kissed her and treated her with such tenderness that she thought they were going to be together for life. Instead, the minute they got home from New York, he made a beeline for his latest conquest. He probably hadn't given Ivy a second thought. Maybe he even thought of the way he'd taken care of her as an act of mercy.

She closed her eyes. Pain echoed through her nerves.

"Are you all right?" Hayes asked, concerned. They had left the office and were now in the car.

She forced a smile. "I'm fine. Tell me about this Minette."

He seemed reluctant. "She owns the Jacobsville newspaper. You know that."

"But I've never met her," she pointed out.

He shrugged. "She lives with her aunt and two siblings, a half brother and a half sister. She's off today because there was a fire in the office and they had to call in a cleaning crew to pick up the mess and deal with the fire damage."

"Was it an accidental fire?" she asked.

"I don't know. She's been running some articles about

the drug trade. I warned her that her new ace reporter was going to bring down some heat on the paper, but she wouldn't listen. The eager-beaver reporter is fresh out of journalism school looking for his first shrunken head to flaunt."

"If he points a finger at the wrong people, he'll get her sued."

"Been there, done that," he murmured. "She got Kemp to represent her and won the suit. But she's letting the kid push the wrong people. Sooner or later, there's going to be a tragedy. I tell her so, but she won't listen."

"She's a crusader," she mused.

He gave her a tight glare. "She's showing me that she doesn't take advice if it comes from my general direction. It may get her killed, in the end."

"You should find her some protection," she pointed out. "If she's trying to shut down the drug lords, you and Cash Grier might thank her for the help."

"You don't understand," he growled. "She isn't doing any of us any good. She's pointing out possible hiding places for the influx of illegal drugs and hammering home that foreign nationals are financing the traffic."

"They are."

"Ivy," he said heavily, "at the same time she's hammering the drug trade, she's holding out olive branches to illegal immigrants. She's making enemies on both sides of the drug issue."

Ivy's face softened. "You know Mario Xicara, don't you?"

He slowed for a turn. His lips thinned. "Yes."

"And his wife, Dolores, and their four little kids?"

"I know the family."

"In the village they came from in Guatemala, one man turned in a drug dealer and his whole family was gunned down. To punctuate the threat, they killed six other families as well. Mario escaped with his wife and children, but his parents and grandparents were among the dead, along with their new baby who was in the house when the drug dealer's minions came in firing."

"I know that, but..."

"They're applying for citizenship," she continued. "But now they have to be sent back to Guatemala until they can get temporary papers. The drug dealers are still around their village."

He grimaced. "There are always two sides to every issue," he reminded her.

"I know." She smiled. "But people are more than statistics."

He gave a turn signal. "I'll talk to Homeland Security. I know a man who works in ICE," he said with resignation, naming the enforcement arm of the immigration service.

"Thanks, Hayes."

"Any other small favors I can do you?" he teased.

"I'll make a list. Hayes, this isn't the way to my boardinghouse," she announced suddenly, as she realized they were heading out of town in the wrong direction.

"I know. I've got an idea."

10

Minette Raynor was twenty-four. She was managing editor of the weekly *Jacobsville Times,* the newspaper of Jacobs County. Her mother had inherited the paper from Minette's grandfather, and she ran it until her death. After that, her father and stepmother ran it. He'd died three years previously. Minette had grown up knowing how to sell ads, write copy, set type and paste up copy in the composing room. It was easy for her to step into her parents' shoes and run the paper. She was tall, slender, dark-eyed and blond, with a scattering of freckles over her nose. Her hair was her most incredible asset. It looked like a thick flow of pale gold that inched down her back almost to her waist. It was much longer than Ivy's.

From a deceased uncle, she'd inherited a ranch that raised steers for beef, and it was ramrodded by her late father's wrangler and two part-time cowboys who were students at the local community college. Her great-aunt Sarah lived with her and helped take care of Minette's half brother, Shane, who was eleven, and her half sister Julie, who was five. Minette's mother had died when she was ten, and her father had married Dawn Jenkies, a quiet librarian who adored him and Minette. Over their years together, she presented Dane with a son and a daughter, upon whom Minette doted. When Dawn died, and her father soon after of a heart attack, Minette was left to raise the children. It seemed to be a labor of love.

Hayes pulled up at her front steps, where she and the children were wielding paintbrushes, touching up the fading white of the door facing and wood trim. Minette, in jeans and a sweatshirt, got up, glaring at Hayes.

He glared back. "I need to ask a favor."

She looked furious. "I don't owe you any favors, Sheriff Carson," she said icily.

"I know that. But I have to put Ivy someplace where she'll be safe. Drug dealers may be after her."

Minette's eyes narrowed. She seemed to be biting her tongue.

Carson just looked uncomfortable. "The county will pay for her upkeep," he said curtly. "It's only for a few days."

Minette looked worriedly at her siblings.

"I'm going to have one of my deputies stay here, too," he added. "If you don't mind."

"I always wanted to open a hotel," Minette told him irritably. But when she saw Ivy's consternation, she went to her and smiled. "I'm sorry. You may have noticed that the sheriff and I don't get along. But you're welcome to stay. Aunt Sarah would love the company. I'm at work most days until late." She looked at Hayes viciously. "When I'm not overdosing men, that is."

"Cut it out," he bit off, avoiding her eyes.

Ivy knew at once that Merrie York was out of luck where Hayes was concerned. Something powerful was at work between these two. And it wasn't business.

The little girl, Julie, walked over to Hayes and looked up at him. "Do you got any little kids?" she asked softly.

"Careful, baby," Minette said softly, eyeing Hayes. "Rattlesnakes bite."

He glared at her. She glared back.

He looked down at Julie, who was blond like her half sister. "No, I don't have any kids," he said a little stiffly.

The child cocked her head at him. "That's very sad," she replied, sounding very grown up. "My sister says little kids are sweet." She frowned. "You don't look like a rattlesnake."

"Julie, would you get me a rag from the kitchen, please?" Minette asked her.

"Okay, Minette!" She ran up the steps and into the house.

"You're very welcome to stay with us," Minette told Ivy, her smile welcoming.

"I'll run you back to the boardinghouse to pack a bag," Hayes said.

Ivy hesitated. "Listen, are you sure this is necessary?"

"Mrs. Brown isn't going to be much protection if Rachel's boyfriend comes looking for you," he said.

She grimaced. "All right, then." She smiled at Minette. "I can cook," she said. "If you need help in the kitchen."

The other woman laughed. "Always. Aunt Sarah and I share kitchen duty, but neither of us is overly skilled. Still, we haven't poisoned anyone."

"Yet," Hayes enunciated coldly.

She stood up, eyes blazing. "Someday," she said slowly, "the truth is going to bite you in the neck! I didn't kill your brother. He killed himself. That's what you can't accept, isn't it, Hayes? You want a scapegoat…!"

"You bought the drug for him that he overdosed on!" Hayes shot back.

Minette stood erect, her face pale. "For the twentieth time, I never used drugs, or got drunk, or put a foot out of line in my life," she said proudly. "So how exactly do you think I'd know where to find illegal drugs in this town?"

He looked odd.

"Never mind," she continued. "I'm tired of beating a dead horse. Ivy, we'll get a room ready for you. The one thing we do have plenty of in this white elephant," she indicated the two-story Victorian house, "is room."

"Thanks," Ivy replied. "Hayes?"

He was staring at Minette, frowning. "What? Yes. We'll go now. Minette, I'd like to speak with Marsh."

"He's out in the barn, fixing a saddle."

Hayes took Ivy to the car, and he went to the barn. He was back in a couple of minutes. He got in the car and drove away.

Ivy didn't ask about his feud with the other woman, but she gathered that it had something to do with his brother's death. Everyone knew that Bobby Carson had died of a drug overdose three years earlier, just before Rachel went to New York. Why he thought Minette was responsible was curious. She was known locally for her hard stand on drug use and her support of antidrug programs in the schools.

"She's very nice," Ivy began.

Hayes didn't answer. "You'll be safe. Marsh will keep you safe. Nobody would think of looking for you out there, but even if they did, you'd see them coming a mile away. Not that I think the boyfriend will come all the way down here, since he isn't sure you've got that journal. But it's best to be cautious." He glanced at her. "I still think Merrie and Stuart would have let you stay with them."

She didn't answer him, either.

The next day, she authorized Hayes to open the safe-deposit box in the Jacobsville bank, with Police Chief Cash Grier and DEA Agent Alexander Cobb as witnesses. He picked her up and brought her to the bank.

It was a haul. Rachel had names, locations, dates, quantities of drugs shipped and the point of origin for a huge cocaine shipment. Implicated in the drug trafficking were her boyfriend, a local Jacobsville resident and two men who sat on Jacobsville's city council two years earlier.

"This is great." Cash Grier spoke for the other men as he read through the documentation. "This is enough evidence to shut down one of the biggest pipelines of illicit drugs in south Texas."

"We can certainly use it," Cobb agreed.

"Amen." Hayes smiled at Ivy. "Rachel made up for a lot with this," he said. "Regardless of her motive."

Ivy wondered about that motive. She didn't say it aloud, but she had a feeling that Rachel had been blackmailing somebody. She probably never expected to die, or to have played a big part in shutting down the drug trade in Jacobs County. It was the one noble act of Rachel's life.

It was decided that Ivy would stay at Minette's house. When she packed up her few things and told Mrs. Brown and Lita what was going on, they both tried to get her to stay.

"I have my father's old shotgun," Mrs. Brown said.

"I'm not afraid of drug dealers," Lita added.

"I know that, but it's going to take professionals to keep this from escalating," Ivy told them. "I don't want either of you in danger. Okay?"

They agreed, reluctantly.

Ivy left Rachel's ashes in her room for the time being. Once the fear of retribution from Rachel's boyfriend was past, she could take care of the funeral.

She was given a room next to Minette's, and she became part of the family overnight. Aunt Sarah, a tiny little woman with white hair, was a live wire. The children had sweet, loving natures. Minette had a wicked sense of humor.

"I'm surprised that Hayes would bring you here," she commented over steak and biscuits. "He really hates me."

"Maybe that's why," Ivy chuckled. "He seems to think

I might be a target." She shook her head. "If anything happened to the kids," she added worriedly.

"Don't you worry," Minette assured her. "We have Marsh Bailey out in the bunkhouse. He was an IPSIC shooter. That's pistol competition," she clarified. "He worked for the U.S. Marshal's Service, and he never misses. God help the outlaw who shows up here uninvited."

"I hope he won't," Ivy said. "But Rachel's boyfriend has more to lose than most people. He might figure out that I have the journal she left, and come after me."

"I don't think he's that stupid," Minette ventured, sipping coffee. Her soft eyes pinned Ivy's across the supper table. "Think about it. There's a journal floating around that has names and addresses and the potential to explode the local drug trade. You don't know who's got it or where it is, but you know you'll get blamed if the authorities find it. Would you walk into the arena, or would you run for your life?"

Ivy felt better. "You know," she said, "I think I'd run."

Minette smiled. "I think I would, too."

For the next two days, Ivy stayed with the Raynors. She got her ledgers from the boardinghouse and drove her little VW back to Minette's house. Hayes came by to check on her and mentioned that they'd heard nothing from their informants about the New York connection to the drug trade. However, he did say that the baker had been arrested and charged with drug trafficking. Julie Merrill was still on the loose, however, and nobody, including her father, had any idea where she'd gone.

"We did phone the Brooklyn precinct that worked your sister's death," he added. "It seems that her boyfriend was involved in an accident yesterday. He's in the hospital and not expected to live."

"What happened to him?" she exclaimed.

"It seems he walked into an elevator shaft in his own apartment building," Hayes told her. "There were two eyewitnesses. They have mob ties, of course. The word on the street is that Smith was trying to trespass on another drug dealer's territory."

"Tough," Ivy said, without any real regret. The man who'd helped Rachel feed her habit had gone the same way she had. It was a fitting sort of end. She said so.

"I have to agree."

"Then, do you think I could go home?" she ventured.

He hesitated. "I can't stop you. Smith won't be a problem, but there are some shadowy members of the drug cartel still on the loose. You won't know who they are."

"I have an answer to that," she replied.

"What?"

"Let Minette do a story about the Jacobsville drug

link and say that all Rachel's records are now in the hands of law enforcement," she suggested. "That should put a kink in their operation—and keep them out of Jacobsville."

He began to smile. "I like the way you think. Okay. I'll talk to her about it."

"And I can go home? I still have Rachel's funeral to arrange."

He nodded. "Go ahead. If you need me, you know where I am."

"Yes, I do. Thanks, Hayes."

"No problem."

She did go back to the boardinghouse, but she was nervous, even under the circumstances. She didn't want to endanger Mrs. Brown and Lita. On the other hand, she hadn't felt right about endangering Minette's young siblings. If only Stuart was still speaking to her. She agonized over his defection to the pretty debutante. He'd just dropped Ivy like a rock, and when she needed him most. If she only knew why!

The next day, she drove out to the cemetery, where the funeral home director and his assistant were waiting. The trees were all bare. It was a gray day. It was misting rain as well. It looked such a forlorn place with the cold wind whipping Ivy's hair around.

A small grave had been dug next to her father's, to receive Rachel's urn. There wasn't anyone there except herself. She had thought of putting the obituary notice in the paper, but Rachel had left plenty of enemies in Jacobsville, and few friends.

She was wearing a long gray dress with an equally long tweed coat. The wind was crisp and cruel. She'd been awake half the night thinking about Stuart and wondering what she'd done to make him stay away. They'd been so close in New York. Now, he didn't seem to remember her at all. At least when he'd disliked her, she'd seen him from time to time. She ached to be with him. Even just the sight of him at a distance would feed her hungry heart. But apparently that wasn't going to happen.

The wind blew coldly around her as she stared at the bronze urn that contained the only human remains of her sister. She'd never felt so alone.

The funeral director's assistant, who was also a lay minister, said the words over Rachel's ashes. As Ivy listened, she was sorry that her sister's life had been so wasted, so full of selfish greed. If only Rachel had been different. If only she'd cared about Ivy. She closed her eyes as the prayer ended, hoping that it had helped the older woman in her path to the other side of life.

When she looked up, she was astonished, delighted, shocked to see Stuart York striding toward her. He wasn't smiling. His wide-brimmed dress hat was pulled down low over his eyes. He was dressed in city clothes, a gray suit that made him look distinguished. He paused at the graveside and looked down at Ivy, who couldn't hide her delight, or her wounds.

"I'm sorry I'm late," he said curtly. "I couldn't find out what time you were having the service. If I'd known, Merrie would have come down, too."

"I didn't think anyone would come," she said simply.

His eyes narrowed. "You didn't think, period," he said shortly. His big hand caught her small one and held it tight. She looked up at him, feeling suddenly safe and confident, and tears misted her eyes.

The funeral home director gave Ivy his condolences, along with the lay minister, and then beckoned to the workman to put the urn in its resting place.

"Do you want to stay for this?" Stuart asked.

She nodded. "It's such a sad way to die," she said.

His hand tightened. He didn't say anything.

He walked with her to her vehicle, and his eyes said what he thought of it. "You'd be safer riding a one-wheeled bicycle," he said flatly.

"It doesn't look like much," she agreed, "but it does run. Mostly."

He turned her to him, taking her gently by the shoulders. "I saw you ride off with Hayes Carson the morning after we got in," he said coldly. "You were with him again the next day."

"Yes," she said, surprised, "because he and Chief Grier…"

"…had to oversee the opening of the safe-deposit box," he finished for her, dark eyes flickering. "You could have called and told me that, Ivy."

"Yes?" Her own eyes began to glitter. "And you could have called me, instead of riding around town with your pretty debutante visitor!"

The hard look on his face melted. He began to smile. "Were you jealous?" he taunted softly.

"Were you?" she shot right back.

He laughed. It was a wicked sort of laugh.

It made her cheeks color. She lowered her eyes to his chest. "I thought you'd had second… I mean, I thought…"

He put his forefinger gently across her lips. "So did I," he whispered.

She met his eyes and couldn't look away. He bent and drew his lips tenderly across her soft mouth. She started to reach up, but he caught her arms and held them down.

"No," he whispered. "Not in a cemetery."

She cleared her throat. "You started it."

"And you have no willpower," he teased. "I love it."

She laughed shyly.

"Why did you go out to Minette Raynor's house with Hayes?"

"How did you…?"

"Two thousand pairs of curious eyes live in this town," he said with affection. "The druggist and the clerk at the bank mentioned it, even before Cash Grier told me the whole story. Which you could have done," he added shortly.

She started to argue, but she realized that he was right. She moved restlessly and didn't look at him. "My pride was hurt, when I heard about you riding around with that woman."

"She was visiting her uncle. I'm doing a business deal with him. She needed a ride to town, and I obliged." He tilted her chin up. "Which I could have let Chayce do. But I'd seen you with Hayes and I figured somebody would see me with her. In fact," he added wickedly, "I drove right by Hayes Carson's office with her. He saw us."

"Rachel gave us enough information to hang the local drug lords out to dry," she said. "Maybe, in one way, she redeemed herself. How about the jewelry?" she added.

"I flew up there yesterday and had the millionaire's attorney meet me at the bank," he told her. "He was astonished that you'd want to give him back what amounted to a king's ransom. He wants to give you a reward."

"I wouldn't take one," she said.

He smiled. "I told him that. Know what he said?"

"What?"

"That you were one in a million, and I was a very lucky man."

"You weren't thinking that, I bet."

"Not at the time, no." He frowned. "You haven't said why you went to Minette's with Hayes. He hates her. Everybody knows he thinks she gave his brother the drugs that killed him."

"He said that Marsh would watch out for me, and that the place was situated so that you could see someone coming two miles away. There's no way to sneak up on it."

"He's right, there—Marsh was a federal agent. But so was Chayce, who works for me. You'll be safer at my house."

"Are you sure about that?"

He grimaced and took a long breath. "I asked Merrie if she could take a few days off and come home to chaperone me with a woman. She laughed her head off when I had to admit that it was you."

"She would."

He brought her hand to his mouth and kissed the palm. "I'll follow you to your boardinghouse. You can leave your car there and come with me in mine."

She hesitated. "I've only just come home from Minette's place, and I've been worried about my boardinghouse friends. Rachel's boyfriend is on his way out of the world," she added, pausing to explain what had happened. "But it's still possible that one of the cartel people could come looking for me. If they see my car there, it might put Mrs. Brown and Lita in danger," she cautioned.

"Suppose we leave it at Hayes's office?"

"Would he mind?"

"Hell, no. Hayes only lives for the adrenaline rushes his job gives him. That's why he's never married. No woman in her right mind would marry him."

"He and Minette are like flint and steel together," she commented.

"Yes, I know," he replied. "One day, there's going to be a fearful explosion between them, and anything could happen. That's why I've discouraged Merrie."

"Merrie isn't stupid, you know," she said gently.

"Well, not in most ways. Come on. Let's go."

Life was sweet again. Ivy forgot the cartel, Rachel's burial, everything as she and Stuart dropped her car off at the sheriff's office.

"I wondered why she wasn't staying with you," Hayes

commented to Stuart. "She and Merrie have been friends forever."

"We had a misunderstanding," Stuart replied. He caught Ivy's hand in his, to make the point, just in case Hayes had missed it. "But we've cleared things up. Merrie's coming home for a few days, too. Chayce and I, and the boys, will make sure Ivy's safe."

Hayes grinned wickedly. "What about the pretty debutante?"

Stuart raised an eyebrow. "Her fiancé is waiting for her back in Houston."

"Oh," Hayes remarked, with a speculative look at Ivy, who flushed.

"Thanks for letting me keep my car here," Ivy said. "I was worried about leaving it at my boardinghouse."

"No problem," Hayes said. "It might work to our advantage if they think you're staying here in my office." He grinned. "In fact, I hope they do think it. I'll call Cash and tell him, too."

"Let me know if you catch anyone," Ivy asked.

"Of course."

"Will he really call me, do you think, if he catches somebody?" Ivy asked as they drove to Stuart's house.

"I imagine so. You're involved, whether you want to be or not." He took her hand in his and held it tightly.

"I found out something else in New York that I didn't share with Hayes."

"What?" she asked, certain that it was something unpleasant.

"The millionaire was concerned enough to hire a private detective. He shadowed Rachel before she took the overdose. She led him to one of the bigger names in drug distribution in the country. The detective said that she was blackmailing the man with information she'd gleaned from her boyfriend. She'd hidden the evidence, and nobody could find out where."

"Did they kill her?" she asked worriedly.

"It wouldn't have been wise to do that, considering that they didn't know exactly what she had on them, or where it was kept."

"She'd used drugs for years," she argued. "She wouldn't have taken an overdose deliberately."

"There were no signs of force on her body," he replied. "I checked with the medical examiner."

"Then, how…?"

"They did a toxicology screen, though," he added. "The stuff she injected was a hundred percent pure. She used too much."

"Did she have help using too much?" she asked warily.

"Her boyfriend was right in the middle of her schemes," he said. "It's possible that he deliberately gave her the pure drug, instead of the drug that had been cut, to save himself. He might not have known about the evidence she had. He might have thought she was bluffing. She would have used her regular dose, which was fatal because of the substitution. It would still look like suicide."

"Tough luck for him, if it's true," she said curtly. "Because when the drug pipeline gets shut down by the DEA, they're going to want to punish someone, and he's the only one left alive that they can get to. If he lives, he may wish he'd died."

"Yes." He glanced at her. "Poetic justice, you might say."

She had to agree that it was. "Poor Rachel," she said, shaking her head. "She was always greedy."

"Always." He squeezed her hand. "She was at that party with Hayes's brother Bobby, you know," he added. "She knew the dealers and where to get the drugs, and she had a case on Bobby at the time because he was rich. She might have thought she was doing him a favor, so when it went bad, she put it around that Minette did the dirty work."

"That would be like her," she agreed. "But Hayes still thinks Minette did it."

"God knows why," he said. "Minette sings in the choir at church, teaches a Sunday school class and she's never had so much as a speeding ticket. She never even knew any kids who were on the wrong side of the law."

"Hayes is blind when it comes to her," she said.

He smiled. "Men tend to be that way when they're afraid of being caught," he told her. "Freedom becomes a religion when you're over thirty."

"I guess most men don't want to settle down."

"Oh, we do, eventually. Especially when we realize that some other man might be poaching on our territory." He glanced at her. "I was ready to punch Hayes."

She felt her cheeks go hot. She smiled. "Were you?"

"Are you sure there's nothing between you?" he persisted.

"I'm very sure," she replied, linking her fingers closer into his.

He smiled.

Merrie was already at the house when they got there, to Ivy's faint disappointment. She'd hoped to have some time alone with Stuart.

He got out and opened her door, helping her out. He led her up the steps, leaving the car in the driveway.

"I didn't believe him when he told me," Merrie teased, hugging her friend.

"I still can't," Ivy confessed, with a shy glance at Stuart.

"Come on in," Merrie said. "Mrs. Rhodes has already made some tea cakes and coffee for us."

"I'd love something hot to drink," Ivy replied. "It was cold at the cemetery."

"I would have been there, too, if I'd known," Merrie said gently. "I just got here about twenty minutes ago. I'm sorry about Rachel."

"Me, too," Ivy replied. "I wish she'd made better choices in her life."

"I hope that information she furnished helps close doors around here for the drug trade," Stuart said as he sat beside Ivy on the sofa. "It's more dangerous than ever when you have two factions fighting for supremacy."

"Rachel actually turned informant?" Merrie exclaimed.

"She did," Ivy replied, and told her the whole story, interrupted briefly by Mrs. Rhodes bearing a silver tray with coffee and tea cakes, milk and sugar and china.

"But why did Hayes take you to Minette's house?" Merrie asked curiously. "He hates her."

"I wouldn't take any bets on that," Stuart replied, munching on a tea cake.

"They're very explosive together," Ivy said warily.

Merrie sighed. "I had a feeling about that," she confessed. She grinned. "I had a real crush on Hayes when I was about sixteen, but I'm not stupid enough to think we'd do well as a couple. We're too different. Besides," she confessed with a shy smile, "there's a very handsome divorced doctor I work with at the hospital."

"Tell me all about him," Ivy coaxed.

Stuart finished his coffee and stood up. "I'll pass," he said with a grin. "I have things to do. Don't go away," he told Ivy.

"I won't," she promised.

He winked at her, leaving her flushed and delighted.

"I still can't believe it!" Merrie exclaimed when he'd gone out of earshot. "You and my brother! I thought you hated each other!"

"So did I," Ivy confessed. "I've loved him since I was eighteen."

"I think he feels something similar. He was livid about seeing you around town with Hayes. No man gets that mad about a woman he hates." She laughed. "You can't imagine how relieved I was! I was sure you were falling for Hayes, and I knew that he and Minette were passionate about hating each other. One day, mark my words, there's going to be an explosion between the two of them. I didn't want you to be hurt," she added gently.

Ivy felt the relief all the way to her toes. She just smiled. "Thanks. But I wasn't kidding when I said Hayes was a friend. I've loved Stuart forever, it seems. I can't believe he feels the same."

Merrie chuckled. "I can."

Ivy leaned forward. "Well, now that we've got Hayes out of the way, tell me about this sexy doctor you work with!"

After supper, Merrie discreetly went upstairs to watch a movie on pay-per-view with Mrs. Rhodes while Stuart went into his study with Ivy and closed the door. As an afterthought, he locked it behind him.

Ivy was nervous and delighted, all at once, as he drew her into his arms.

"I'm starving," he whispered as his mouth covered hers.

She realized quickly that he wasn't talking about food. She held on for dear life and kissed him back with her whole heart. She felt him lift her, carry her, to the long leather sofa. He put her down on it and joined her, drawing her completely against his powerful body.

She shivered at the sensations that rose like a flood, almost searing her as passion consumed them both.

He ground her hips into his, groaning when she jerked and gasped into his demanding mouth. She made no protest at all when she felt his lean hands go under her blouse, against her bare skin.

"Your body is softer than silk," he breathed into her mouth. "Warm and sweet to touch. I want you, Ivy."

She wanted him, too, but they were getting in over their heads and she was an old-fashioned woman. She grew more nervous as his ardor increased. Helpless, she stiffened.

He hesitated, lifting his head to look down into her wide, apprehensive eyes. His own narrowed. "Yes," he whispered. "You want me. You'd give in, if I asked you to. But you don't want it to happen like this, do you?"

She swallowed, knowing she might lose him forever if she told the truth. "I… I was raised to believe that some things are still wrong even if the whole world says they're right."

She looked up at him nervously, waiting for him to get up and walk out, or just to make some sarcastic comment. He was a worldly man in his thirties. He'd said he wasn't a marrying man, and she wasn't capable of sleeping with him out of wedlock. Her heart fell to her knees. She couldn't go on living if she lost him, now. What would she do? Her eyes pleaded with his as the silence grew around them. It was, truly, the moment of truth.

11

And then, when Ivy was certain she'd lost, Stuart began to smile. It wasn't a sarcastic smile, either. He rolled over onto his side and traced patterns on her soft, swollen mouth. His shirt was open and her fingers were tangled in the thick hair that covered his chest. She didn't remember unfastening buttons, but she must have. Her own blouse and bra were down around her waist.

"I told you, I don't seduce virgins," he whispered deeply.

"I remember," she whispered back.

"I do, however, marry them," he murmured against her lips.

Her eyes widened. "You want to…to marry me?"

He kissed her eyelids closed. "Of course I do," he replied huskily. "I wanted you when you were just eighteen. I've gone almost out of my mind wanting you since then, and hating myself for it. You're so young, Ivy," he told her, hugging her close. "But I can't live without you."

She clung to him, burying her face in his warm throat. "I can't live without you, either, Stuart," she confessed on a broken sob. "I love you…!"

His mouth stopped the words. He kissed her until her mouth was sore and they were both on the verge of surrender.

Whether it was by accident or by design, a loud knock at the door announced Merrie.

"Who wants cake and ice cream?" she called.

Stuart laughed. "Both of us!" he called back, winking at Ivy, who was delightfully flushed.

"Coming right up. You two coming out to get it?"

Stuart made a face. "Sure," he replied.

"Okay! Five minutes!"

Her footsteps died away.

Stuart's eyes began to glitter wickedly as he eased Ivy onto her back and slid over her. "Five whole minutes," he murmured against her soft mouth. "Let's make the best of them, sweetheart."

They did, too.

Amid plans for a big, society wedding that Ivy really didn't want, Chief Cash Grier and Sheriff Hayes Carson came to talk to Ivy. Stuart had gone out onto the ranch because there was a problem with some equipment, and Merrie was in town ordering invitations and a wedding cake.

Mrs. Rhodes led them into the living room, where Ivy was making a list of people she wanted to invite to the wedding.

"What can I do for you?" she asked them, smiling as she offered them chairs around the big, open fireplace that was blazing, cozy and warm in the large room.

"We thought you might like to know how things are going since we got Rachel's packet of information," Hayes told her.

"Would I ever!" she replied.

"It turns out that her boyfriend's main supplier was from Jacobsville," Cash Grier said. "Do you remember back last year when two of my patrol officers arrested a drunk politician and his daughter slandered me in the press?"

"Everybody remembers that," she said.

"Well, his daughter, Julie Merrill, was up to her neck in drug trafficking, along with the two commissioners who resigned from the city council and vanished."

"Julie was arrested and accused of arson for trying to burn down Libby Collins's house, wasn't she?" she replied. "And then she skipped bond and vanished, about the same time that Dominguez woman took over Manuel Lopez's old drug territory."

"Good memory, Ivy," Hayes chuckled.

"Better than mine," Cash agreed, grinning. "Anyway, we couldn't find her anyplace and, believe me, we looked. So this information Rachel left pointed to a hotel in downtown San Antonio where one of her drug-dealing boyfriend's contacts lived. Guess who the contact turned out to be?"

"Julie Merrill?!"

"The very same," Cash told her. "We've got her in custody. She's lodged in the county jail awaiting arraignment."

"Will that shut down the drug trade locally?" Ivy asked. "And what about those two councilmen?"

"They're still hiding out somewhere," Hayes drawled. "But we'll turn them up sooner or later. Meanwhile, Dominguez has a successor."

"Do you know who it is?" she asked.

Cash and Hayes glanced at each other and some silent message passed between them. "We have an idea," Cash said. "We're working on proof. One of Cy Parks's old friends is going to help us out. He's a Mexican national with some long-held grudges."

"Rodrigo Ramirez," Ivy murmured thoughtfully.

"How do you know about him?" Cash asked suspiciously.

"I know Colby Lane's new wife, Sarina," she said. "She mentioned that Colby and Rodrigo had some, shall we say, problems during the time they were working on breaking the Dominguez case."

"Translated," Hayes said with a droll smile at Cash, "that means that Colby and Rodrigo could hardly stay in the same room together without exchanging threats of violence."

"Well, Rodrigo and Sarina had been partners for three years, after all," Cash pointed out.

"Yes, well, Colby and Sarina had been married and had a child together. Anyway," Hayes continued, "we have a lead on where Dominguez's lieutenant, who's taking over the Culebra cartel, is hiding out. Rodrigo's going to infiltrate it."

"What's Sarina going to say to that?" Ivy asked. "She and Rodrigo worked together busting up Dominguez's operation. Sarina's DEA, too, you know."

Cash chuckled. "Cobb doesn't want to let her resign. He says she can go undercover as Rodrigo's contact. Colby wants her to work for me. So do I," he added. "I only have one investigator, and it's a big county. I was hoping that she'd start right away. But Cobb offered her this peach of a case and she walked right over Colby and took it."

"Colby's really crazy about her," Ivy mentioned.

"Yes, and vice versa," Cash said. He sighed. "Well, maybe one day Colby will find a way to convince her to resign. Meanwhile, he and Bernadette hold down the fort on their ranch in Jacobsville while Sarina works nights."

"Is he still teaching tactics for Eb Scott?" she asked.

They nodded. "There was one other confession in Rachel's papers," Cash added slowly. "We thought you ought to know. She admitted that she gave Bobby Carson the drug that killed him."

Ivy's gasp was audible. She glanced at Hayes, whose face was as closed as a clam shell. "She confessed? But why?"

"Who knows?" Cash replied. "Maybe she had a premonition. Whatever her reason, she made amends for a lot of bad things she'd done in her life."

"Was there anything about me?" Ivy wanted to know. She hadn't even asked to read the papers, certain that they were all about drug trafficking and not about personal matters.

Cash hesitated.

"No," Hayes replied quietly. "She just noted that she guessed all her things would go to her sister at her death.

It wasn't a will. She wasn't planning to die. But she knew that blackmailing drug lords is an iffy business. I guess she wanted to make the point."

Ivy felt her heart sink. She'd hoped for more than that.

"Don't lie to her," Cash said coldly. "Telling the truth is always the best way, even if it seems brutal." He looked at Ivy. "She said she'd told her boyfriend that you'd have all the blackmail information in case something happened to her."

"Dear God!" Ivy exclaimed, feeling sick.

"That wasn't necessary," Hayes said curtly.

"It was," Cash disagreed. "Mean people don't usually change, Ivy," he added. "If anything, they get meaner. She put you in the line of fire deliberately by telling Jerry Smith she'd given you the evidence."

"I'm not surprised," she said sadly. "She always hated me, from the time I was old enough to know who she was. My life was hell when I was a child."

Hayes pursed his lips. "Not anymore," he mused. "I noticed that Merrie York was at the engravers ordering wedding invitations this morning for you and Stuart."

She burst out laughing. "There's no such thing as a secret in Jacobsville."

"Damned straight," Cash agreed. "Are we getting invited?"

"Everybody's getting invited," Ivy replied with a

smile. "I would have liked to elope, but Stuart says we're going to have all the trimmings."

"I love weddings," Hayes said. "It's the only time I get decent cake."

"No fair," Ivy protested. "Barbara makes wonderful cakes at her café."

"I eat on the run, mostly," Hayes said.

"Are Jerry's friends going to come after me, when they know about Rachel's confession?" she worried.

"Not likely," Cash said with a grin. "Jerry survived his fall, against all the odds, and he's turning state's evidence. He pointed out his management-level supplier, who was picked up in New York City this morning and charged with drug trafficking. It seems this supplier had enough methamphetamine and crack cocaine in a rented, vacant apartment to qualify him for superdealer status. Federal charges," he continued, "and they carry long prison sentences. Cobb and the DEA had already picked up the ex-state senator's daughter in San Antonio, and we hear that the two ex-councilmen implicated in the scheme are trying to make it to Mexico."

"If they do, Rodrigo will push them back across the border and yell for the police," Hayes chuckled.

"I'm just glad it's over," Ivy said quietly. "It's been a long week."

"It certainly has," Hayes agreed.

Ivy wondered how he'd taken the news that Minette had never given his little brother the drugs that cost him his life. He might not believe it just yet. His vendetta against the woman had gone on for some time. Maybe he liked hating her.

They left a few minutes later, and she went back to her list.

The wedding, predictably, was the social event of the season. The church was decorated in white and red poinsettias, because it was only a few weeks before Christmas. Ivy wore a white gown with a train and a trailing veil that Stuart had bought for her at Neiman Marcus. She looked in the mirror and couldn't believe that this was her. She'd never dreamed that Stuart would want to marry her one day, when she was cocooned in her daydreams. She smiled at her reflection, flushing a little with happiness.

She walked down the aisle alone. She'd had offers from townspeople to give her away, but it seemed right to make the walk all by herself. You couldn't really give people away in these enlightened times, she'd told Stuart. If anything, she was giving herself.

Stuart stood at the beautiful arbor of poinsettias where the minister was waiting. He looked down the aisle as Ivy walked toward him and the look on his face was fascinating to her. This worldly, experienced man looked very much like a young boy on his first date. His eyes were eloquent.

She stopped beside him with her bouquet of white roses and lily of the valley and faced him shyly, with her veil draped delicately over her face, while the minister read the vows.

Finally the ring was on her finger, and on his. He lifted the beautiful lacy veil to look upon her for the first time as a bride.

"Beautiful," he whispered, as he bent to kiss her with exquisite tenderness. "Mrs. York," he added, smiling.

She beamed. She could have walked on air. She was the happiest woman in Texas, and she looked it.

Everyone in town was there. The big families, the little families, friends and acquaintances filled the church and flowed out into the yard.

"At least," she whispered to him at the reception, "nobody started a mixer, like they did at Blake Kemp's wedding to his Violet."

"It's early, yet," he cautioned, nodding toward a fuming Minette Raynor glaring up at a taciturn Hayes Carson.

"He doesn't believe she wasn't responsible, does he?" she mused.

"He doesn't want to believe it," he corrected. "Here, precious, take a bite of the cake so the photographer can make us immortal."

She flushed at the endearment and nibbled the white cake as the flash enveloped them. The camera captured similar exquisite moments until the happy couple finally climbed into a waiting white limousine and sped away toward the airport.

Jamaica, Ivy thought as she lay exhausted in Stuart's strong arms, was a dreamy place for a honeymoon. Not that they'd seen much of it yet. The minute the bellboy had deposited their luggage, received his tip and left the room, they'd ended up in the bed.

Ivy knew the mechanics of it, from her romantic novels and blunt articles in women's magazines. But reading about it and doing it were two very different things.

The sensations Stuart drew from her untried body were so powerful that they frightened her. She lost control of herself almost at once. His mouth and his hands coaxed a response out of her that would make her blush afterward. He teased her, encouraged her, praised her as he drew her with him from one peak to an even higher one.

There was one tiny flash of pain, and then nothing except sheer heat and passion that built on itself until she was shivering, exploding with pleasure, begging for relief from the tension that pulled her poor body so taut that it felt likely to explode.

And it did, in a maelstrom of excited delight that was beyond rational description. She cried out endlessly as her body arched up to receive his in helpless trembling thrusts.

He found his own relief just as she did, and then collapsed over her. She cradled him in her arms, drunk on ecstasy, blind with satiation.

After a few breathless minutes, he managed to lift his head and look down into her misty, happy eyes.

"Now I know you're disappointed," he said dryly, "that we rushed it like this. But later, I promise, I'll torture you with passion and make you scream like a wildcat when I satisfy you."

"Dis…appointed?" she asked, blank-eyed.

He pursed his lips. "You're not disappointed?"

"Good Lord, Stuart!" she exclaimed, barely able to breathe even now. "I thought I was going to die!"

He chuckled. "I must be better than I thought I was," he told her. He bent and kissed her eyelids. "I wanted to go slow, but I just lost it. I've waited so long for you, little one. Years and years. For the past year or so," he added huskily, "I've been as celibate as a man stranded on a desert island. I wasn't able to want anyone but you. So I couldn't draw it out the way I meant to, tonight."

She was delighted with the confession. Her long legs curled around his and her eyes half-closed in satisfaction. If she were a cat, she mused, she'd be purring. "I don't have a single complaint."

"It didn't hurt?" he persisted.

"Only a little. Mostly, I was too busy to notice."

He nibbled her lower lip. "I'm good," he drawled.

She grinned and punched him in the ribs. "Very good. I think. My memory seems to be slipping." She glanced up at him, drawing her fingers through the thick hair on his chest. "Could you do all that again, do you think, so I can make up my mind?"

"Darlin'," he whispered into her parting lips, "I would be delighted…!"

The next day, holding hands and walking along the beach while the waves crashed on the sand beside them, she wondered if anyone had ever been as happy as she was right now.

She leaned her head against his bare shoulder and kissed it. "Did I mention that I loved you?" she asked softly.

"I believe you did," he replied, and pulled her close. He looked down into her wide, radiant eyes. "But I didn't." He traced a path down her soft cheek, and his eyes were solemn. "I could have told you anytime in the past two years that I loved you. I still do. I always will."

It was powerful, hearing the words. She could hardly breathe. "Really?"

"Really." He bent and kissed her eyelids closed. "We've had a nice breakfast and some comfortable exercise. What would you like to do next, Mrs. York?"

She grinned wickedly, tugged his head down and whispered in his ear.

His eyebrows arched. "Do you know, that's exactly what I'd like to do next, too!"

She pulled away, laughed and went running back down the beach. Stuart gave a shout of laughter and ran after her.

Years later, she could still draw a smile from him when she reminded him of that bright, sweet morning on a Jamaican beach, when their lives together were just beginning. It was, she thought, the best morning of her life.

* * * * *

Catlleman's Choice

For Alicia
And for Arizona's Stephanie, Ellen,
Trish and Nita

1

At first, Mandelyn thought the pounding was just in her head; she'd gone to bed with a nagging headache. But when it got louder, she sat up in bed with a frown and stared at the clock. The glowing face told her that it was one o'clock in the morning, and she couldn't imagine that any of the ranch hands would want to wake her at that hour without cause.

She jumped up, running a hand through the glorious blond tangle of her long hair, and pulled on a long white robe over her nightgown. Her soft gray eyes were troubled as she wound through the long ranch-style house to the front door that overlooked the Chiricahua Mountains of southeastern Arizona.

"Who is it?" she asked in the soft, cultured tones of her Charleston upbringing.

"Jake Wells, ma'am," came the answer.

That was Carson Wayne's foreman. And without a single word of explanation, she knew what was wrong, and why she'd been awakened.

She opened the door and fixed the tall, blond man with a rueful smile. "Where is he?" she asked.

He took off his hat with a sigh. "In town," he replied. "At the Rodeo bar."

"Is he drunk?" she asked warily.

The foreman hesitated. One corner of his mouth went up. "Yes, ma'am," he said finally.

"That's the second time in the last two months," she said with flashing gray eyes.

Jake shrugged, turning his hat around in his hands. "Maybe money's getting tight," he guessed.

"It's been tight before. And it isn't as if he doesn't have options, either," she grumbled, turning. "I've had a buyer for that forty-acre tract of his for months. He won't even discuss it."

"Miss Bush, you know how he feels about those condominium complexes," he reminded her. "That land's been in his family since the Civil War."

"He's got thousands of acres!" she burst out. "He wouldn't miss forty!"

"Well, that particular forty is where the old fort stands."

"Nobody's likely to use it these days," she said with venom.

He only shrugged, and she went off to change her clothes. Minutes later, dressed in a yellow sweater and designer jeans, she drew on her suede jacket and went out to climb in beside Jake in the black pickup truck with the Circle Bar W logo of Carson Wayne's cattle company emblazoned in red on the door.

"Why doesn't anybody else ever get called to go save people from him?" she asked curtly.

Jake glanced at her with a faint smile. "Because you're the only person in the valley who isn't scared of him."

"You and the boys could bring him home," she suggested.

"We tried once. Doctor bills got too expensive." He grinned. "He won't hit you."

That was true enough. Carson indulged her. He was fiery and rough and lived like a hermit in that faded frame building he called a house. He hated neighbors and he was as savage a man as she'd ever known. But from the first, he'd warmed to her. People said it was because she was from Charleston, South Carolina and a lady and he felt protective of her. That was true, up to a point. But Mandelyn also knew that he liked her because she had the same wild spirit he possessed, because she stood up to him fearlessly. It had been that way from the very beginning.

They wound along the dusty ranch road out to the highway. There was just enough light to see the giant saguaro cacti lifting their arms to the sky, and the dark mountains silhouetted against the horizon. Arizona was beautiful enough to take Mandelyn's breath away, even after eight years as a resident. She'd come from South Carolina at the age of eighteen, devastated by personal tragedy, expecting to find the barren land a perfect expression of her own emotional desolation. But her first sight of the Chiricahua Mountains had changed her mind. Since then, she'd learned to look upon the drastically different vegetation with loving, familiar eyes, and in time the lush green coastline of South Carolina had slowly faded from memory, replaced by the glory of creosote bushes in the rain and the stately stoicism of the saguaro. Her cultured upbringing was still evident in her proud carriage and her soft, delicately accented voice, but she was as much an Arizonian now as a Zane Grey character.

"Why does he do this?" she asked as they wound into the small town of Sweetwater.

"Not my business to guess," came the reply. "But he's a lonely man, and feeling his years."

"He's only thirty-eight," she said. "Hardly a candidate for Medicare."

Jake looked at her speculatively. "He's alone, Miss Bush," he said. "Problems don't get so big when you can share them."

She sighed. How well she knew that. Since her uncle's death four years before, she'd had her share of loneliness. If it hadn't been for her real estate agency, and her involvement in half a dozen organizations, she might have left Sweetwater for good just out of desperation.

Jake parked in front of the Rodeo bar and got out. Mandelyn was on the ground before he could come around the hood. She started toward the door.

The bartender was waiting in the doorway, wringing his apron, his bald head shining in the streetlight.

"Thank God," he said uneasily, glancing behind him. "Mandelyn, he's got a cowboy treed out back."

She stopped, blinking. "He's what?"

"One of the Lazy X's hands said something that set him off. God knows what. He was just sitting quiet at the table, going through a bottle of whiskey, not bothering anybody, and the stupid cowboy…" He stopped on an impatient sigh. "He busted my mirror, again. He broke half a dozen bottles of whiskey. The cowboy had to go to the hospital to get his jaw wired back together…."

"Wait a minute," she said, holding up a hand. "You said he had the cowboy treed…"

"The cowboy whose jaw he broke had friends," the bartender sighed. "Three of them. One is out cold on the floor. Another one is hanging from his jacket on a hook where Carson put him. The third one, the last one, is up in a tree out back of here and Carson is sitting there, grinning, waiting for him to come down again."

Carson never grinned. Not unless he was mad as hell and ready for blood. "Oh, my," Mandelyn sighed. "How about the sheriff?"

"Like most sane men, he gave the job of bringing Carson in to his deputy."

Mandelyn lifted her delicate eyebrows. "And?"

"The deputy," the bartender told her, "is in the hall closet, asking very loudly to be let out."

"Why don't you let him out?" she persisted.

"Carson," the bartender replied, "has the key."

"Oh."

Jake pulled his hat low over his eyes. "I'm going to sit in the truck," he said.

"Better go get the bail bondsman out of bed first, Jake," the bartender said darkly.

"Why bother?" Jake asked. "Sheriff Wilson isn't going to get out of bed to arrest the boss, and since Danny's locked in the closet, I'd say it's all over but the crying."

"And the paying," the bartender added.

"He'll pay you. He always does."

The bartender made a harsh sound in his throat. "That doesn't make up for the inconvenience. Having to order mirrors…clean up broken glass…it used to be once every few months, about time his taxes came due. Now it's every month. What's eating him?"

"I wish I knew," Mandelyn sighed. "Well, I'd better go get him."

"Lots of luck," the bartender said curtly. "Watch out. He may have a gun."

"He may need it," she told him with a cold smile.

She walked through the bar, out the back door, just in time to catch the tail end of a long and ardent string of curses. They were delivered by a tall man in a sheepskin coat who was glaring up at a shivering, skinny man in the top of an oak tree.

"Miss Bush," the Lazy X cowboy wailed down at her. "Help!"

The tall, whipcord-lean man turned, pale blue eyes lancing at her from under thick black eyebrows. He was wearing a dark ranch hat pulled low on his forehead, and his lean, tough face needed a shave as much as his thick, ragged hair needed cutting. He had a pistol in one hand and just the look of him would have been enough to frighten most men.

"Go ahead, shoot," she dared him, "and I'll haunt you, you bad-tempered Arizona sidewinder!"

He stood slightly crouched, breathing slowly, watching her.

"If you're not going to use that gun, may I have it?" she asked, nodding toward the weapon.

He didn't move for a long, taut minute. Then he silently flipped the gun, straightening as he held the butt toward her.

She moved forward, taking it gently, carefully. Carson was unpredictable in these moods, but she'd been dealing with him for a long time, now. Long enough to know how to handle him. She emptied the pistol carefully and stuck it in one coat pocket, putting the bullets in the other.

"Why is that man in the tree?" she asked Carson.

"Ask him," Carson said in a deep drawl.

She looked up at the thin cowboy, who was young and battered-looking. She recognized him belatedly as one she'd seen often in the grocery store. "Bobby, what did you do?"

The young cowboy sighed. "Well, Miss Bush, I hit him over the back with a chair. He was choking Andy, and I was afraid he was going to do some damage."

"If he apologizes," she said to Carson, who was slightly unsteady on his feet, "can he come down?"

He thought about that for a minute. "I guess."

"Bobby, apologize!" she called up.

"I'm sorry, Mr. Wayne!" came the prompt reply.

Carson glared up toward the limb. "All right, you..."

Mandelyn had to grit her teeth as Carson went through a round of unprintable words before he let the shivering cowboy come down.

"Thanks!" Bobby said quickly, and ran for it, before Carson had time to change his mind.

Mandelyn sighed, staring up at Carson's hard face. It was a long way up. He was tall and broad shouldered, with a physique that would have caught any woman's eye. But he was rough and coarse and only half civilized, and she couldn't imagine any woman being able to live with him.

"Jake with you?" he bit off.

"Yes. As usual." She moved closer and slowly reached out to catch his big hand in hers. It was callused and warm and it made her tingle to touch it. It was an odd reaction, but she didn't stop to question it. "Let's go home, Carson."

He let her lead him around the building, as docile as a lamb, and not for the first time she wondered at that docility. He would have attacked any man who tried to stop him. But for some reason he tolerated Mandelyn's interference. She was the only person his men would call to get him.

"Shame on you," she mumbled.

"Button up," he said curtly. "When I want a sermon, I'll call a preacher."

"Any preacher you called would faint dead away," she shot back. "And don't give me orders, I don't like it."

He stopped suddenly. She was still holding his hand and the action jerked her backward.

"Wildcat," he said huskily, and his eyes glittered in the dim light. "For all your culture and polish, you're as hard as a back-country woman."

"Sure I am," she replied. "I have to be, to deal with a savage like you!"

Something darkened his eyes, hardened his jaw. All at once, he turned her, whipped her around, and bent to jerk her completely off the ground and into his hard arms.

"Put me down, Carson!" she said curtly, pushing at his broad shoulders.

He ignored her struggles. One of his arms, the one that was under her shoulders, shifted, so that his hand could catch her long blond hair and pull her head back.

"I'm tired of letting you lead me around like a cowed dog," he said in a gruff undertone. "I'm tired of being called a savage. If that's what you think I am, maybe it's time I lived down to my reputation."

His grip on her hair was painful, and she only half heard the harsh words. Then, with shocking precision, he brought his hard mouth down on her parted lips and took possession.

It was the first time he'd touched her, ever. She went rigid all over at the unfamiliar intimacy of his whiskey-scented mouth, the rasp of whiskers that raked her soft skin. Her eyes, wide open and full of astonished fear, looked up at his drawn eyebrows, at the thick black lashes that lay against his hard, dark-skinned cheek. He made an odd sound, deep in his throat, and increased the pressure of his mouth until it became bruisingly painful.

She protested, a wild sound that penetrated the mists of intoxication and made his head slowly lift.

His chiseled lips were parted, his eyes as shocked as her own, his face harder than ever as he looked down at her. His hard gaze went to her lips. In that ardent fury his teeth had cut the lower one.

All at once, he seemed to sober. He put her gently down onto her shaky legs and hesitantly took her by the shoulders.

"I'm sorry," he said slowly.

She touched her trembling lips, all the fight gone out of her. "You cut my mouth," she whispered.

He reached out an unsteady finger and touched it while his chest lifted unsteadily.

She drew back from that tingling contact, her eyes wide and uncertain.

He let his hand fall. "I don't know why I did that," he said.

She'd never wondered before about his love life, about his women. But the feel of his mouth had fostered an unexpected intimacy between them, and suddenly she was curious about him in ways that unsettled her.

"We'd better go," she said. "Jake will be worried."

She turned, leaving him to follow. She couldn't have borne having to touch him again until some of the rawness subsided.

Jake opened the door, frowning when he saw her face. "You okay?" he asked quickly.

"Just battle-scarred," she replied with a trace of humor. She climbed in, drawing her knees together as a subdued Carson climbed in beside her and slammed the door shut.

"Get going," he told Jake without looking at him.

It was a horrible ride back home for Mandelyn. She felt betrayed. In all their turbulent relationship, she'd never once thought of him in any physical way. He was much too coarse to be an object of desire, too uncivilized and antisocial. She'd vowed that she'd never love a man again, that she'd live on the memory of the love she'd lost so many years ago. And now Carson had shocked her out of her apathy with one brutal kiss. He'd robbed her of her peace of mind. Tonight, he'd changed the rules, without any warning, and she felt empty and raw and a little afraid.

When Jake pulled up at her door, she waited nervously for Carson to get out of the truck.

"Thanks," Jake whispered.

She glanced at him. "Next time, I won't come," she said curtly.

Leaving him to absorb that, she jumped down from the cab and walked stiffly toward the front door without a word to Carson. As she closed the door, she heard the pickup truck roar away. And then she cried.

2

When dawn burst over the valley in deep, fiery lights, Mandelyn was still awake. The night before might have been only a dream except for the swollen discomfort of her lower lip, where Carson's teeth had cut it.

She sat idly on the front porch, still dressed, staring vacantly at the mountains. It was spring, and the wildflowers were blooming among the sparse vegetation, but she wasn't even aware of the sparkling early morning beauty.

Her mind had gone back to the first day she'd ever seen Carson, when she was eighteen and had just moved to Sweetwater with her Uncle Dan. She'd gone into the local fast-food restaurant for a soda and Carson had been sitting on a nearby stool.

She remembered her first glimpse of him, how her heart had quickened, because he was the only cowboy she'd seen so far. He was lean and rangy looking, his hair as unruly then as it was now, his face unshaven, his pale eyes insolent and intimate as he lounged back against the counter and stared at her with a blatant lack of good manners.

She'd managed to ignore him at first, but when he'd called to her and asked how she'd like to go out on the town with him, her Scotch-Irish temper had burst through the restraints of her proper upbringing.

Even now, she could remember his astonished look when she'd turned on the stool, coldly ladylike in her neat white suit. She had glared at him from cold gray eyes.

"My name," she'd informed him icily, "is Miss Bush, not, 'hey, honey.' I am not looking for some fun, and if I were, it would not be with a barbarian like you."

His eyebrows had shot up and he'd actually laughed. "Well, well, if it isn't a Southern belle. Where are you from, honey?'

"I'm from Charleston," she said coldly. "That's a city. In South Carolina."

"I made good grades in geography," he replied.

She'd given a mock gasp. "You can read?"

That had set him off. The language that had followed had made her flush wildly, but it hadn't backed her down.

She'd stood up, ignoring the stares of the astonished bystanders, walked straight over to him, and coolly slapped him with all the strength of her slender body behind her small hand. And then she'd walked out the door, leaving him staring at her.

It was days later that she learned they were neighbors. He'd come to talk to Uncle Dan about a horse, and that was when she'd found out who Carson Wayne was. He'd smiled at her, and confessed to her uncle what had happened in town, as if it amused him. It had taken her weeks to get used to Carson's rowdy humor and his unpolished behavior. He would slurp his coffee and ignore his napkin, and use language that embarrassed her. But since he was always around, she had to get used to him. So she did.

Later that first year, she'd gone to the rodeo, and Carson had been beating the stuffing out of another cowboy as she was coming out of the stands. Obviously intoxicated, he was throwing off the men who tried to stop him. Without a thought of defeat, she'd walked over to Carson and touched him lightly on the arm. He'd stopped hitting the other man immediately, looking down at her with dark, quiet eyes. She'd taken his hand, and he'd let her lead him around the corral, to where Jake was waiting nervously. After that, Jake went looking for her whenever his boss went on a spree. And she always went to the rescue. But after last night, she'd never go again.

With a long sigh, she walked back into the house and put on a pot of coffee. She fixed a piece of toast and ate it with her coffee, checking the time. She had a meeting at nine with Patty Hopper, a local woman who'd just come back home fresh out of veterinary school and needed an office. Then, after lunch, she had to talk to the developer who was interested in Carson's forty-acre tract. It was going to be another long day. The man had insisted on seeing Carson personally, but after last night, it was going to be heavy going. Mandelyn didn't particularly relish the thought.

Patty met her at the vacant house Mandelyn wanted to show her. The small, dark-eyed woman had light brown hair and a broad, sweet face. She and Mandelyn had been on the verge of friendship when Patty went away to college, and they still met occasionally when the younger woman was home on vacation.

"Well, what do you think?" Mandelyn answered her. "Isn't it a great location, just off the town square? And I can help you get a great interest rate if you want to finance it over a twenty-year period."

"I'm speechless." Patty grinned warmly. "It's exactly what I wanted. I've got space for an operating room here, and enough acreage out back to put in fences for runs.

This gigantic living room will make a perfect waiting room. Yes, I like it. I like the price, too."

"I just happen to have all the paperwork right here," Mandelyn laughed, producing an envelope from her large purse. "Then you can meet with James over at the bank and convince him you need the loan."

"James and I went to school together," Patty told her. "That won't be any problem at all. I've saved up a hefty down payment, and I'm a good credit risk. Just ask all my classmates who loaned me money!"

"I believe you." Mandelyn smiled as she watched Patty sign the preliminary agreement. "This is a sunny office. I can see you making your fortune right here."

"I hope you're right." Patty stood up, folding her arms over the tan sweater she was wearing with casual jeans. "Wow! All mine."

"Yours and the bank's, at least," came the dry reply.

"You're a jewel, Mandy," Patty told her. She glanced curiously at Mandelyn's lip. "I heard you were riding around with Jake in the early morning hours."

"Small towns," Mandelyn said gruffly. "Yes, I was. Carson had the local bar in an uproar again."

Patty laughed. "Just like old times," she said, and looked oddly relieved. "Carson's a bearcat, isn't he? I'm on my way out there next, on a large animal call. He's got a sick bull."

"Don't get too close, he might make a grab for you," Mandelyn teased.

"Me? Not Carson, he's too polite."

"That's rich!" Mandelyn laughed bitterly. "He's a savage. Something right out of ancient history."

"He's always been polite to me," Patty said. "Strange, isn't it, that he's never married?"

Mandelyn felt her blood boil. "It doesn't seem strange to me. He's too uncivilized to get a woman. He'd have to kidnap one and point a gun at her to get a wife!"

"I thought he was your friend," Patty said.

"He was," Mandelyn said coldly. She turned. "Well, I've got a developer coming round in about an hour. I'd better go and have my lunch. I'm glad you liked the office."

"Me too," Patty said, laughing. "Say, do you really think Carson would be all that bad in bed?" she added curiously. "He's awfully sexy."

Mandelyn couldn't meet her friend's eyes. "If you say so. I'll give you a call later about the details of the agreement, okay?" she said with a forced smile.

"Sure," Patty said. "Thanks again."

"My pleasure."

Mandelyn had a salad at the local cafe, but she didn't enjoy it. Her thoughts kept returning to Carson and to Patty's disturbing remarks about him. Afterward, she went back to her office where the developer was pacing back and forth, waiting for her. She made a sly wink at Angie, her new secretary.

"Hello, Mr. Denton," she said pleasantly, extending her hand. "Sorry I'm late. I was finalizing another deal."

"Perfectly all right," he returned, a tall, dignified man in a gray suit. "I'd like to go out to the ranch, if you're ready?"

She hesitated. "I'd better check with Mr. Wayne first," she said.

"I had your secretary do that," he said curtly. "He's waiting for us. I'll drive my car."

She didn't like his high-handedness, but she couldn't afford to antagonize a potential client, so she ground her teeth together in a false smile and followed him out the door.

"Sorry," Angie mouthed at her.

Mandelyn gave her a shrug, and winked again.

All the way to the ranch, Mandelyn felt as if her stomach was tied in knots. She glanced out across the grassy valley rather than ahead to the ramshackle house nestled in the cottonwood trees with the mountains behind it. She didn't want to see Carson. Why was fate tormenting her this way?

His black Thunderbird was sitting near the house, covered with dust and looking unused. The pickup truck

Jake had driven the night before was parked by the barn. The corral was deserted. The front door was standing open, but she couldn't see through the screen.

"This is where he lives?" Mr. Denton asked in astonishment as he pulled his green Lincoln up in front of the rough wood house.

"He's rather eccentric," she faltered.

"Crazy," he muttered. He got out of the car, looking neat and alien in his city clothing, and Mandelyn fell reluctantly into step beside him. She was wearing a blue knit suit, with her hair in a bun. She looked elegant and cool, and felt neither. She'd tried to disguise her swollen lip with lipstick, but it was raw where her tongue touched it.

As they started up the steps, Carson walked out onto the porch with quick strides. He looked even taller in his work boots. He was wearing faded denim jeans and a blue chambray shirt half unbuttoned over his broad, hair-roughened chest. He looked tired and hung over, but his blue eyes were alert and at least he seemed approachable.

"Mr. Wayne?" the developer said, putting on his best smile. "Nice place you have here. Rustic."

Carson bent his head to light a cigarette, pointedly ignoring the developer's outstretched hand.

"You won't take no for an answer, will you?" Carson asked him with a cold blue glare.

Denton looked a little ruffled but he withdrew his hand and forced the smile back onto his thin lips. "I got rich that way," he replied. "Look, I'll up my previous offer by two thousand an acre. It's a perfect tract for my retirement village. Lots of water, flat land, beautiful view..."

"It's the best grazing land I've got," Carson replied. "And there's a fort on the place that dates back to the earliest settlement."

"The fort could be moved. I'd be willing..."

"My great-grandfather built it," came the cold reply.

"Mr. Wayne," the developer began.

"Look," Carson said curtly, "I don't like being pushed. This is my place, and I don't want to sell it. I told you that. I told her that," he added, glancing toward Mandelyn. "I'm tired of talking. Come out here again and I'll load my gun."

"You can't threaten me, you backwoods...!" the developer began.

"Oh, no," Mandelyn ground out, covering her face with her hands. She knew even as Carson began cursing what was going to happen. She flinched at the first thud, the shocked cry, the heavy sound of a body landing on hard ground. She peeked between her fingers. The developer was trying to sit up, holding his jaw. Carson was standing over him with calm contempt, smoking his cigarette. He didn't even look rumpled.

"Get off my land, you…" He tacked on a few rough words and bent to lift the other man by the collar. He frog-marched him to the Lincoln, tossed him inside, and slammed the door. "Vamoose!" he growled.

Mandelyn stood there, frozen, while the Lincoln jerked out of the yard. She stared for a long minute and then, with a sigh, started after it.

"Where the hell do you think you're going?" Carson asked.

"Back to town."

"Not yet. I want to talk to you."

She whirled and glared at him. "I don't want to talk to you."

He took her arm and half led, half dragged her up the steps and into the house. "Did I ask?"

"No, you never do!" she shot back. "You just move in and take over! He made you a very generous offer. You've cost me a fortune…!"

"I told you not to bring him out here."

"You told my secretary he could come!" she floundered.

"Like hell I did. I told her to tell him he could come if he felt lucky."

And poor little Angie hadn't realized what that meant.

"Angie's new," she muttered, standing still in the dim living room. He didn't even have electricity. He had kerosene lanterns and furniture that she didn't want to sit on. It looked as if it were made with leftover gunnysacks.

"Sit," he said curtly, dropping into a ragged armchair.

She shifted uncomfortably on her feet. She'd only been in this house once or twice, with her uncle. Since his death, she'd found excuses to stay on the porch or in the yard when she stopped by to talk business with Carson.

His face hardened when he saw the look she was giving the sparse furniture. He got up, furiously angry, and walked into the kitchen.

"In here," he said icily. "Maybe the kitchen chairs will suit you better."

She felt cruel. She hadn't meant to be rude. With a sigh, she walked past him and sat down in one of the cane-bottomed chairs around the table with its red-checked oilcloth cover. "I'm sorry," she said. "I wasn't trying to be rude."

"You didn't want to soil your designer clothes on my filthy furniture," he laughed through narrowed eyes. He sat down roughly and leaned back in the chair, glaring at her. "Why pussyfoot around?"

She stared at him unblinkingly. "What do you want?"

"There's a question," he replied softly. His blue eyes

wandered slowly over her face, down to her lips, and hardened visibly. "Hell," he breathed at the swollen evidence of his brutality. He pulled an ashtray toward him with a sigh and crushed out his half-finished cigarette. "I didn't realize how rough I'd been."

"I'll put it down to experience," she said curtly.

"Do you have much?" he asked, holding her gaze. "Did you fight because you were afraid?"

"You were hurting me!" she said, red with embarrassment and bad temper.

His nostrils flared as he breathed. He paused a moment, and his next words took her completely by surprise. "You told Patty I was too savage to get a woman."

Her mouth flew open. She just sat and stared, hardly able to believe Patty's betrayal.

"I…I never dreamed…"

"That she'd tell me?" he asked coolly. He pulled another cigarette from his pocket and lit it with an impatient snap of his lighter. "She was kidding around, she didn't mean anything. I guess you didn't either." He stared at the cigarette. "I've been thinking about it a lot lately, about getting older, being alone." He looked up. "When Patty said that this morning, it made me mad as hell. Then I realized that you were right, that I don't even know how to behave in polite society. That I'm not…civilized."

"Carson…" she began, at a loss for words.

He shook his head. "Don't apologize. Not for telling the truth." He sighed, stretching, and the hard, heavy muscles of his chest were evident beneath his shirt. Her eyes were drawn to the mat of dark hair visible in the opening, and she felt a sensation that shocked her. "I didn't sleep," he said after a minute, watching her. "I'm sorry I cut your lip, that I manhandled you. I guess you knew I was drinking."

"You tasted of whiskey," she said without thinking, and then flushed when she remembered exactly how he'd tasted.

"Did I?" His eyes dropped to her swollen lip. "I don't know what came over me. And you fought me…that only made it worse. You should have known better, little debutante."

"I've been fighting you for years," she reminded him.

"Verbally," he agreed. "Not physically."

She glared at him. "What was I supposed to do, lie back and enjoy it?" she challenged.

His eyes darkened. His chest rose and fell roughly. "All right, I'm sorry," he growled. "For God's sake, what do you expect? I never knew my mother, never had a sister. My whole life revolved around a man who beat the hell out of me when I disobeyed…."

She stood quietly, forcing away her bad temper, hearing him without thinking until the words began to penetrate. She turned slowly and stared up at him. "Beat you?"

He drew in a slow breath, then glanced down at her bare arm where his strong, tanned fingers held it firmly. His thumb moved on the soft skin experimentally. "My father was a cattleman," he said. "My mother couldn't live with him. She ran away when I was four. He took me in hand, and his idea of discipline was to hit me when I did something he didn't like. I had a struggle just to get through school—he didn't believe in education. But by then, I outweighed him by fifty pounds," he added with glittering eyes, "and I could fight back."

It explained a lot of things. He never talked about his childhood, although she'd heard Jake make veiled references to how rough it had been.

Her eyes searched his hard face curiously.

He lifted his hand to her face and touched her lip gently. "I'm sorry I kissed you like that."

She went flaming red. She felt as if his eyes could see right through her.

"I've never been gentle," he said, "because I never knew what it was to be treated gently. And now, I'm thirty-eight years old, and I'm lonely. And I don't know how to court a woman. Because I'm a savage. This," he sighed bitterly, tracing her swollen lip, "is proof of it."

She stared up at him, searching his eyes quietly as his hand dropped. "Didn't you have any other relatives?" she asked.

"Not one," he said. He turned away and went to stand by the window. "I ran away from home once or twice. He always came after me. Eventually I learned to fight back, and the beatings stopped. But I was fourteen by then. The damage had already been done."

She studied his long back in silence, and then shifted, looking around the messy kitchen until her eyes found a facsimile of a coffeepot. She got to her feet. "Mind if I make some coffee?" she asked. "I'm sort of thirsty."

"Help yourself." He watched her with a familiar, unblinking scrutiny. "You look odd, doing that," he remarked.

"Why?" she asked with a laugh. "I'm very domestic. I cook, too, or don't you remember those dinners Uncle used to invite you to?"

"It's been years since I've eaten at your table."

She stared down at the pot she was filling. How could she possibly confess that she was too uneasy with him to enjoy his company? He disturbed her, unsettled her and she didn't understand why. Which only made it worse.

"I've been too busy for guests," she said. Her eyes went up to the tattered curtains at the window. "You could use some new curtains."

"I could use a lot of things," he said curtly. "This house is falling apart."

"You're letting it," she reminded him. She put the pot on to boil, grimacing at the grease that had congealed and blackened on top of the once-white range.

"There hasn't been any reason to fix it up before," he said. "Just me, living alone, not much company. But I've hired a construction firm to do some renovations."

That was startling. She turned to face him, her gray eyes wide and curious. "Why?" she asked without thinking.

"It has something to do with the reason I brought you in here," he admitted. He finished the cigarette and crushed it out. "I need some help."

"You!" she burst out.

He glared at her. "Don't make jokes."

"Okay," she sighed. "What do you want me to do?"

He hesitated uncharacteristically. His face hardened. "Hell, look at me," he growled finally, ramming his hands into the pockets of his worn, faded jeans. "You told Patty I was too savage to get a woman, and you were right. I don't know how to behave in civilized company. I don't even know which fork to use in a fancy restaurant." He shifted restlessly, looking arrogant and proud and self-conscious all at once. "I want you to teach me some manners."

"Me?" Mandelyn exclaimed in shock.

"Of course you," he shot back. "Who else do I know with a cultured background? I need educating."

She blinked away her confusion. "After all these years, why now?"

"Females," he said angrily. "You always have to know it all, don't you? Every single damned thing…all right," he sighed roughly, running a hand through his thick hair. "There's a woman."

She didn't know whether to laugh or cry. She stood there like an elegant statue, staring at him. Patty! she thought. It had to be Patty! It was the only possibility that made sense. His unreasonable anger about what Mandelyn had said to Patty, his sudden decision to renovate the house coinciding with Patty's return to Sweetwater. So that was it. The invulnerable man was in love, and he thought Patty had become too citified to like him the way he was. So he was making the supreme sacrifice and having himself turned into a gentleman. Pygmalion in reverse.

"Well?" he persisted, glaring at her. "Yes or no?"

She lifted her shoulders. "Surely there's someone else."

"Not someone like you," he returned. His eyes wandered over her, full of appreciation and something much darker that she missed. "You're quality. A real, honest-to-God lady. No, there's no one else who could teach me as well as you could."

She dropped her eyes to the coffeepot and watched it bubble away.

"Look on it as a challenge," he coaxed. "Something to fill your spare hours. Don't you ever get lonely?"

Her face lifted and she studied him. "Yes," she said. "Especially since Uncle died."

"You don't date?" he said.

She shifted uncomfortably. There was a reason for that, but she didn't want to discuss it with him, not now. "I like my own company."

"It isn't good for a woman to live alone. Haven't you ever thought about getting married?"

"I've thought about a lot of things. What do you want in your coffee?"

She poured it out and braved the refrigerator for cream. Inside there was a basket of eggs, some unsliced bacon, some moldy lumps and what appeared to have been butter at one time.

"I don't have any milk, if that's what you're looking for," he muttered.

She gaped at him. "You have hundreds of cows on this ranch, and you don't have any milk?"

"It isn't a dairy farm," he said.

"A cow is a cow!"

"If you want the damned milk, go milk one of them, then!"

She put her hands on her hips and glared at him. He scowled back. Eventually, she gave in with a sigh and put the cups on the table.

"That's what I like most about you," he said as she sat down gingerly in one of the rickety old chairs.

Her eyes came up. "What?"

He smiled slowly, and his blue eyes darkened, glittered. "You fight me."

Her skin tingled at the way he said it. Before she thought, she said, "You didn't like it last night."

His smile faded. He sighed and lifted the cracked mug to his lips. "I was drunk last night."

"Why?"

He shrugged. "Things got on top of me. I started thinking about how alone I was…." His eyes shot up, pinning hers. "I didn't expect to see you today. I thought you'd never speak to me again."

She fidgeted uncomfortably. "We all get depressed sometimes, even me. It's all right, no harm done." She touched her lower lip with her tongue. "Well, no permanent harm, anyway," she added dryly.

"What you told Patty was true," he said.

"I didn't really mean that, or what I called you last

night," she said, watching him. "You're not an unattractive man, Carson."

"Pull the other one," he said curtly and put his cup down to light another cigarette. "I've finally got a little money, and I'm working on some investments that will pay a good dividend. But there's nothing about me that would attract a woman, physically or intellectually, and you know it."

She caught her breath. Did he really believe that? Her eyes wandered slowly over the lean, tough length of him, the powerful muscles of his arms and chest, the narrow flat stomach and long legs. He was devastating physically. Even his craggy face was appealing, if it were shaved and his hair trimmed. She remembered suddenly what Patty had said about how he'd be in bed, and she turned crimson.

He looked up in time to catch that blush and he frowned. "What brought that on?"

She wondered what he'd say if she admitted that she and Patty had been wondering how he was in bed. "Nothing," she said, "just a stray thought."

"Twenty-six, and you still blush like a virgin," he murmured, watching her. "Are you one?" he asked, smiling faintly.

"Carson Joseph Wayne!" she exclaimed.

His blue eyes searched her gray ones. "I didn't realize you knew my middle name."

She toyed with her coffee cup. "It was on the deed, when I sold you that ten-acre parcel that used to be part of Uncle's land."

"Was it?" He sipped some more of his coffee. "You still haven't answered me. Will you teach me?"

She went hot all over at the way he said it. "Carson, any woman who wanted you wouldn't mind the way you are..." she began diplomatically.

"This one would," he said harshly.

She was suddenly jealous and didn't know why. How ridiculous! She touched her temple with a long finger. "Well..."

"I'm not stupid," he said shortly. "I can learn."

"Oh, all right," she said with equal curtness.

He seemed to relax a little. "Great. Where do we start?"

Her eyes wandered over him. God help her, it would take a miracle. "You'll need some new clothes," she said. "A haircut, a shave..."

"What kind of clothes?"

"Shirts and slacks and jeans, and a suit or two."

"What kind? What color?"

She grimaced. "Well, I don't know!"

"You'll have to come with me to Phoenix," he said. "There are some big department stores there."

"Why not Carter's Men's Shop in Sweetwater?" she protested.

His jaw tightened. "No way am I going in there with you, while old man Carter laughs in his whiskers watching us."

She almost laughed at the fierce way he said it. "Okay. Phoenix it is."

"Tomorrow," he added firmly. "It's Saturday," he reminded her when she started to protest. "You can't have any business that won't wait until Monday."

"That sounds as if I'd better not," she laughed.

"You work too hard as it is," he said. "Tomorrow you'll have a holiday. I'll even buy you lunch. You can teach me some table manners at the same time."

It looked like this was going to be a fulltime job, but suddenly she didn't mind. The project might be fun at that. After all, Carson did have distinct possibilities. His physique was superb. Why hadn't she ever noticed that? She lifted her cup and sipped her coffee while Carson slurped his.

"That's the first thing," she said, indicating the cup. "Sip, don't slurp."

And when he tried it, unoffended, and succeeded, she grinned at him. He grinned back and a wild flare of sensation tingled up her spine. She'd have to be careful, she told herself. After all, she was revamping him for another woman, not herself. And then she wondered why that was such a depressing thought.

3

If it had sounded like a simple thing, helping Carson buy clothes, Mandelyn soon lost her illusions.

"You can't be serious," he told her, glaring as she tried to convince him that a pale blue pinstriped shirt with a white collar was very trendy and chic. "The boys would laugh me out of the yard."

She sighed. "Carson, it's a whole new world. Nobody has to go around in white shirts anymore unless they want to."

"What kind of tie would I wear with that…thing," he asked shortly, while the small salesman hovered nearby chewing on his lower lip.

"A solid one, or something with a small print."

"God save us," Carson burst out.

"And with a solid colored shirt—say, pink—you'd wear a striped tie."

"I'm not wearing pink shirts," he retorted. "I'm a man!"

"A caveman," she agreed. "If you don't want my advice, I'll go buy a tube of lipstick."

"Hold it," he called as she started to walk away. He stared down at the packaged shirt. "All right, I'll get it."

She didn't smile, but it took an effort. Her eyes went over him. He was wearing a beige corduroy jacket and a worn white turtleneck shirt and tan polyester slacks. He'd had a haircut and a shave, though, and already he looked different. In the right clothes, he'd be an absolute knockout, she realized.

After a few minutes, she convinced him that striped shirts weren't at all effeminate, and he bought several more in different colors and ties to match. Then she coaxed him toward the suits.

The salesman took him to the changing rooms, and when he came back minutes later in a vested blue pinstriped suit wearing a blue shirt and burgundy tie, she almost fell off her chair. He didn't look like Carson anymore, except for the rigid features and glittering blue eyes.

"Oh, my," she said softly, staring at him.

His expression softened just a little. "Will I do?" he asked.

"Yes, you'll do," she agreed, smiling. "Women, look out!"

He smiled reluctantly. "Okay, what else do I need?"

"How about something tan?" she asked. "One of those Western-cut suits."

He tried one on, with similar results. He had just the physique to look good in a suit, and the Western cut showed it off to perfection. She let the salesman point him toward some sports coats and slacks, and then after he had paid for his purchases, she talked him into two pairs of new boots and a gray Stetson and a brown one to top it all off.

Just before they left the store she remembered some items they hadn't shopped for. She turned, but she lost her tongue immediately when she tried to say what was on her mind.

His eyebrows arched. "Something wrong?"

"Something we forgot," she said hesitantly.

A corner of his mouth pulled up. "I don't wear pajamas."

"How about things to go under them?" she said finally, averting her eyes.

"My God, you're shy," he laughed, astonished.

"So what?" she returned, her whole stance belligerent. “I’ve never gone shopping with a man before. And do you have socks?”

“I guess I’d better go back, hadn’t I?” He put the parcels in the car. Then he opened the passenger door and helped Mandelyn inside.

“Will you be all right here until I get back?” he asked.

“Sure,” she said.

“Won’t be a minute.”

She watched him walk away, and smiled. Transforming him was getting to be fun, even if it did have its difficult moments.

Her eyes went over the interior of the car. It was spotless, and she guessed that he’d had the boys give it a cleaning for him, because it had never looked so clean. Her hand reached out to touch the silver arrowhead he had suspended from the rear-view mirror and she frowned slightly as she realized what it was attached to. It was a blue velvet ribbon, one she remembered having lost. She’d worn it around her hair in a ponytail one day years ago when Carson had come to see Uncle Dan. She remembered Carson tugging the ponytail, but she hadn’t looked back, and later she’d missed the ribbon. It was odd, that a man as unsentimental as Carson would keep such a thing. Perhaps he liked the color, she thought, and turned her eyes back toward the store. It was hot, and there was no shade nearby. She fanned herself with her hand.

Minutes later, he came back, tossed his parcels into the trunk and climbed in beside her.

"I'm sorry, honey," he said suddenly, studying her flushed, perspiring skin. "I didn't expect to be so long. There was a crowd."

She smiled. "I'm okay."

He studied her eyes for a long moment, and his face seemed to go rigid. "Oh, God, you're something," he said under his breath.

The passion in his soft words stirred something deep inside her. She stared back at him and couldn't drag her eyes away. It was a moment out of time. Her eyes dropped involuntarily to his hard mouth.

"Don't," he laughed roughly, turning back to twist the ignition key savagely. "Keep those curious glances to yourself, unless you want me to kiss you again."

He'd shocked her, and her face showed it. She wondered if he wanted her. Then she remembered Patty and went cold. Her eyes gazed out the window. If he had any emotion in him at all, it would naturally be for Patty. Wasn't the object of this whole crusade to make him into a man Patty would want? She crossed her long legs with a sigh and stared out over the city.

"Hungry?" he asked after a minute.

"I could eat a salad," she agreed.

"Rabbit food," he shot back. "You can get that any day."

Her eyebrows arched. "That sounds like you're taking me someplace special," she said, glancing at him with a grin. "Are you?"

"Do you like crepes?" he asked.

Her eyes lit up. "Oh, yes!"

He smiled faintly. "A cattleman I know told me about a place. We'll give it a try."

It turned out to be a hotel restaurant, a very classy one. Mandelyn had definite misgivings about how this was going to turn out, but she'd never be able to teach Carson any manners without going into places like this. So she crossed her fingers and followed him in.

"Do you have a reservation, monsieur?" the maître d' asked with casual politeness, his shrewd eyes going over Carson's worn jacket and polyester trousers. "We are very crowded today."

There were empty tables, Mandelyn could see them, and she knew what was going on. She touched Carson's arm and whispered, "Give him a tip."

"A tip?" Carson growled, glaring down at the shorter man with eyes that threatened to fry him to a crisp. "A tip, hell! I want a table. And I'd better get one fast, sonny, or you and your phony French accent are going right out that front door together." He grinned as he said it, and Mandelyn hid her face in her hands.

"A table for two, monsieur?" the maître d' said with a shaky smile and a quick wave of his hand. "*Mais oui!* Just follow me, *s'il vous plait!*"

"Tip him, hell," Carson scoffed. "You just have to know the right words to say."

She didn't answer. All around the exclusive dining room, people were staring at them. She tried to follow some distance behind him; maybe she could look as if she were alone.

"Don't hang back there, for God's sake, I'll lose you," Carson said, gripping her arm to half drag her to the table the maître d' was indicating. "Here. Sit down."

He plopped her into a chair and jerked out one for himself, "How about a menu?"

The maître d' turned pink. "Of course. At once."

He signaled a waiter with almost comical haste. "Henri will take care of you, monsieur, mademoiselle," he said, and bowing, beat a hasty retreat.

Henri moved to the table and presented the menus with a flourish. "Would monsieur and mademoiselle like a moment to peruse the menus?" he asked politely.

"Hell, no, we want these crepes," Carson said, pointing at the entry on the menu. "I'll have about five. Get her two, she needs fattening up. And bring us some coffee."

Mandelyn looked under the table, wondering if she might fit beneath it if she tried hard enough.

Henri swallowed. "*Oui,* monsieur. Would you care for a wine list?"

"Hell, what would I do with that?" Carson asked, glaring belligerently at the waiter. "I don't give a damn what kind of wine you've got. Want me to give you a list of my herefords, lot numbers and all? I've got several hundred…."

"I will bring the coffee, monsieur!" the waiter said quickly, and exited.

"This is easy," Carson said, smiling at Mandelyn. "And they say it's hard to get service in fancy restaurants."

She covered her face with her hands again, trying to get her mind settled so that she could explain it to him. But meanwhile, he'd spotted a fellow cattleman across the room.

"Hi, Ben!" he yelled in that deep, slow drawl that carried so well out on the range—and even in this crowded restaurant. "How's that new bull working out? Think your cows will throw some good crossbreeds next spring?"

"Sure hope so, Carson!" the cattleman called back, lifting his wineglass in a salute.

Carson didn't have anything to salute back with, so he raised a hand. "So that's what the wine's for," he told Mandelyn. "To make toasts with. Maybe I better order us a bottle."

"No!" she squeaked, grabbing his hand as he started looking around for Henri.

He stared pointedly at her long, slender hand, which was wrapped around half of his enormous, callused one. "Want to hold hands, do you?" he murmured drily. His fingers caught hers, and all at once the rowdy humor went out of him. He searched her gray eyes. His fingers smoothed over her skin, feeling its texture, and her heart went wild.

"Soft," he murmured. "Soft, like your mouth." He stared at her lower lip for a long moment. "I'd like to kiss you when I was sober," he said under his breath, "just to see how it would feel."

Her fingers trembled, and he felt it. His hand contracted and brought hers to his mouth. "You smell of perfume," he breathed huskily. "And you go to my head like whiskey when you look at me that way."

She tried to draw her hand back, but he wouldn't let go of it.

"You said you'd teach me," he reminded her with a slow smile. "I'm just getting in some practice."

"I said I'd teach you manners," she replied in a high-pitched tone. "You don't threaten maître d's and waiters and yell across classy restaurants, Carson."

"Okay," he said, smoothing the backs of her fingers against his hard cheek. "What else shouldn't I do?"

"What you're doing right now," she whispered.

"I'm only holding your hand," he said reasonably.

But it didn't feel that way. It felt as if he were reaching over the table and taking possession of her, total and absolute possession of her mind and her heart and even her body.

"Mandelyn," he whispered, as if he were savoring the very sound of her name, and she realized with a start that he'd hardly ever said it. It was usually some casual endearment when he spoke to her. He made her name sound new and sweet.

She watched his dark head bend over her hand with wonder, watched his chiseled lips touch it, brush it with a tenderness she hadn't imagined him capable of. Her breath caught in her throat and tremors like the harbingers of an earthquake began deep in her body.

"Carson?" she whispered back.

His eyes lifted, as if he'd heard something in her voice that he wasn't expecting.

But before he could say anything, the waiter was back with the coffee.

"Where are my crepes?" Carson asked curtly.

"It will be only a minute, monsieur, just a minute," Henri promised with a worried smile and a fervent glance toward the kitchen.

Carson stared after him. "It had better be," he said.

Henri retreated, and Mandelyn had to smother a grin. "You do come on strong, don't you?" she managed with a straight face.

"I learned early that it was the only way to come out on top," he returned. "I don't like being put down. Never did."

"They aren't trying to put you down," she began.

"Like hell," he said, smiling coldly.

She moved restlessly in her chair. "Lifestyles among the well-to-do are different."

"You and I are pretty far apart, aren't we?" he asked quietly.

"Oh, I don't know," she murmured. "I used to think I'd enjoy going fishing once in a while, in a pair of old dungarees and a worn-out shirt."

"Did you? I could take you fishing sometime, if you like."

She looked up, half amused, and it dawned on her that she hadn't ever seen him smile as much as he had this one day. "Could you?"

He let his eyes run slowly over her. "I could loan you some old jeans and a shirt, too." He leaned back and lit a cigarette. "After all, you ought to get something out of this deal. You teach me what I need to know. And then I'll teach you a few things." He was looking straight at her when he said it, and she tingled all over.

Henri came back with the crepes seconds later, and Mandelyn was able to damp down her suddenly intense awareness of Carson while she instructed him in the use of flatware.

"Why don't they just give you a fork and let it go at that?" he grumbled when she'd explained the formal arrangement of knife, forks and spoons.

"Because it's etiquette," she told him. "Besides, you can't very well eat soup without a soup spoon, or sweeten tea without a teaspoon, or..."

"I get the idea," he sighed. "I suppose you'd never forgive me for eating peas on my knife.'

She laughed softly. "I think you might make a record book or two for managing that."

"It's easy," he returned. "All you have to do is get mashed potatoes on the knife and dip it in the peas."

She burst out laughing at the mischief in his eyes. "I give up."

"Not yet, you don't. Eat your crepes. You could use a few extra pounds. You're too thin."

Her eyebrows arched. "I never would have expected you to notice something like that."

He didn't smile. "I notice a hell of a lot about you, Mandelyn."

Once again, the way he said her name made her head swim, and she actually blushed. Her gaze fell back to her plate while Carson slowly cut his crepes.

Minutes later, after a companionable silence and a second cup of coffee, they sampled the restaurant's strawberry crepes.

Mandelyn licked whipped cream from her upper lip and Carson watched the action with an expression she didn't understand. She lifted her eyes to his and felt tremors along her spine.

"It's sexy, don't you know?" he said under his breath as he read the question in her eyes.

"Eating whipped cream?" she laughed nervously, deliberately misunderstanding him.

"Don't play dumb. You know exactly what I mean."

She ignored him and her quickened heartbeat, and finished her crepe.

"How about a movie before we go back to Sweetwater?" he asked.

"Sorry," she laughed. "I have some paperwork to do before I go to bed."

He didn't like that. His eyes glittered across the table at her. "Do you work all the time?"

"Don't you?" she returned. "I can't remember a time in the past few years when you actually took a vacation."

"Vacations are for rich men," he said, dropping his eyes to his coffee cup. He toyed with it idly. "Maybe everyone's right. Maybe I'm not cut out to be a rancher."

"What else could you be?" she teased.

"What do you mean, that I'm too crude and stupid to be anything but a cattleman?" he asked coldly. His voice carried so that people at the other tables immediately looked to see if he fit his own description of himself.

"That's not what I meant at all, and will you please lower your voice?" she asked in a squeaky tone.

"Why should I?" he asked curtly. He threw his napkin down on the table and stood up, glaring around him. "And what are you people staring at?" he asked haughtily. "Who wrote the rules and said that you have to keep your eyes down and speak in whispers and never do anything out of the ordinary in a snobby restaurant? Do you think the waiters here drive Lincolns—is that why you're so afraid of them? Do you think that head waiter has a villa on the Riviera and owns stock in AT&T?" He laughed coldly while Mandelyn seriously considered hiding under the tablecloth. "These people that wait on you are no better or worse than any of you, and you're paying to be here just like I am, so why are you all letting these stuck-up dudes push you around?"

The cattleman a few tables over who was a friend of Carson's burst out laughing.

"Hell, yes, why are we?" he burst out, grinning. "You tell 'em, Carson!"

A lady closer to their table glared at Carson. "It's amazing the kind of people they allow in these restaurants," she said with hauteur.

Carson glared back at her. "Yes, isn't it?" he agreed with a speaking glance. "And it's amazing how many people think they're better than other people because of what they've got, right, lady?"

The lady in question turned red, got up and left.

"Please sit down," Mandelyn pleaded with Carson.

"You sit. I'm leaving. If you're coming with me, come on. And where the hell is the check?" he demanded of a trembling Henri. "I want it now, not when you get around to it."

Henri was writing it as he came, his hand shaking. "Here, monsieur!"

Carson took it and stormed out toward the cashier, leaving Mandelyn to fend for herself. She got up quietly and walked slowly out of the dining room, her poised serenity drawing reluctant admiration. She was Miss Bush of Charleston from her head to her toes.

But serene was the last thing she felt when she caught up with Carson in the parking lot.

"You hot-tempered, ill-mannered, overbearing son of Satan," she began, her small fists clenched at her sides, her eyes throwing off silvery sparks, her hair glinting with blond fire in the sunlight.

"Flattery won't work with me," he assured her, grinning at her display of temper. "Get in, firecracker, and I'll take you home."

"I've never been so embarrassed…!" she began.

"Why?"

"Why!"

He stared at her as she stood rigidly beside the car, not opening her door. "Well, get in," he repeated.

"When you open the door for me," she said icily. "Women's lib or not, it is good manners."

With a resigned sigh, he went around and made an elaborate production of opening the door, helping her inside the car and closing it again.

"I'll never go anywhere with you again as long as I live," she fumed when he'd climbed in beside her and turned the key in the ignition.

"You started it," he reminded her as he pulled out onto the highway. "Making that crack about my ignorance…"

"I did no such thing," she shot back. "I simply asked what else you'd do. You love cattle, you always have. You'd be miserable in any other job and you know it.'

"You meant that I wasn't capable of doing anything else," he returned, his eyes growing fiery again.

"I can't talk to you!" she ground out. "You're always on the defensive with me, you take everything I say the wrong way!"

"I'm a savage, remember?" he asked mockingly. "What else do you expect?"

"God knows," she said. She turned her eyes out the window to the long, arid stretch of land that stretched toward the horizon. "None of this was my idea," she reminded him. "I don't care if you eat peas off your knife for the rest of your life."

There was a long, pregnant silence. He lit a cigarette and smoked it quietly as the miles went by. Eventually, she glanced at him. His face was rigid, his eyes staring straight ahead. He looked unhappy. And she felt guilty about that, guilty about losing her temper. He wanted Patty, and without some polishing, he'd never get her. He must know that and the knowledge was eating him alive.

"How far did you get in school?" she asked suddenly.

He took a deep, slow breath, and wouldn't look at her. "I have a bachelor's degree in business administration, with a minor in economics."

She felt shocked, and it showed.

"I got my education while I was in military service,

in the Marines," he told her bluntly. "But that was a long time ago. I've lived hard and I've worked hard and I haven't had time for socializing. I hate pretense. I hate people lying to each other and cutting at each other and pretending to be things they aren't. Most of all," he added hotly, "I hate places that put you down on the basis of your bank account. God, how I hate it!"

He must have spent a good part of his youth being looked down on, humiliated. Her heart thawed. She reached out and touched his sleeve very gently, and he tensed even at that light touch.

"I'm sorry," she said. "Sorry that I lost my temper, that I yelled at you."

"I have scars," he said quietly. "They don't show, and I try to forget them. But they're pretty deep."

She dropped her eyes to his stubborn, square chin. "Still want to take me fishing?"

"I reckon."

"How about Monday?"

He hesitated, and her eyes came up.

"You work on Monday," he reminded her, and there was a strangely puzzled look about him, as if he hadn't expected her to take him seriously.

"So I'll play hookey." She grinned.

He laughed softly. "All right. So will I."

She settled her head back against the seat with a sigh.

"If you'll put the worm on the hook," she added. "I'm not committing homicide on any helpless worms."

Later, she thought about that sudden decision to take a day off—something she never did—and go fishing with Carson, of all people. How odd that he'd never mentioned that business degree he held, almost as if he was ashamed of it. She felt vaguely sorry for him. Carson wasn't a bad man. He had wonderful qualities. He'd stayed two nights with old Ben Hamm and his wife on their ranch when the couple had the flu. He'd fed them and taken care of them, and then paid their utility bills for the month because Ben had been unable to work for a week and had gotten behind. Then there was the poor family that he'd "adopted" for Christmas. He'd bought toys for the kids and had a huge turkey with all the trimmings delivered to their home. Yes, Carson was a caring man. He just had an extremely hard shell, and Mandelyn decided that he probably had plenty of reasons for it. What would it be like to know the man beneath the shell? She fell asleep on the thought.

4

Bright and early Monday morning she called Angie at home and told her she wasn't coming in to the office.

"I'm going fishing. I'll call in later to see if there are any messages," she told the younger woman.

"Fishing?" Angie burst out.

"Why not?' she replied.

"Excuse me, Miss Bush." Angie cleared her throat. "It's just that I never thought you'd like fishing."

"Well, we'll both find out after this morning. Have a good day."

"You, too."

Mandelyn didn't own a pair of old jeans. She wore a slightly worn pair of designer jeans with a colorful striped pullover shirt and sneakers, and left her hair long. She looked a little less proper than usual, she decided finally.

Carson wasn't outside when she drove up, and she hesitated at the front door when he called for her to come inside. It was a little unnerving to be totally alone with him, but she chided herself for her continuing feeling of uneasiness with him and went inside anyway.

"Just be a minute," he called from the back of the house. The bedrooms must be located there, but she'd never seen them.

"Take your time," she replied. She sighed over the worn furniture and bare walls. With a little paint and love, this house had great possibilities. It wasn't all that old, and it was built sturdily. She pursed her lips, studying it. The room was big, but it could be comfortable, and there was a huge rock fireplace that would be a showpiece with a little cleaning up. The windows were long and elegant, and the floor would have a beauty all its own if it were varnished.

"You won't find any sidewinders under the rug, if that's what you're looking for," Carson taunted from the doorway.

She turned and had to force herself to look away again. He'd obviously just come from a shower. He was fully dressed except for the shirt he was shrugging into, a blue printed one that matched his eyes. She got a wildly exciting glimpse of broad, tanned muscles and a thick pelt of hair running down past the buckled belt around his lean hips, and her heart started beating unexpectedly hard. She'd seen Carson without a shirt before, for God's sake, she told herself, why was it affecting her this way all of a sudden?

"You look elegant even in jeans," he murmured drily. "Couldn't you find anything worn?"

"This is worn." She pouted, turning to find him closer than she'd expected. She took a slow breath and inhaled the scent of a men's cologne that was one of her particular favorites. "You smell good," she blurted out.

"Do I?" He laughed softly.

His hands had stilled on the top buttons of the shirt and he looked down at her in a way that threatened and excited all at the same time. His chiseled mouth was smiling in a faint, sexy way and his blue eyes narrowed as they studied her.

"Why are you so nervous?" he asked with his head lifted, so that he was looking down his crooked nose at her. "You've been alone with me before."

"You were always dressed before," she said without meaning to.

"Is that it?" He watched her face and deliberately flicked open the buttons he'd fastened. "Does this bother you?" he asked in a deep, lazy tone, moving the shirt aside to let the hair-roughened expanse of his chest show.

Her breath caught and she didn't understand why. Her lips went dry, but she barely noticed.

He lifted her hands with slow, easy movements, and brought her fingers to his cool skin, letting her feel the hard muscles.

"No flab," she laughed unsteadily, trying to keep things light between them, but her legs felt shaky.

"Not a bit," he agreed. "I work too hard for that." He pressed her fingers hard against him and moved them in a slow, sensuous pattern down the center of his chest and back up again. "I don't suppose you brought a fishing pole?"

"I don't...own one," she replied. Incredible, that they were conducting an impersonal conversation while what they were doing was growing quickly more intimate.

His chest rose and fell unevenly. He pressed her palms flat against his hardened nipples and she could hear his heartbeat, actually hear it. He moved, so that he was closer than ever, and his breath stirred the hair at her temples.

She couldn't look up, because she wanted his mouth desperately, and she knew he'd see it. She didn't understand her own wild hungers or his unexpected reaction to her nearness and her touch. She didn't understand anything.

The room seemed dark and private. There was no

sound in it, except for his breathing and the loud tick of the mantel clock.

He drew his open mouth tenderly across her forehead, his breath hot, his chest shuddering with the harshness of his breathing. Impatiently, he took her hands in his and guided them down the hard muscles of his chest and around to his lean hips. She protested, a stiff little gesture.

"Don't fight me," he whispered unsteadily, moving her hands down the sides of his legs and back up to his hips. "There's nothing to be afraid of."

But there was! Her own reaction to him was terrifying. She felt his legs touch hers and she made an odd sound in her throat, one that he heard.

His head moved nearer. Her eyes closed and she felt his warm breath at her forehead, her nose, the open softness of her mouth. Unaware of her response, she opened her mouth to invite his, tilted her head back to give him full access. And waited, breathing in his scent as his mouth came closer. Would it be gentle this time, she wondered, or would he hurt…?

"Mr. Wayne!" The loud call was like a gunshot. Carson's head jerked up. He looked dazed, and his eyes were a dark blue, haunted, hungry as they met hers for just an instant before he moved away.

"What is it, Jake?" he asked curtly, buttoning his shirt as he went out onto the porch.

Mandelyn heard the voices with a sense of unreality. She was still trembling, and her mouth was hungry for the kiss she hadn't gotten. Her misty eyes searched for Carson and found him standing outside the door. She looked at him with open wonder, letting her rapt eyes wander down the superb masculinity of his back and hips and legs. She remembered the feel of his skin, the smell of him. Her breasts ached and as she crossed her arms, she felt the nipples' hardness.

She licked her dry lips and ground her teeth together as she tried to get her rebellious body back under control. It wanted him. God, it wanted him, all of him, skin against skin, mouth against hungry mouth. She almost moaned aloud at the force of that wanting, at the urgency she'd never felt before. Her sweet memories of the man in her past had faded completely away during that passionate onslaught, had been replaced with a different emotion. With a wildness that she'd never known, a violent need.

How in the world could she face Carson now, after giving herself away so completely? He was still a man, he wouldn't hesitate to take anything that was offered, despite their long friendship. If she acted like a temptress, what could she expect? He was human.

She cleared her throat as he came back into the room. If only she could find an excuse to go home.

"I'll find you a pole," he said good-humoredly, grinning at her. "Got a hat?"

"No."

"Here." He reached into the closet and tossed her a straw one that just fit. "It belonged to me, years back. Well, let's go."

He herded her out the door before she had a chance to protest, and minutes later they went bumping over his pasture in the pickup truck toward the stream where the swimming and fishing hole spread out invitingly past some cottonwood trees.

"We used to swim here," he told her as they sat on upside-down minnow buckets in the cool shade. "Some of the boys still do, but it's a good fishing spot, nevertheless. Here."

He handed her the bait can and she stared at it distastefully.

"Please?" she asked softly, looking up at him.

His eyes remained on hers for a minute before he turned them back to the bait can. "I'll show you how."

"But, Carson…"

"Just watch."

He threaded worms onto the hook while she grimaced. "Soft-hearted little thing," he chided. "I'll never take you rabbit hunting, that's for sure."

She stuck out her tongue at him. "Well, I wouldn't go, so don't ask me."

"Patty's having a party next Friday night," he said as he threw her line into the stream. The red cork bobbed gaily against the murky water. He glanced at her.

"Is she?" she asked in a breathless tone.

He threaded worms onto his own hook. "Kind of a social gathering, I think, so folks can get acquainted with her and tour her new office."

"She's really proud of it," she murmured.

He threw his own line in and leaned his elbows on his knees, holding the pole between them. Nearby birds were calling, and crickets made pleasant sounds in the underbrush.

She glanced at him. "Are you going?"

He laughed shortly. "You know I don't socialize."

She looked down at the ground. "I could…teach you."

His eyes glanced sideways. "Could you?"

"You've got the clothes now," she reminded him. "All you need to know is some of the new dance steps and how to talk to people."

He stared at her for a long moment. "Yes."

She shifted on the bucket. "Well, do you want to?"

"Want to what?" he asked huskily.

She looked up into his eyes and felt herself going hot

all over. She dragged her gaze back to the water. "Uh, do you want me to teach you?"

"I think you may be the one who needs teaching," he said.

Her face flamed, because she knew exactly what he was talking about. She felt like a girl on her first date, tongue-tied and expectant.

"I know how to dance," she said.

"Deliberately misunderstanding me again?" he said with a soft laugh.

"I thought we came here to fish?"

"I am."

"Do you want to learn to dance or not?" she asked impatiently.

"I guess so."

"You can come over tomorrow night, if you want to," she said. "I'll make supper."

He studied her for a long moment. "All right."

She tingled from head to toe in a new, exciting way. She smiled, and he watched the movement of her lips with an expression that it was just as well she didn't see. It would have frightened her.

She studied the bobbing red cork with drowsy, contented eyes, hardly aware when it went straight under. When she felt the tug on the line and realized what was happening, she jerked too soon. The hook came flying up on the bank, straight into her shirt and caught there.

"My God, were you trying to send the fish to the moon?" Carson drawled. "You caught something at least."

She glared at him. "My favorite shirt," she moaned, letting her eyes fall to the hook sticking through the soft fabric just above the peak of her tiptilted breast.

"Hold still and I'll get it out for you," he said. He put down his pole and knelt beside her.

She hadn't realized how intimate it was going to be. In order to extricate the barbed hook, he had to slide one lean, work-roughened hand into the V-neck of the shirt. And Mandelyn wasn't wearing a bra. That discovery made Carson start violently.

His eyes met hers. She could see the dark blue circles around his lighter blue irises, and the black thickness of his lashes. But what she was feeling was the touch of his knuckles on her bare breast, and her body was reacting noticeably to it.

"Carson, I can get it out," she said too quickly.

"Let me," he whispered. But he was holding her eyes when he said it, and his fingers were moving very delicately on bare skin. She trembled.

He smelled of wind and fir trees and desert. And his

skin was rough against her softness, but it was a natural roughness, like sand against silk, or bark against water.

Even the crickets seemed to have gone mute. There was silence all around them in the little glade. Nothing existed except Mandelyn's awed face and Carson's hard one, and the sound of his breathing as he closed his eyes and tenderly cradled Mandelyn's head in one big hand.

She jerked a little in reaction, but he shook his head slowly and lowered his face toward her.

"Sit still, Mandy," he whispered as his lips stroked her mouth. "I just want to see how you taste when I'm sober."

"Carson, your hand..." she whispered half-heartedly, and her slender fingers touched his hairy wrist in token protest.

"Shh," he breathed. His mouth was like a teasing breeze, brushing at her lips. His fingers stroked over the soft curve of her breast, edging toward the hard tip with every movement, teasing her body as he teased her mouth.

She stiffened, moved. Her eyes opened, her breath quickened. His face was so close that all she could see was his mouth. He'd shaved. That registered. And he tasted of smoke and coffee and mint. But his hand...!

She caught it just as his thumb and forefinger found the hard tip, and her nails bit into him helplessly and she moaned. It took every ounce of will power she had to move his hand away. She was afraid of the new sensations she was feeling. She was afraid of Carson.

"All right," he said softly, not offended at all. Her flushed face and wide, frightened eyes told him everything he needed to know. His hand brushed the long strands of hair away from her cheeks, and he looked at her with such reverence that she couldn't seem to move.

"The hook," she reminded him.

"Yes," he murmured, smiling faintly. "Later. I want that kiss, honey."

Her heart was beating so wildly that she could barely breathe at all. His head bent and she waited for his mouth, no protest left in her, only a sense of anticipation.

His lips were warm and hard and exquisitely tender. She closed her eyes with a soft sigh and let him do what he wanted. He eased between her trembling lips, letting her feel the texture of his own. Her hands dug into the hard muscles of his shoulders in an agony of wanting.

But still he teased her, rubbing his closed lips between her open ones, nibbling at her soft mouth. And then he stopped. She moaned aloud as he got to his feet and reached down to bring her body into the hard curve of his.

"It's all right," he murmured, wrapping her securely in his arms. "I only want to feel you while we kiss."

She reached up, hesitant, and touched his hard face.

"Carson," she whispered.

His chest rose and fell roughly. "I've waited years for you to say my name that way," he murmured unsteadily as he bent again. "Years, centuries..."

"Hard," she pleaded, trembling. "Hard, please...!"

A tremor ran through him, probably of shock, she thought dizzily as he took her open mouth. She'd shocked herself with the whispered demand. She tasted him, experienced him with every sense she had as he gently crushed her breasts into his hard chest and his mouth merged roughly, intimately with her own. His tongue stabbed between her teeth, into the dark warmth of her mouth, tangling with her tongue in a wild, exquisite exploration.

He groaned against her mouth. A faint tremor shook his arms, and she arched into his body. She wanted him. Her body told her that, it screamed at her to end this sweet torment. She wanted to feel his skin against hers, she wanted the driving power of his body to overwhelm her, possess her. She wanted his open mouth on her soft breasts....

When he lifted his head abruptly, it was like being thrown to the ground. She shivered.

His darkened blue eyes searched hers quickly, intensely, and although he'd loosened his grip, he still held her by the arms. He started to draw back and her shirt came with him.

"Oh, hell," he muttered, looking down. The hook that had gone through her blouse had caught in the thick pocket of his shirt.

She started laughing as reaction set in. Her twinkling eyes sought his. "I've hooked you," she teased.

He stared at her for a long moment. "I haven't seen you laugh before. Not like this."

"I haven't felt like this before," she blurted out. "I mean, being relaxed and going fishing and…and being myself."

"Stand still while I get us untangled," he said, and reached down, frowning as he tried to extract the barbed end of the hook from his pocket. "Damn, I'll have to cut it," he muttered. He dove into his pocket and dragged out an old pocket knife, expertly extracting the blade and slicing deftly through the fabric. His eyes glanced at her apologetically. "Sorry, honey, but this is the only way. I'll buy you another blouse."

"You don't have to do that. It was my fault, after all," she said breathlessly.

"Stand still, so I don't nick you," he said softly and slid his hand under the fabric again, against her bare skin.

She felt wildly female at the feel and sight of that dark-skinned, tough hand inside her blouse. Her lips parted and she studied the face so close to hers with wide, fascinated eyes.

He felt the stare and looked down into her eyes. His hands paused in their task and he watched her for a long moment. "Why didn't you want me to touch you?" he whispered.

Her lower lip trembled a little. "I…haven't been touched…that way since I was eighteen, Carson," she said unsteadily.

"If I'd persisted a minute longer, you'd have let me, though, wouldn't you?" he asked.

She licked her dry lips and her wide gray eyes searched his blue ones with uncertainty. "I didn't expect that," she whispered.

"Why not? I'm human, Mandy. I may be rough and half-civilized, but I'm capable of wanting a woman."

"Oh, I didn't mean it like that," she said, touching his hard mouth with her fingers. She searched his eyes curiously. "Carson…you…you've had women, haven't you?"

Time seemed to hang suspended between them. "Yes," he said quietly.

Her breath shuddered out of her throat. Her fingers traced his lips unsteadily, with helpless pleasure. "I've never been to bed with a man," she breathed.

His nostrils flared. His chest rose and fell raggedly. "You're twenty-six."

She smiled nervously. Having him this close was affecting her wildly. "Yes, I know. Do you think I might get in the record books?"

"Not," he sighed heavily, "if you keep touching me that way."

"Oh!" Belatedly she realized just how intimate her fingers had grown on his face. She moved them back down to his arm. "Sorry."

"You excite me," he admitted, turning his attention back to the hook. He sliced the fabric gently, not unaware of her hot blush or the increasing pressure of her fingers. "So watch out."

That wasn't going to be easy, she realized, feeling his warm fingers being slowly removed from her blouse. "Thank you," she said as he removed the hook as well.

"My pleasure," he murmured drily.

"Carson, I didn't mean to..." she began, losing her train of thought when he looked down into her eyes. "I didn't know...I wasn't..."

"Hush." He handed her the fishing pole with a warm, knowing look. "I haven't been with a woman in a long time," he said slowly. "It was a moment out of time, that's all. Nothing to be afraid of."

"Of course." She managed to get a worm on the hook and began talking real estate, out of nervousness. She'd reacted to Carson's lovemaking like a shy young girl, and she knew now that while he might need lessons in deportment, he'd never need them as a lover. He knew exactly what to do with a woman. And now she was more afraid of him than ever. In all the years she'd known him, she'd never thought of him as a lover. Now it was impossible to think of him any other way.

He followed her lead in conversation, and they talked about general things for a long time while the day moved lazily by. After they had caught a good number of fish, they packed up their gear and went back to the house.

"I've enjoyed today. Thank you," she said. She was reluctant to leave him, and that was odd. In the past she'd always been glad to get out of his sight.

"So have I," he replied. He studied her for a long moment. "Want to stay for supper? We can cook the fish together."

She should have said no. But she didn't. Her face lit up and she smiled. "Sure!"

He chuckled. "Want to clean them for me?"

She frowned. "Carson, I hate to be a drag, but I don't think I know how. Uncle didn't fish, you know."

"Yes, and cleaning fish isn't something you learn in finishing school, is it, little lady?"

He didn't say it in an insulting way. She searched his hard face. "Does it bother you, my background?"

"No," he said firmly. "If you want to know, I think

a lot of you. Until you came along, I'd never met a real lady."

"You wouldn't think I was one at times, though," she murmured, smiling at him as she followed him into the kitchen.

"You're a firecracker sometimes, all right," he agreed. He caught her by the waist after he'd put down the string of fish, and jerked her against his body. "But I like you that way, Mandy. A woman with a temper," he murmured, bending, "is usually pretty passionate…."

His mouth crushed down against hers and she moaned, the sound unusually loud in the confines of the room as she savored his strength, the urgency of his hard kiss.

He lifted his head, his eyes glittering with some new emotion. "Why did you moan?" he asked roughly. "Fear or pleasure?"

Her lips trembled and, embarrassed, she pulled away. "I'll get started on the fish."

He watched her for a minute speculatively and then he smiled. "I'll get some potatoes to fry."

It was a quiet supper. She enjoyed her crisp fish, but Carson seemed preoccupied.

"Want to call it off?" she asked.

His head came up. "What?"

"Tomorrow night."

He shook his head. "No. I want to learn to dance."

His eyes dropped to her soft mouth. "With you," he added softly.

Her chest felt tight. He was doing it again, using that wicked charm that she hadn't known he possessed.

"I have to practice on somebody, don't I?" he asked when he saw her hesitation. "I thought teaching me how to make love went part and parcel with teaching me to court a woman," he added with a wicked smile.

She flushed. "You don't need teaching in that department, and well you know it," she said.

His eyebrows arched. "I don't?"

She looked up. Her wide eyes pleaded with him. "Don't take advantage, will you?" she asked softly. "I'm afraid of you, a little."

"Yes, I know you are," he replied, his voice deep and quiet in the stillness of the room. He reached across the table and took her small hand in his, rubbing his thumb over the silky skin. "Haven't you ever wanted a man, or was it that exclusive upbringing that kept you innocent?"

"That exclusive upbringing is the downfall of a lot of girls," she murmured drily. "Most of the others were quite experienced."

"Didn't you date?"

That brought back painful memories, and she didn't want to face them. She shrugged. "I was terribly shy in those days. It was hard for me to talk to men at all."

"Not when you got out here," he chuckled. "I'll never forget the first time I saw you."

"I slapped you," she recalled with a wicked smile. "I didn't know at the time how dangerous that was."

"I would never hit you back," he said. "I'd cut off my arm first."

"That's what Jake knows, that's why I always get rousted out of bed to come and save the world from you," she laughed.

He studied her hand. "Jake isn't as blind as you are, I guess."

"Blind?"

"It doesn't matter." He let go of her fingers and lit a cigarette. His eyes searched hers. "Getting dark. You'd better go home, before somebody makes a remark about your being here alone with me after dark."

"Would that bother you?"

"Yes," he said simply. "I don't want any blemish on your reputation. I'd fire any one of my men who suggested that anything improper went on here."

"It did this afternoon," she blurted out and then flushed.

He searched her eyes slowly. "I wanted to see if I could make you want me," he explained quietly.

She got up from the table in such a rush that she almost knocked over her chair. "I'd better go," she faltered.

He got up, too, and walked along behind her at a slow, steady, confident pace.

"Was that too crude a remark for a gentleman to make?" he murmured drily. "Sorry, Mandy, I don't always think before I say things to you. Look on it as getting some sexual experience. You seem to be pretty backward yourself in that department."

She turned at the front porch and met his stare levelly. "Are you sorry? Would you rather I was experienced?"

He reached out and put his knuckles against her lips. "I'd like, very much, to let you get that kind of experience with me," he said quietly. "Because the way I'd take you, even the first time would be good. I'd make sure of it."

She could hardly walk, her knees felt so weak. She headed for her car in a daze, wondering at the explosive quality of their changing relationship.

"Hey," he called as she opened her car door.

"What?" she asked.

"What time tomorrow night?"

She swallowed and looked back. He was standing on the porch, leaning against a post. The soft light of the kerosene lanterns outlined his superb physique. He looked devastating, and she wondered what he'd do if she walked back up on that porch and kissed him.

"Oh...about six," she faltered.

"Do I dress?"

"You'd better," she said, "if we're going to do the thing properly."

"By all means," he murmured drily. "'Night, honey."

"Good night, Carson."

She drove off, jerking the car as she never had before. Carson was getting to her! She must be off her rocker to let him get under her skin that way. She was the teacher, not Carson. At least, it had started out that way. She had to be careful. Her memories of love were too sweet to let reality interfere with them. She'd learned the hard way that loving was the first step to agony. She didn't want to go through it again. She couldn't! From now on, she'd just keep Carson at arm's length. It was safer that way.

5

Mandelyn went home and paced the floor until bedtime. And then she tossed and turned for hours, remembering vividly the touch of Carson's lean fingers on her breast, the fierce hunger of his mouth on her own. She felt on fire for him, and part of her hated the reaction.

It had been years. Years, since she'd felt passion. She hadn't wanted to give herself over to it again, and yet Carson had kindled an emotion in her that overwhelmed her tenderest memories of the past. She'd never felt so violent, so hungry. She rolled over onto her back and stared at the ceiling. Perhaps it was her age. Perhaps she'd reached the brink of spinsterhood and was feeling alone, as Carson felt alone.

She could picture him, blue eyes devouring her face, dark-skinned hands so gentle on her body….

Of course, it could just be infatuation. He was her creation, after all, she was teaching him. Yes, that could be it. She could be like Svengali, overcome by pride. But if that was it, why did she tingle when she thought about Carson? She closed her eyes and thought about birds.

Patty came by the office the next day at lunchtime with some documents from the bank. "Here are the loan papers," she said with a grin. "What time do we meet with that attorney?"

"Today at five," Mandelyn said. "Happy?"

"Just ecstatic," came the reply. "I've got to run out to Carson's and see about that bull. Want to come along, and we'll swing by the barbecue place and have lunch on the way back?"

"Yes, I'd like that," Mandelyn said. "Angie, just close up at noon when you get your own lunch, okay?"

Angie nodded. "Have fun."

Fun! Mandelyn's heart was racing wildly as she climbed into the red pickup truck beside Patty. She didn't really want to see Carson, but he was coming to her house for dinner that night so she couldn't very well avoid him.

Carson wasn't at the house when they drove up. The door was closed and locked.

"I wonder where he could be?" Patty asked, nibbling on her lip. "Surely to goodness he knew I was coming?"

"Maybe he's in the barn," Mandelyn suggested.

Patty sighed. "Boy, am I sharp, not to have thought of that. Maybe I should try another profession...yep, look, there's the ranch pickup."

They walked down to the barn. Mandelyn wished she hadn't worn the spiked high heels that went so well with her jaunty little two-piece blue and white suit. But when she entered the barn and saw the frank appreciation on Carson's face, she decided it was worth a little discomfort. He was half kneeling beside his bull, with Jake at his side, and he couldn't seem to take his eyes off her.

Both men got to their feet, and Mandelyn couldn't help noticing how animated Patty suddenly became. She was wearing jeans and a T-shirt, and had her hair pulled back in a bun, but she still looked feminine and cute, and Carson gave her a big grin and hugged her.

"There's my best girl," he said, and Mandelyn felt suddenly murderous.

"How's my patient?" Patty asked, hugging him back while Jake looked at them with an expression Mandelyn couldn't quite describe.

"Well, he's about the same," Carson sighed, staring down at the bull. He still had an arm around Patty, and Mandelyn found she resented it.

Patty got down beside the big animal, a Hereford, and checked him over with professional thoroughness. "We'll try another dose of the same, and see if that won't do it. He's improved some, Carson, I think we can save him."

"If you don't, I may never speak to you again," Carson assured her. "And I'll guarantee at least five of my cows will die of broken hearts, judging by the way they've behaved since he's been out of action."

Mandelyn flushed, but Patty only laughed. "We'll restore him to his former vigor. Let me get my bag. Mandy, you aren't in a rush to get back, are you?"

"No," came the quiet reply. "I don't have anything pressing."

"Here, I'll help with that bag," Jake said curtly, and walked out of the barn behind Patty with a determined stride. Mandelyn had never actually seen the easygoing foreman move so quickly.

Carson studied Mandelyn with narrow, thoughtful eyes, hands on his hips, powerful legs apart. "You're quiet. And you won't look at me. Why?"

Her eyes glanced off his and back down to the bull. "What's the matter with the bull?" she asked nervously.

He moved closer, ignoring the question. So close that she could smell him, feel him, touch him if she chose. His shirt was half unbuttoned, and she wanted to reach out and rip it open....

His fingers tilted her oval face up to his eyes, and he

looked at her for a long time. “Shy, Mandy?” he asked softly.

She flushed and tried to look away, but he wouldn’t let her. Her lips parted on a rush of breath.

“Tonight,” he whispered, making a promise of it as he searched her wide eyes.

Her lips trembled and he started to bend toward them, his eyes intent, his lean hand moving to the back of her head to position her face where he wanted it. And just as his open mouth started to touch hers, the truck door slammed.

He laughed. “I seem to spend my life trying to kiss you without interruptions, don’t I, honey?”

She managed a nervous laugh, too, but her eyes were wary. She didn’t miss the speculative look he sent toward Patty and Jake, or the way he moved quickly back to his bull. Was he trying to make the other girl jealous?

She didn’t say another word until Patty was ready to go, and then she all but ran for the truck. Carson made her nervous, he intimidated her. She sat there listening as Patty told him what else to do for the sick bull. And all the while Mandelyn never actually looked at him. She was frightened of what her eyes might tell him.

“You sure were quiet today,” Patty remarked as they ate a hamburger at a local restaurant known for its barbecue. “You and Carson have a fight or something?”

"Oh, nothing like that," Mandelyn said. "We, uh, I just couldn't think of anything to say, that's all. I don't know a lot about animals."

"I love them," Patty sighed. "I always did. There was never anything I wanted to be more than a vet." She glanced suspiciously at Mandelyn. "What was going on in the barn when Jake and I walked in, by the way? You were hot and bothered like I've never seen you. Carson make a pass?"

"You know I don't feel that way about Carson," Mandelyn said nervously, making a jerking motion with her hand that knocked over her cup of soda.

Patty ran for more napkins, and Mandelyn sat there in the ruin of her suit wondering if it would be undignified to scream.

The rest of the day was no better. She didn't make a single sale, although she did show one undecided young couple six houses only to learn that at least one major thing was wrong with each. She stopped by the attorney's office for the closing on Patty's new building, and then locked up her own office with a weary sigh. She still had to think of something to fix for supper. And Carson was coming!

She jumped in her car and made a wild rush home to see what she had to cook. Thank goodness there was some chicken she could fry and some vegetables. She took off her suit, put on jeans and a loose shirt, and got to it. She didn't even think about what lay ahead; it made her too nervous. Things were getting entirely out of hand with him, and she didn't know what to do anymore. What had begun as a simple etiquette course now promised to be a full-fledged affair if she didn't watch her step. It occurred to her that he wanted her, physically. But she knew that he could feel that way and still be in love with Patty. It wasn't the same with men as it was with women. Which made her even more nervous about her own survival instincts. They didn't seem to work with Carson.

Just before six, she tried on five outfits before deciding on a demure little yellow sundress. She left her hair down and brushed it to silky perfection, and then stared at herself in the mirror and hoped she didn't look too eager or too dressed up. She hadn't been so excited in years, and over Carson, of all people!

He got there five minutes early, just as she'd finished dishing up the chicken and vegetables. She ran to the door to let him in, and smiled in helpless appreciation at the way he looked.

He was wearing one of the new outfits they'd bought him—tan slacks with a patterned shirt and a casual white and tan plaid blazer. He was freshly shaven and his hair, under his Stetson, was well-groomed. He smelled of fine cologne and he looked good enough to eat.

"Well?" he asked impatiently.

She stood aside to let him in, sensitive to the sweeping glance he gave her. "You look very nice," she murmured.

"So do you. Good enough to be the main course, in fact."

She grinned. "I'd give you a rash."

"Think so?" He tossed his hat onto the chair and there was a sudden sharp gleam in his eyes.

She knew what he was thinking, and it frightened her. She went hurriedly ahead of him into the dining room, where the table was already laid, including iced tea in tall glasses.

"I'd just finished," she explained. "Shall we start?"

He sighed. "I guess so," he said with a wistful glance in her direction.

She stood by her chair while he sat down and shook out his napkin.

"Ahem!" she cleared her throat.

He glanced up. "Something wrong with your throat?"

"I'm waiting for you to seat me."

"Oh." He got to his feet, frowning. The gleam came back into his blue, blue eyes. He pulled out her chair and bent and lifted her in his hard arms. "Like this?"

he asked softly, putting her down in the chair with his mouth hovering just above her own.

"N-not exactly," she whispered back. Her eyes fell to his mouth, and she wanted it. Wanted it…!

He seemed to know that, because he straightened with a purely masculine smile on his face and went back to his own chair.

"This looks good," he murmured while she tried to get her heart to settle down, her lungs to work again.

"I hope it tastes that way," she said tautly. "It was a rush job. I had a long afternoon."

"So did I."

"How's your bull?" she asked, handing him the platter of chicken.

"He'll make it. He was better after that second shot. Poor old critter, I felt sorry for him."

"I thought it was the cows you felt sorry for," she murmured demurely.

He studied her downbent head for a long moment before he dished out some mashed potatoes onto his plate. "You ought to come over when I turn him back out into the pasture," he said drily. "You'd learn a few things."

She all but overturned her tea glass, and he threw back his black head and laughed uproariously.

"All right, I give up, you're out of my league," she burst out. "You terrible man!"

"You need to spend some time around Patty," he remarked. "She'd put you on the right track soon enough. A girl after my own heart."

Which was probably true, she thought miserably. Patty would suit him to a tee. He might want Mandelyn, but Patty appealed to his mind and heart. How terrible, to be wanted only for her body.

"You put out salad forks," he remarked. "Why? You didn't make a salad."

"I meant to," she said.

"Etiquette," he scoffed. "I'll be damned if I understand any of it. A bunch of rules and regulations for snobs, if you ask me. Why dress up a table like this when all you do is eat, anyway? Who the hell cares which fork you eat what with?"

"Ladies and gentlemen do," she said, biting down hard on a roll.

"I'm not much of a gentleman, am I?" he sighed. "I don't suppose if I worked at it all my life, I'd improve a hell of a lot."

"Yes, you will," she said softly. She studied his craggy face, liking its hardness, its strength. Her eyes fell to his slender hand and she remembered how tender it had been on her bare skin. She dropped her fork noisily against her plate and scrambled to pick it up.

"Do I make you nervous, Mandelyn?" he murmured wryly. "That's a first."

She shifted in her seat. "I'm not used to entertaining men here," she admitted.

"Yes, I know that."

He was watching her, the way he always did, and that made her more nervous than ever. They finished the meal in silence, and he helped her carry the dishes into the kitchen. Not only that—he insisted on helping as she washed them. He dried them, smiling at her confusion.

"I'm handy in the kitchen," he reminded her. "I have to be or I'd have starved to death years ago. I don't have women over to cook my dinner."

She lifted her eyes to his hard face and searched it curiously.

He looked down at the curious expression on her flushed face. "Yes, once in a while they come over for other purposes," he said softly. "I'm a man, not a plaster saint, and I have all the usual needs."

Her face colored slowly and he grinned. She tore her eyes away, but her hands trembled and she hated that giveaway sign.

"You're such a little greenhorn," he murmured. "You don't know anything about men and women, do you?"

"I'm not ignorant," she muttered.

"I didn't say you were. Just innocent." He finished

drying the last dish and put it to one side. "I like that. Your being innocent, I mean. I like it a lot."

She couldn't meet his eyes. He made her feel shy and young and all thumbs.

"Why hasn't there been a man?" he asked quietly.

"Let's start your dancing lessons, shall we?" she began nervously. She started past him, but he caught her.

"Why, Mandelyn?" he persisted.

"Carson..."

His big hands caught her waist and crushed her body against his. "Why, damn it?" he burst out, his patience at an end.

Her vulnerability to his nearness shocked her. She panicked and suddenly tore away from him as if she couldn't bear for him to touch her. She stood with her back to him, shivering.

She knew he hadn't liked her withdrawal, not one bit. But she couldn't help it, he terrified her. She was getting in over her head, and she didn't know how to stop him, how to handle him. Carson was more man pound for pound than she'd ever seen.

She swallowed down a rush of shyness and turned back to face him. He was preoccupied, as if he was thinking deep thoughts. He came close again, his gaze intent.

"Suppose you show me how to dance," he said at last. "Then next week comes culture. I've bought tickets for a ballet in Phoenix. I thought you might come along and explain it all to me."

She laughed. "You, at a ballet?"

He glared at her. "Stop that!"

"Yes, Carson," she said demurely.

"Turn on that damned stereo, will you?"

A moment later the music flowed sweetly into the silence. Mandelyn went easily into his arms and showed him how to hold her, not too tightly, not too loosely. Then she taught him what to do with his feet. He was a little clumsy at first, but an apt enough student.

"Why do I have to hold you so far away?" he asked. "I've seen couples practically making love on the dance floor."

"Not in polite company," she said huskily, staring at her feet.

"Yes, in polite company," he murmured. His hands brought her gently closer, until she was standing right up against him, so close that she could feel his heartbeat against her breasts. "Like this. Here." He brought one of her hands up to his neck and slid his arm further around her, resting his chin on her head. "Mmm," he murmured, "much better."

That depended on one's point of view, she thought nervously. She felt stiff, because her body was reacting to his like wildfire.

"Don't panic," he said softly. "We'll just dance."

But she was all too close to him, and something had happened to his body that she'd never experienced before. She tried to edge a little away from him, but he held her fast.

"Carson," she protested weakly.

"Mandelyn, I know you're a virgin," he said quietly. "I'm not going to make a wild grab for you."

"Yes, I know, but...but..."

"But you can feel me wanting you and you're frightened, isn't that it?" He lifted his head and searched her eyes. "I'm not embarrassed. Why should you be? It's a man's very natural reaction to a lovely woman."

She'd never heard it put like that. She studied his hard face.

"I've spent my life working with animals," he said, his voice quiet, deep. "I don't find anything distasteful about reproduction, about sex. You shouldn't either. It's God's way of perpetuating the species, and it's beautiful."

She flushed, but she didn't look away. "You make it sound that way," she said softly.

His eyes searched hers intimately. "I don't like the idea of one-night stands and affairs, or people living together without marriage. I'm old-fashioned enough to want a woman with principles when I marry, and not a woman who'll proposition me just because she feels liberated."

Her eyebrows arched. “Has that ever happened to you?” she asked.

He laughed softly. “As a matter of fact, yes, at a cattle convention, of all places. She was a little rodeo rider and as pretty as a picture. She came up to me, touched me in a way I won’t even tell you about and invited me to spend the night with her.”

She hesitated. “Did you?” she asked in a tiny voice, all eyes.

He studied her mouth for a long moment. “Shame on you. A well brought up young woman like you, asking a man that kind of question….”

“Did you sleep with her?” she persisted.

“No, as a matter of fact, I didn’t,” he chuckled. “I like to do the chasing.”

“Yes, I imagine you would,” she replied, but she felt relieved all the same.

His hand slid down her back to the bottom of her spine and pushed her just a little closer, and she caught her breath and froze.

“Too intimate?” he murmured. “Okay, I get the message. The kind of girls I’m used to don’t mind being held like that. But I guess I’ve got a lot to learn about civilized behavior.”

She nuzzled her face against his chest with a sigh.

"I've got a lot to learn about the reverse," she said with a smile. "No one's ever held me this way."

His hands contracted on her waist, and she gasped. "Hey, not so tight," she laughed. "That hurts!"

"Why don't you go out with anyone?"

That was a good question, but it wasn't the time for confessions. "I like my own company," she said after a minute.

"You'll need a man one day."

"No," she protested. "I don't want anyone."

His hand caught suddenly in the thick length of her hair and tugged sharply. She gasped at the twinge of pain and stared at him as if he were a stranger.

"You can't live alone forever," he said harshly, his eyes glittering down into hers. "You need more than your work."

"What do I need, since you're such an expert on the subject?" she challenged hotly.

He pulled her hair, more gently now, forcing her head down onto his shoulder while the music played on, forgotten. "You need to be dragged into a man's bed and loved all night long. That's what you need."

"Not with you," she protested, pushing against his hard chest. "You've got a woman already!"

He wouldn't let go. "I have?"

"Of course," she grumbled, pushing harder. "The one

we're remodeling you for, remember? The one who's too stuck up to like you the way…you are…will you let go of me, damn it!" She stood still, hating the slow, sweet stirrings of her own body as he held her and she felt his heartbeat merging with her own.

His chest rose and fell with gathering speed, and the hand holding her long hair released it and began a caressing motion.

It dawned on her that the music was still playing, a sultry tune that only made more dangerous an already flammable situation.

"Dance, don't fight," he whispered deeply. "Don't fight me."

Her legs were trembling as he drew her into a rhythm that was more like making love to music than dancing. His hard thighs brushed her own and never in her life had she felt weaker or more vulnerable.

"I'm afraid." She didn't know that she'd said it out loud, or that Carson's pale blue eyes glittered like diamonds when he heard her.

"Yes, I know," he breathed into her hair. His fingers slid between hers caressingly. "I won't hurt you."

Her nails pressed unconsciously against his chest and he stiffened. She frowned, drawing back so that she could see his face. What she found there disturbed her.

His nostrils flared, his jaw clenched. "No, you aren't the only one who's vulnerable," he said curtly.

Her fascinated eyes searched his. Her rebellious hands liked his visible reaction to them. They opened the top button of his shirt, and his breath caught, but he didn't make a move to stop her.

Her lower lip trembled. "I…Carson?" she whispered questioningly.

"Go ahead," he breathed. "Do it."

"But…"

His open mouth touched her forehead. "Do it."

He was trembling already. By the time she fumbled open the shirt and eased the edges aside, his quickened breathing was visible as well. Fascinated, she put her hands flat on the hair-roughened flesh and began to caress him with slow, tentative movements. He seemed to like what she was doing, if the intent hardness of his expression was any indication.

She slid her hands around to his muscular back and laid her hot cheek against his bare skin and closed her eyes. He smelled clean and sexy, and she drew her cheek, then her lips, against his body with dreamy motions.

His fingers tangled in her hair and turned her face, so that her mouth was against him.

"Kiss me," he whispered. "No, honey, not like that.

Open your mouth and do it. Yes," he groaned unsteadily, and his hands grew rough. "Yes."

She drew her mouth over every hard inch of his chest, up to his shoulders, his throat, his chin. But even on tiptoe, she couldn't reach his mouth.

"Carson," she moaned protestingly, tugging at his thick hair.

"Do you want my mouth?" he whispered.

"Oh, yes," she whispered back. She moved her body against his slowly. "Oh, yes, I want it very, very much!"

He bent and touched her lips with his, savoring them for a few taut seconds until her mouth opened. His arms drew her close, his hand held the back of her head still, and the kiss became explosive and hot. He groaned as he felt her quick, fervent response to it. His hands moved down to her hips and pushed them against his, and this time she didn't protest.

Her hands worshipped him, running hungrily up his spine, to his shoulder blades, around to his hard ribs and, daringly, to the muscular stomach above his belt.

He shuddered and lifted his head. She stared up at him with dazed, misty eyes and a swollen mouth.

"Shouldn't I touch you like that?" she whispered.

"I like letting you touch me like that," he replied huskily. "Unfasten it."

She flushed. "No, I couldn't!"

He held her hands against him, tenderly. "It's my body, isn't it?" he whispered. "If I don't mind, why should you? Aren't you curious?"

She was. She'd never wanted to touch a man that way, not even Ben when she was eighteen, and the realization shook her to her very shoes.

"Mandy," he said quietly, "I wouldn't seduce you. You'd have to want it, too, before I'd go that far."

"But..."

"But what, honey?" He bent and brushed his lips across her eyebrows, her closed eyes.

"Why...are you making love to me?"

His mouth smiled. "Because it feels good. Because I've never made love to a virgin."

She drew back and studied him curiously. "Never?" she whispered.

He shook his head, smiling. "You're my first."

She felt young and shy and a little embarrassed. Her eyes fell to his bare chest and she tingled just looking at it. "You're...my first," she confessed. "I never let anyone..."

"Never let anyone what, baby?" he whispered.

"Touch me...the way you did yesterday," she said finally.

"Here?" he asked softly, and brushed his knuckles over her soft breast.

"Y...yes," she faltered. She pressed close to him, shivering a little. He made her feel the wildest hungers.

His hands smoothed down her back and around to her hips. He moved her body lazily against his and caught his breath at the rush of sensation.

"Don't faint," he teased when she stiffened. "Think of it as private tutoring, Mandy. You're teaching me to be a gentleman. Let me teach you how to be a woman."

"I'm afraid!"

"I won't force you, precious," he whispered. "I won't ever force you. Let me show you what magic two people can make. Let me show you how sweet it can be."

He lifted her gently in his arms and looked down into her hungry gray eyes while his own blazed with pale blue flames. "I've got to have more of you than this," he whispered. "I want to feel you under me, just once, just for a few seconds."

"Carson...!" she moaned against his suddenly devouring mouth.

"Sweet," he whispered unsteadily, biting at her open, pleading lips. "God, you're so sweet...."

She felt him moving, but his mouth was seducing hers, and she clung to him and closed her eyes. She knew he was taking her to the bedroom. She knew, too, that once he had her down on the mattress and could feel her body yielding under the hard pressure of his own that no power on earth was going to stop him from taking her. Despite all the promises, he was on fire for her. And she was on fire for him. It was going to happen, and she wasn't even sorry. She sensed something in him that calmed her, that made her relax and return his tender caresses.

He carried her into the dark bedroom and laid her down on the soft coverlet. His hand traveled down from her shoulder, tracing her breasts, her waist, her stomach, the long line of her legs.

"I won't make you pregnant," he promised tautly, "and I won't hurt you. Okay?"

She trembled a little as she realized what he was saying, how explosive the passion between them had become. She felt his hands easing her dress down to her waist, over her hips. There was nothing under it but her briefs, and very gently he removed those, too, so that she was nude.

"You're trembling," he whispered as one big, warm hand rested on her belly. "You've never been nude with a man, either, have you?"

"No," she managed weakly.

"Your body feels like cream, Mandelyn," he said softly. He ran his hands over her, letting her feel their rough tenderness as he learned the soft contours of her body.

"Slender, and beautiful, and soft to touch. Honey and spice and cotton candy..."

He bent and his mouth touched her stomach. She cried out, shocked by the intimacy of his lips there and by her own violent reaction to it.

"Hush, baby," he whispered in the darkness. "Hush now, there's nothing to be afraid of. I know what I'm doing."

"Yes, I know," she laughed shakily, "that's why I'm frightened. You...you said you wouldn't..."

"I want you," he whispered. "I've wanted you for so long, Mandy. I look at you and ache. Couldn't you pity me enough to give me one night?"

She wanted that night, too, but pity wasn't what was motivating her. She saw his head bend, his face a pale blur in the darkness and a piercing sweetness washed over her. Carson. He was Carson, and as familiar as her own face in the mirror, and no part of him was repulsive to her. She wanted him, too.

"Yes," she breathed. "Oh yes."

He seemed to freeze for a moment, and then he crushed her to him. "Let me turn on the light," he whispered hoarsely. "Let me watch you when it happens."

His hand went out before she could respond. He turned on the bedside lamp, flooding the room with light. She shrunk from him slightly in embarrassment.

But he wasn't looking at her. His eyes were on the large color photograph in the ornate silver frame on the bedside table. His face paled. He reached out a hand and picked it up and stared down at the boyish face through the glass and his hand shook.

"Who?" he asked, his voice sounding dazed.

Her eyes barely focused. "It's Ben. Ben Hammack. He…was my fiancé."

6

"Your fiancé?" He spoke as if he wasn't sure he'd heard her in the first place, and his eyes were riveted to the photograph.

The lovely, sultry sweetness between them had been dissipated by the stark light, and she fumbled with the coverlet, drawing it quickly over her body.

"You were engaged?" he persisted. "When?"

"Before I came out here," she faltered.

He stood up, replacing the photograph. His hand ran roughly through his disheveled hair, and she stared up at him helplessly. His shirt was still open and his mouth was faintly swollen from the pressure of the kisses they'd given each other. His eyes still bore traces of frustrated passion when they burned down into hers.

"Why didn't you tell me about him before?" he demanded. "When I asked if you'd ever wanted a man before...."

She shivered at the accusation in his tone.

"It was when I was eighteen, Carson," she said, tugging the coverlet closer.

"Stop that," he growled. "I know every inch of you now, so stop behaving like a little prude. Was that a lie, too, are you really a virgin?"

"I haven't lied to you!"

"By omission!" he returned. "You never said anything about a fiancé! So where is he now? Did he throw you over? Are you still hung up on him, is that it?"

"Will you calm down?"

"Calm down, hell!" he ground out, glaring at her as he fumbled to light a cigarette. "I hurt all over. How could you let me make love to you with the image of another man sitting right here beside the bed...!"

She dropped her eyes, clutching the coverlet, embarrassed. "I was out of my head," she said miserably.

"So was I. I've never in my life wanted a woman so much. And if I hadn't turned on that damned light, we wouldn't be talking now. I'd be loving you."

The way he said it caused shimmers of sensation all over her bare body. "Yes, I know," she whispered.

"You'd have hated me for it," he added curtly.

"Would I?" she murmured.

His face hardened and he turned away from her to smoke the cigarette. "Where is he, this ex-fiancé?"

She sighed and stared down at her hands, unconsciously letting the coverlet slide a little. "He's dead."

That seemed to startle him. He turned around and came back to her, sitting down on the bed beside her. "Dead?"

She drew in a slow breath. "He was killed in a plane crash, on his way to a banker's convention in Washington, D.C. It was a small plane and it crashed into a hillside. You see, they…picked him up in pieces…."

He caught her hand reluctantly, and held it firmly in his. "I'm sorry. That would have made it worse."

She nodded. Her hand clung to his. "He was twenty-three, and I loved him with all my heart." Her eyes went past him to the photograph, and Ben looked very young to her now, with his blond hair tousled and his green eyes wicked and mischievous. "He came from a very old Charleston family. We had the same background and our families were friendly. He was brilliant, cultured and he could have gone to the moon. I could hardly believe it when he asked me to marry him. I wasn't his usual kind of girl at all. I was shy and quiet and he was so outgoing…." She shrugged and the coverlet, unnoticed, slipped again. Carson's eyes dropped as she spoke, his face going rigid as he stared at the soft, exposed curves. "After he died, I very nearly went crazy. Uncle had inherited the real estate office here and the ranch, and he'd planned to resell it. But when he saw what was happening to me, he moved us out here instead. I think it probably saved my sanity. I couldn't stop thinking about the way Ben died. It was killing me."

He forced his eyes back up to hers. "That's why you didn't date," he said suddenly.

"Of course." She stared at the photograph. "I loved him so much. I was afraid to try again, to risk losing anybody else. I went out with one or two clients over the years, in a strictly platonic way. But most men won't be satisfied with just companionship, and when I realized that, I just gave up on it completely."

"Now it makes sense," he murmured.

She looked up. "What does?"

"The way you've been with me," he said quietly. "As if you were starving to death for a little love."

Her mouth trembled. "I'm not!"

"Aren't you?" He reached out, and slowly peeled the coverlet back, letting it drop to her waist. And he looked down at her creamy, hard-tipped breasts with an expression that pleased her almost beyond bearing. "You see?" he said. "You like it when I look at you."

She did. Her hands trembled as she jerked the coverlet back in place, her face red, her eyes wild. "I don't!"

"Deny it until hell freezes over, but you would have given in before I turned on the light," he said hotly. "You wanted me, damn you!"

Her eyes closed and her hands trembled, clutching the fabric. She couldn't answer him, because he was right and they both knew it.

He got up abruptly and turned away. "God, this is rich," he said, a note of despair in his voice. He paced, smoking like a furnace. "I thought it was because you were a virgin, that being made love to was new and you were learning things about me that you liked. And all the time, I was substituting for a ghost."

That shocked her. "No," she began, because she couldn't let him believe that. It just wasn't true.

"A dead man. A shrine." He seemed to get angrier as he went along. His eyes burned when he whirled suddenly to glare down at her. "Why did you let me bring you in here?" he burst out.

She shivered a little at his tone. "I don't know."

He lifted the cigarette to his lips jerkily and his eyes went involuntarily to the photograph. "You were still mourning him when we met, weren't you?" he asked. "That's why you got so mad at me when I made a pass."

"I couldn't bear the thought of another relationship," she hedged, staring down at the coverlet.

"Hell! You mean, you couldn't bear the thought of

some ruffian wanting you. I didn't measure up, did I? I wasn't fit to wear his shoes!"

"Carson, no!" she said fiercely. "No, it isn't like that!"

"I'm rough and hard and I've got no manners," he ground out. "I don't come from a socially prominent family and I didn't go to Harvard. So I'm not even in the running. I never was. You've built him into a little tin god and you keep his picture by your bed to remind you that you've climbed into the grave with him, isn't that it!"

She got up, dragging the cover with her, and went to stand in front of him, her eyes wide, her heart aching. He was hurting, and she'd done that to him. All because of a past she couldn't let go of.

"Carson," she said softly, reaching out to touch his hard arm.

The muscles contracted. "Don't do it, honey," he cautioned in a dangerously soft voice. "I'm feeling pretty raw right now."

"Well, so am I," she burst out. "I didn't want you to start pushing your way into my life, to back me into a corner! I didn't start kissing *you…!*"

"As if you ever would have," he said quietly. His eyes were bleak, his face pale and hard. "I guess I've been dreaming. You're as far out of my league as I am out of yours. It's just as well that you aren't civilizing me for yourself, isn't it?"

Her smooth shoulders lifted and fell. "I guess so." She stared down at his boots.

"We'd better forget the dancing lessons," he said coldly. "And before you start getting the wrong idea about what happened tonight, I told you once that I've been without a woman for a while. You went to my head, that's all."

That hurt. She had to fight down a flood of tears. Her eyes lifted proudly to his. "Same here," she said curtly.

"Yes, I know that," he said with a mocking smile. He nodded toward the photograph. "Why don't you take that to bed with you, and see if it makes you burn the way I did."

She lifted her hand, but he caught her wrist and held it easily, letting her feel his strength.

It brought her to her senses like a cold shower of rain. "You can let go," she said defeatedly. "I won't try to hit you."

He dropped her wrist as if it had scorched him. "Hadn't you better put your clothes on? You might catch cold—if ice can."

Her eyes flashed at him. "I wasn't cold with you," she said fiercely.

The hasty words seemed to kindle something in him.

His eyes narrowed and glittered. He reached out and caught the back of her head and before she could turn her mouth, his lips crushed down on it. He twisted her mouth under his, hurting her for an instant, before he lifted it again and glared into her eyes.

"Firecracker," he said heavily, "if you weren't worshipping a damned ghost, I'd throw you down on that bed and make you beg for my body. But as things stand, I'd say we both had a lucky escape."

He let her go and strode out of the room. Seconds later, the door slammed, and she heard his car start and roar away. The house was so still that she could hear the clock in the living room, like a bomb. Tick. Tick. Tick.

She hardly slept at all that night. Her eyes had been well and truly opened by Carson's cutting remarks. She hadn't realized just how much she'd been living in the past until he'd accused her of making a shrine for Ben. Of trying to climb into the grave with him.

With a cup of coffee in her hand the next morning, she sat on the edge of her bed and stared at the photograph. Ben looked impossibly young. And as she gazed at his picture, she remembered how things had been all those years ago. It hadn't been a great love affair. He'd been a handsome, eligible bachelor with a magnetic personality, and she'd been young and shy and flattered by his attention. But over the years, she had built his image into something unrealistic. It had taken Carson's feverish lovemaking to teach her that.

She flushed remembering how it had been between them the night before. He'd been so tender, so achingly tender and patient. And if he hadn't seen that photograph…

She got to her feet, frowning, and paced the floor. Her eyes went involuntarily to the bed and her mind traced, torturously, every wild second she'd spent on it the night before. Carson, kissing her with such sweet hunger, Carson touching her in ways no one else ever had. Carson, looking at her with eyes that ate her. Loving her.

Her eyes closed. It had been loving, of a kind. He'd wanted her quite desperately, and not for the first time last night. He'd wanted her for a long time; perhaps from the very beginning. But he hadn't let her know it. Not until he asked her for those "lessons." And now she had to wonder if that had been only a means to an end. If he'd decided it was past time to do something about his violent hunger.

Did he care, though? That was the thing that tortured her. Was it just a physical hunger that he was trying to satisfy, or did he feel something for her? And did it matter to her?

She put her cup back in the kitchen and got dressed to go to work. It probably was a moot point now, she thought miserably. If the way he'd looked and talked last night was any indication, he'd never want to see her again.

Angie had several messages from prospective clients which Mandelyn took to her office and stared at blankly. It was an hour before she could get into the mood to work, and even then she did it halfheartedly. She spent the day staring at the phone, hoping that Carson would call. But by five o'clock, he hadn't, and she realized that he probably wouldn't want to. She went home in a daze and spent the evening staring at the walls.

Friday came dragging around, finally, and Patty stuck her head in the door of the real estate office to remind Mandelyn about coming to her party that night.

"The party?" Mandelyn felt sick all over. Carson had been going to take her. "I…I don't know, Patty."

"You've got to come," she prodded. "Carson said he was bringing you."

Mandelyn's heart jumped. "Recently?" she asked hesitantly.

"This morning, when I went out to give his bull the all-clear." Patty grinned. "He was in a foul mood until I mentioned that the Gibson boys were coming to play for me. He used to sit in with them years ago. He's a heck of a good guitarist, you know."

"No, I didn't," Mandelyn said slowly. There were a lot of things she didn't know about Carson, it seemed.

"Anyway, they'll probably jam for a while. It's going to be lots of fun. See you about six!"

"Okay," she replied with a wan smile.

"I wish I could come," Angie sighed when Patty was gone. "I've got to babysit my sister's kids. Three of them. All preschoolers. Patty was going to introduce me to a guy who'll be there. Now I'll have to load a gun and look for my own. All on account of my sister's bridge game."

Mandelyn almost laughed at the younger woman's miserable look. "I'd offer to stand in for you, if I could," she said, and really would have considered it. She wasn't looking forward to spending an evening around Carson, whom she was certain hated her.

"I'd almost let you," Angie replied. "But don't worry, I'll survive. I was a girl scout."

"I guess that would help.

"Survival training usually does, with preschoolers," Angie murmured, and reached for the phone, which was ringing off the hook. She pressed the "hold" button. "It's for you. Mr. Wayne."

Mandelyn's heart tried to reach into her throat. She was tempted to have Angie tell him she couldn't come to the phone. Amazing, how he brought out these cowardly instincts of hers.

"Okay," she said, and wandered slowly back into her office. She picked up the phone with trembling hands. "Hello," she said professionally.

"Can you be ready by five-thirty?" Carson asked coldly, and without any preliminaries.

The sound of his voice made her ache. She closed her eyes and wrapped the cord around her fingers. "Yes," she said.

"Patty's idea," he reminded her. "I'd as soon have gone alone."

"Well, if you'd rather…!" she began, feeling hurt and hating him.

"Hell, yes, I would, but I won't give this whole town something to gossip about by refusing to go with you. And neither will you. Be ready." And he slammed the phone down.

Mandelyn slammed her own receiver down, gave a furious groan and heaved a telephone directory at the door.

Angie, shocked, rushed to the doorway. "Are you okay?" she asked, her eyes wide and fascinated. She'd never seen the very proper Miss Bush throw things.

"No," Mandelyn said with blazing eyes. "No, I'm not. I'll kill him one day. I'll shoot him through the heart. I'll feed him cactus branches. I'll…

"Mr. Wayne?" Angie gasped. "But you're friends."

"Me? Friends with that animal?"

Angie stood quietly, fishing for the right words.

"I'm going home," Mandelyn said. She grabbed up her purse and stormed out the door. "Close up, will you?"

"Sure. But…"

"I'll put alum in his punch," Mandelyn was muttering. "I'll put burrs under his saddle…."

Angie just shook her head. "It must be love," she murmured drily, and then laughed at the thought. Miss Bush and Carson Wayne would be the mismatch of the century. Miss Bush was cool and proper and Carson was a wild man. She couldn't picture the two of them in love. Not in a million years. She went back to her desk and started clearing it.

Mandelyn sped home at such a rate that she attracted the attention of Sheriff's deputy Danny Burton. Considering that Danny hardly ever noticed speeders, that was quite a feat.

She pulled over when she heard the siren, and sat there fuming until the short, dark-headed deputy came around to her window.

"Let's see your license, Miss Bush, and your registration," Danny said drily. "Might as well do the thing properly. Where's the fire—that's the other part of my speech."

"The fire is going to be under Carson Wayne, just

as soon as I can find some wood and matches," she said venomously.

He stared at her. "You're his pal," he reminded her.

"That rattlesnake?" she burst out.

He cleared his throat and took the license and registration from her shaking hands. "He must have done something pretty bad to rile you. Poor old feller."

"Poor old feller? He locked you in a closet, have you forgotten already?"

He grinned. "He's been locking me in closets for six years. I've got used to it. Besides, when he sobers up, he always buys me lunch at Rosie's. He ain't a bad guy." He handed back the license and finished writing up the ticket. "Why were you in such a rush?" he asked.

"Patty's party's tonight," she murmured.

"Oh, yeah. I'm going, too. Looks like it's going to be a real hummer, especially since the Gibsons and Carson will be together again. Damn, that Carson can make a guitar sing!"

Why did everybody know that except her? It made her even madder. She took the ticket with a sigh.

"Now slow down," he cautioned. "If you wreck the car, you can't very well go dancing tonight, can you, Miss Bush?"

She sighed. "I guess not. Sorry, Danny. I'll slow down."

"Good girl. See you later."

"Yes. See you later."

She drove home under a black cloud. Even after she'd dressed in a full red printed skirt and a white peasant blouse, with low-heeled shoes, she still hadn't cooled down. She felt wild. Furious at Carson, furious at the circumstances that forced her to be near him. She only wanted to close him out of her life and forget that he even existed. He was haunting her!

When he drove up, her heart began to race wildly. She didn't want to see him, she didn't want him near her! Her body tingled as she opened the door and looked at him. He was wearing jeans and a red print Western shirt with a red bandana. His brown boots were the new ones they'd bought together in Phoenix. They were highly polished, and matched the tan hat he'd bought to go with them. And he looked so handsome and virile that she ached.

His own eyes were busy, sweeping over her body in the unfamiliar casual clothing. Her hair was loose around her shoulders, and she seemed smaller and much more feminine than before. His teeth ground together and his face grew harder.

"Ready?" he asked curtly.

"When I get my purse and shawl, yes," she returned

icily. She jerked them up from the sofa and locked the door behind her.

He opened the door of the Thunderbird for her, but she hardly noticed. She was still angry at his curtness.

He got in and started the car, then sped out onto the highway.

"Keep that up and you'll get one, too," she said, staring straight ahead.

"Get one, what?" he asked.

"Speeding ticket."

His eyebrows jerked up. "The way you drive, you got a ticket? Sheriff Wilson hire a new man or something?"

She continued to stare out the window. "Danny gave it to me."

"Pull the other one. Danny never stops anybody."

"I was doing ninety-five at the time.'

The car went all over the road before he righted it. "Ninety-five, on these roads?"

"Go ahead, make some nasty remark," she challenged, her eyes glittering up at him. "Go on, I dare you!"

His eyes studied hers for an instant before they went back to the road. "In a temper?"

"You ought to know. Yours isn't so sweet today, either."

"I think I'm entitled to a bad temper, considering how I got it."

She flushed and wouldn't look at him. She wouldn't talk to him, either. He didn't seem to mind. He drove all the way to Patty's house without saying a word.

7

"Carson! Mandy! It's about time you got here!" Patty laughed, rushing forward to grab Carson by the arm. She looked nervous and flustered, and nearby, Jake was talking to a group of cowboys.

Mandelyn had never in her life felt such a violent urge to hit another woman. Patty, blissfully unaware of her friend's reaction, clung closer to Carson's sleeve and grinned.

"The Gibsons have been waiting for you," she teased. "Jack said he wouldn't even play if you didn't come."

Carson laughed, and Mandelyn could have cried, because it seemed that the day was long gone when he would laugh with her that way.

"In that case, I'd better get over there, I reckon. You

look sweet," he added in a soft drawl, glancing down at Patty's blue polka-dotted dress and white shoes.

"Thank you," Patty said, and curtsied. Her eyes flirted with him. "It's nice to have my efforts appreciated."

Her hair was loose tonight, too, and she'd never looked less tomboyish. Jake glanced at her out of the corner of one eye and scowled. Mandelyn was the only one who caught that look, and she wondered for an instant if Jake might be jealous. What an odd idea. Carson's foreman never looked at women.

"Excuse us, Mandy," Patty said politely and dragged Carson away. He went like a lamb, without a backward glance.

Mandelyn felt out of place. She was in no humor to enjoy partying this evening. But Jake seemed to sense that, and excused himself from the other cowboys to join her.

"You look as out of place as I feel, Miss Bush," he said wryly. "I'm not much of a partygoer."

"And I'm not in much of a party mood," she sighed, clasping her hands tightly in front of her. She was watching Carson. He shook hands with the four brothers at the bandstand and accepted a big guitar from one of them. Tossing his hat to Patty, he sat down with them.

"Quite a treat, to hear the boss play," Jake murmured. "He doesn't do that very often these days."

"I've never heard him play," she mentioned.

He glanced down at her. "I'm not much surprised. He probably thinks you'd prefer something classical."

"Everybody seems to know me better than I know myself," she sighed. Actually, she liked Country-Western music very much.

They were tuning up and Carson said something and they all laughed. He seemed so different here, with people he knew. He was relaxed and cheerful and outgoing…a stranger. He seemed to sense her watching him and glanced up, but his eyes weren't smiling. She dropped her own to avoid the accusation and frank dislike in his gaze.

"You two have a falling-out?" Jake asked quietly. "He's been pure hell the past few days."

"I noticed," she said shortly.

Jake shrugged and leaned back against the doorway to listen. The Gibson brother who led the band gave them the beat and they swung into a fast, furious rendition of "San Antonio Rose." The others muted their own instruments, two guitars, a bass and a fiddle, and Carson's lean fingers flew across the steel strings of his guitar with beautiful precision. Mandelyn gaped at him. She'd expected that he'd be passable, but what he was doing with the instrument made her knees weak. He was expert.

"Good, ain't he?" Jake grinned. "I used to fuss because he wouldn't go professional, but he said running all over the country with a band wasn't his idea of fun. He liked cattle better."

She watched Carson with sad, quiet eyes. "He's marvelous," she said softly, and her tone hinted that she didn't mean only as a musician.

Jake glanced at her curiously, puzzled by her rapt expression, by the odd look in her gray eyes. So that was it. He looked back at his boss and smiled slowly.

Patty was standing near him, clapping and laughing. He glanced up at her and grinned as he finished the piece. The band gave the last chord and cheered.

"How about 'Choices'?" Jake yelled.

Carson looked up and frowned when he saw Jake standing beside Mandelyn.

"Yes, how about it?" Patty seconded. "Come on, Carson, do it!"

"He wrote that one," Jake told Mandelyn. "We made him copyright it, but he never would let anyone record it."

She studied the man in the red checkered shirt and couldn't fathom him. He gave in to the prodding finally. What he did to the guitar then was so sweet and heady that Mandelyn felt a rush of emotion. It was a love song, pure and simple. All about two different worlds with no bridge between them. And he sang it in a deep, sultry voice that would have made a dedicated spinster's heart whirl. He had the sexiest voice Mandelyn had ever heard, and she watched, spellbound, while he sang. His eyes lifted once, glanced off hers, and went to Patty. He smiled. And Mandelyn closed her eyes on a wave of pain.

When he finished, there was a moment's pause, and then uproarious applause.

"And he's raising cattle, can you believe it?" Patty burst out. She laughed and bent over to kiss Carson firmly on the mouth. "You're great!"

Mandelyn felt sick. Jake said something rough under his breath. He looked down, noticed her sudden paleness and took her arm.

"Are you okay, ma'am?" he asked gently.

"Just a little wobbly," she laughed nervously. "I've been working hard lately.

"You're not alone. So has boss man."

The band had started to play some dance music now. Jake glanced at his boss, who was glaring in his direction. He glared back.

"Would you dance with me, Miss Bush?" he asked.

"Well..."

"He dared me," he said curtly, glancing past her to Carson. "Two can play that game."

"I don't understand."

He led her onto the dance floor. "Never mind," he

grumbled. He shuffled around, much the way Carson had the night she'd taught him to dance.

Patty was looking at the two of them curiously. Jake gave her a cold smile and whirled Mandelyn around.

Mandelyn looked up, and saw murderous fury in his face. So that was it, she realized, Jake and Carson were competing for Patty!

Her eyes fell to Jake's collar. She sighed miserably. It seemed that she wasn't the only one suffering. So Jake wanted Patty, too. He wouldn't win. She knew instinctively that Carson would beat the younger man in any kind of competition, especially when it came to loving.

"Are you sure you feel okay?" Jake asked quietly.

"Not really," she admitted. "But I'll make it."

He smiled at her. "Yes, ma'am, I imagine you will."

The evening wore on, and Carson never left the brothers Gibson for a minute. He played and Patty stayed by him. Mandelyn sat down after the first dance, leaving Jake to circulate among the other women. There was a large crowd, larger, she suspected, than Patty had anticipated. But everyone seemed to be having a great time.

Patty brought Carson a beer and held it to his firm lips while he played. Mandelyn got more and more morose, until finally she was praying that it would all be over and she could go home. She'd never been more miserable in her life. Watching Patty and Carson ogle each other was more than she could bear.

Eventually, Jake joined her again, squatting down beside her chair to watch with narrowed angry eyes as Carson and Patty talked while the band was preparing to play their closing song.

"Patty looks nice," she said quietly.

He shrugged. His eyes went to a piece of string that he was twisting into a hangman's noose in his hands. "Yeah, I guess so."

She felt a sudden kinship with Jake and impulsively murmured, "You, too, huh?"

He looked up, flushed, and looked down again. "Maybe it's contagious."

"Maybe it's curable."

He laughed reluctantly. "Reckon? If you find an antidote, share it with me."

"Same here."

He glared toward Carson and Patty. "It's disgusting. She's too young for him."

Her eyes widened as she gaped at him. "You're almost Carson's age. She's a little young for you, too, isn't she?"

"What's that got to do with anything?" he grumbled.

She only smiled. He probably felt as miserable as she did. She laid a gentle hand on his broad shoulder. "Don't let it get you down. Take up the guitar and practice."

"I can't even carry a tune," he sighed. He looked up. "You might study veterinary medicine."

"I faint at the sight of blood," she confessed.

He smiled warmly. "I guess we're both out of the running."

"I guess." She smiled back.

It was too bad they didn't look across the room at that moment. If they had, they'd have seen two furious pairs of eyes glaring at them from the bandstand.

Carson hadn't danced one single dance all evening. But as the band launched into the "Tennessee Waltz" he led Patty to the floor and held her close during that last dreamy tune.

He shook hands with the Gibson boys, bent down to brush his lips over Patty's cheek and thanked her for the evening. And then he turned to Mandelyn with such evident reluctance that she wanted to scream and throw things.

"Thanks, Patty," she said with forced politeness. "I had a lovely time."

"Good. I'm glad," Patty said with equally forced politeness. "See you."

Mandelyn shot out the door past Carson and climbed into the Thunderbird with ill-concealed impatience. He sauntered along, taking his time, cocking his hat at a jaunty angle.

"You're in a flaming rush," he remarked as he climbed in beside her and started the car.

"I'm tired," she said. Her gaze went out the window to the ghostly shapes of the saguaro cactus against the sky.

"From what?" he asked. "You only danced once. With Jake."

"Jake dances very well."

"He stepped all over you."

She stared ahead as the headlights penetrated the darkness. She almost said, "So did you the other night." But she wasn't going to fall into that trap. She kept her silence.

"Patty looked good, didn't she?" he remarked. "I haven't seen her let her hair down and wear a dress in years."

"She looked lovely," she said through her teeth.

He glanced at her and away again. "Want to declare a truce? At least until the ballet? It would be a shame to waste those tickets."

"I'm not going to any damned ballet with you," she said vehemently. "And, no, I don't want to declare a truce. I hate you!"

He whistled through his teeth. "Temper, temper."

"I've seen so much of yours lately that it's affected my mind," she said sweetly.

"I thought it was your loving memory of your late fiancé that had done that," he said.

She turned, eyes glittering. "Stop this car and let me out, right now!" she demanded.

Amazingly, he did just that. He stopped the car abruptly. "Okay! If you want to walk, go ahead. It's seven more miles."

"Fine. I love long walks!" She got out, slammed the door violently, and started down the road. He took off, leaving skid marks behind him.

She couldn't believe he'd really done that. She stood gaping at his disappearing tail-lights and tears welled up in her soft gray eyes. She felt lost and frightened, and she really did hate him then. Leaving her alone in the darkness on a deserted highway.

She looked around nervously. She could hardly see her feet at all, and she just knew there were rattlesnakes all around her. Diamondbacks! She began to move gingerly, wishing she had a flashlight, wishing she could have kept her stupid mouth shut. She'd set him off again, just when his temper seemed to be improving.

Her lips trembled. She was really afraid now, and there wasn't a soul in sight. There were no houses, no cars, no nothing. She rounded a curve, shaking, and there was the Thunderbird. Carson was leaning against it, smoking a cigarette.

"Damn you!" she bit off, but she was crying and the words hardly registered.

He said something rough and threw the cigarette to the ground. The next minute, she was in his arms.

He held her much too close, rocking her, his arms warm and hard and protective. And she cried, because of the miserable night she'd had, because of the way things were between them.

"I'm sorry," he said at her ear. "I'm sorry."

She trembled at the deep softness in his voice. "I was afraid," she admitted unsteadily.

His arms tightened slowly. She felt the length of him and something kindled in her own body. Her eyes closed. She clung to him, her hands flat against the rippling muscles of his back, her breasts crushing softly into his chest, her legs brushing the powerful muscles of his. Out on the desert, a coyote howled and the wind blew. And Mandelyn had never felt so safe, or so happy.

"We'd better get home," he said after a minute. "Come on."

He held her hand, led her to the car, and put her in on the driver's side. She slid reluctantly across, wondering what would have happened if she'd stayed close to him. Probably, she thought miserably, he'd have pushed her away.

Driving, it was only a short way from there to her

house. He stopped outside the door, but he didn't switch off the engine.

"I…would you like some coffee?" she offered.

"No, thanks. I've got to get some sleep. We're moving cattle in the morning."

"Oh. Thanks for the ride."

"Sure. Any time."

She opened her door and hesitated. "About the ballet…"

"Since I've already got the tickets, it would be a shame to waste them. I can't take anyone but you with me." He laughed shortly. "Patty would laugh her head off."

Her teeth ground together. "No doubt. What night?"

"Wednesday. We'll need to leave here by five, to get there in time."

"I'll close up early." She got out, hating him more than ever, and slammed the door.

"Mandelyn."

She paused. He'd rolled down the passenger window and was leaning across. "Yes?"

"This will be the last time," he said curtly. "I think when we get through with the ballet, I'll have learned enough to cope."

"Good. It was getting a bit boring, wasn't it?" she asked coldly.

"I'll tell you something, honey," he said quietly. "I've

about decided that I like my world better than I like yours. Mine has the advantage of real people and honest emotions. Yours is an old house with elegant furniture and the warmth of a tomb. Speaking of which, there's yours. Why don't you go and moon over your lost love?"

Her fists clenched by her sides. "If I had a gun, I'd blow you in half," she spat.

"Hell. If you had a gun, you'd shoot yourself in the foot. Good night."

He rolled up the window while she was stomping onto the porch. She jammed the key into the lock and broke it in half as he roared away.

Her eyes widened. The back door had an old lock and she didn't have its key. The windows were down and locked. Now what was she going to do?

With a heavy sigh, she went out and got a big rock. She took it to the side of the house and flung it through the window. The sound of shattering glass made her feel a little better, even though she knew she was going to have an interesting story to tell the repairman in the morning.

Unfortunately, the handyman she had to call was out working on the renovations at Carson's place. He was too busy to come. She managed to talk his wife into giving her the number of a man who put in windows in his spare time. She contacted him and got a promise that he'd do the window first thing Monday morning. Meanwhile she got a locksmith to come out and fix the door. She hadn't asked the handyman's wife how things were going over at Carson's, although she was curious about how the house would look when they got through. Carson's preparations were none of her business. Probably Patty knew, though, she thought miserably.

She went up to Phoenix and spent the rest of the weekend there just to get away. How drastically things had changed in just a few short weeks, she thought. She and Carson had been on the verge of friendship, but those few days together had changed everything. Actually, she decided, that long, hard kiss he'd given her behind the bar had done it. She'd been curious about him after that, and when he'd made a pass, she hadn't had the strength to put him off. She'd wanted to know how he would be as a lover. And now she knew, and the knowledge was eating her up like acid. She'd never known that a man could be so tender, so protective and possessive. She could have had all that, if not for Carson's obsession with changing to suit Patty.

Patty. She went out to the balcony of her hotel room and glared over the city's lights. The wind tore through her hair and she drank in the sounds and smells of the night. He'd kissed Patty at her party. Why had he done that? She closed her eyes and she could almost hear Carson's deep, slow voice as he sang. She leaned her head against the wall and wondered how it would be to sit with him on his porch late on a summer evening while he sang to her. And if there were children, they could sit on her lap....

The thought was intensely painful. She remembered how it had been that night, the night she'd wanted him so much. If only he hadn't turned on the light and seen Ben's photograph.

Dear Ben. Her bastion against emotional involvement. Her wall that kept love out of her life. And now she was twenty-six and alone and she'd lost the only man in the world she wanted to live with.

Of course, she hadn't a chance against Patty. She'd always known that. Carson was too fond of the woman. She turned back into her room. How odd that he wanted to learn cultural things for Patty, though. Especially when Patty seemed to like country things and country people. How very odd.

She went back to Sweetwater late Sunday night, feeling drained and no more refreshed than before. It was going to be another long week.

It didn't help that Patty came into her office early Monday morning with a complaint about the property.

"The roof leaks," she grumbled. "It poured rain here,

and you told me that roof was sound. I had ten half-drowned cats before I thought to check."

"I'm sorry, Mandelyn said formally. "The previous owner assured me he'd had a new roof put on recently. You know I'd never purposely misrepresent a property," she added. "You're going to have trouble finding a roofer. Carson seems to have every workman in town out at his place."

"It's coming along nicely, too," Patty remarked. "He's had new furniture put in the house and carpeting…it's a showplace already. Once they get the new roof on, and the painting finished, it will make most houses in the valley look like outbuildings."

"You'll like that, I'm sure," Mandelyn murmured under her breath.

"I'll call Carson and see if he can loan me his roofer," Patty said suddenly. "Why didn't I think of that myself?"

"Good idea," Mandelyn said with a wan smile.

Patty started out the door and paused. "Uh, Jake spent a lot of time with you at the party," she murmured. "Seen him since?"

"I've been out of town," Mandelyn said noncommittally. "I haven't seen anybody."

"Jake's been out of town, too," Patty said, her smile disappearing. She opened the door and went out, slamming it behind her.

Angie glanced up from her typewriter with a curious stare. "You and Jake…?"

"Oh, shut up," Mandelyn said. "I haven't been anywhere with Jake. She's just mad because Carson isn't running after her fast enough, I suppose. He isn't good enough for her…."

She went into her office and slammed the door, too. Angie shrugged and went back to work.

Mandelyn didn't hear from Carson at all. Wednesday, she went ahead and dressed to go to the ballet, feeling not at all happy about it. She'd rather have stayed home and bawled. It was how she felt. She wasn't even sure that Carson would show up at all. He was getting to be wildly unpredictable.

She chose a floor-length blue velvet gown with white accessories and put her hair up with a blue velvet ribbon. She kept remembering that blue velvet ribbon in Carson's car, and wished she could get it out of her mind. He must not have gotten it from her, after all.

At five-thirty, he still hadn't shown up, and she was on her way back to her bedroom to change her clothes when she heard a car pull up.

She felt as nervous as a girl on her first date. She was probably overdressed, but she'd wanted to look pretty for him. That was idiotic. But she couldn't help herself.

She opened the door, and found him in a tuxedo.

That was one item they hadn't bought together, and she couldn't help but stare. He was so striking that she couldn't drag her eyes away. He had the perfect physique for a tuxedo, and the whiteness of the silk shirt he was wearing made his complexion darker, his hair blacker. His blue eyes were dark, too, as they looked down at her.

"You…look very nice," she faltered.

"So do you," he said, but his eyes were cold. Like his face. "We'd better go."

She followed him outside, forgetting her wrap in the excitement. They were halfway to Phoenix before she remembered.

"My stole," she exclaimed.

"You aren't likely to freeze to death," he said curtly.

"I didn't say I was, Carson," she replied.

He tugged at his tie. "I'll be glad when this is over," he grumbled.

"It was your idea," she said sweetly.

"I've had some pretty bad ideas lately."

"Yes, I know."

His eyes drifted slowly over her. "Was it necessary to wear a dress that was cut to the navel?" he asked harshly.

She wouldn't let him rattle her. "It was the only dressy thing I had."

"Left over from the days when you dated the eligible

banker and were in the thick of Charleston society, no doubt," he said mockingly.

She closed her eyes and wouldn't answer him.

"No retort?" he chided.

"I won't argue with you, Carson," she said. "I'm through fighting. I've got no stomach for it anymore."

She felt that way, too, as if all the life had been drained out of her.

"You, through fighting?" he laughed coldly.

"People change."

"Not enough. They never change enough to suit other people. I'm dressed up in this damned monkey suit going to a form of entertainment I don't understand or even like. And it isn't going to change what I am. I'm no fancy dude. I never will be. I've accepted that."

"Will your fancy woman accept it?" she laughed unpleasantly. "Will she want you the way you are?"

"Maybe not," he replied. "But that's how she'll take me."

"So masterful!" she taunted. "How exciting for her!"

He turned his head slowly and the look in his eyes was hot and dangerous. "You'll push me too far one day.

She turned her gaze toward the city lights of Phoenix.

He pulled up near the auditorium and parked. There was a crowd, and she kept close to Carson, feeling a little nervous around all the strangers.

He glanced down at her, frowning. "Aren't you afraid to get that close to me?" he taunted.

"I'm less afraid of you than I am of them," she confessed. "I don't like crowds."

He stopped dead and looked down at her with narrow, searching eyes. "But you like culture, don't you, honey?"

The sarcasm in his voice was cutting. She looked back at him quietly. "I like men with deep voices singing love songs, too," she said.

He seemed disconcerted for a minute. He turned away, guiding her into the throng with a puzzled frown.

Everything seemed to go wrong. Their tickets were for another night, and Carson was told so, politely but firmly.

"Wrong night, hell," he told the small man at the door. Then he grinned and that meant trouble. "Listen, sonny, they were supposed to be for tonight. I'm here. And I'm staying.'

"Sir, please lower your voice," the little man pleaded, looking nervously around him.

"Lower it? I plan on raising it quite a bit," Carson returned. "You want trouble, you can have it. In spades."

Mandelyn closed her eyes. This was getting to be a pattern. Why did she let herself in for this kind of embarrassment?

"Please go in, sir. I'm sure the mixup is our fault," the small man said loudly and with a forced smile.

Carson nodded at him and smiled coldly. "I'm sure it is. Come on, Mandy."

He guided her into the auditorium and seated her on the aisle beside him. He stuck out his long legs and stared down at the program. He scowled.

"Swan Lake?" he asked, staring at the photos in the printed program. He glanced at Mandelyn. "You mean we came all this way to watch some woman dressed up like a damned bird parading across the stage?"

Oh, God, she prayed, give him laryngitis!

Around them were sharp, angry murmurs. Mandelyn touched his hand. "Carson, ballet is an art form. It's dancing. You know that."

"Dancing, okay. But parading around in a bird suit, and her a grown woman?"

She tapped him on the arm with her program.

"Swatting flies?" he asked.

She hid her face behind her program, slid down in the seat, and prayed for a power failure. There were too many lights. Everyone could see that the loud man was with her.

He continued to make loud comments until the lights went down. Mandelyn almost sagged with relief in the darkness. But she should have known better. The minute the orchestra began to play and the lead ballerina finally appeared, he sat up straight and leaned forward.

"When does the ballet start?" he demanded.

"It just did!" she hissed.

"All she's doing is running around the stage!" he protested.

"Shut up, could you!" the man behind Carson said curtly.

Carson turned around and glared through the darkness. "I paid for my ticket, just like you did. So shut up yourself. Or step outside."

The man was twice Carson's age, and rather chubby. He cleared his throat, trying to look belligerent. But he held his peace.

Carson glanced down at Mandelyn. "Something in your shoe?" he asked. "Why are you hiding?"

"I'm not hiding," she choked, red-faced as she sat back up.

He was staring at the stage. Out came a muscular male dancer, and Carson gaped and caught his breath and burst out laughing.

"Oh, do be quiet," she squeaked.

"Hell, look at that," he roared. "He looks like he's wearing long johns. And what the hell is that between his legs…?"

"Oh, God," she moaned, burying her hands in her face.

"Better not bother Him, lady," the man behind her suggested. "If He hears what that man's saying, He'll strike him dead."

Mandelyn was only hoping for hoarseness, but it didn't happen. Carson kept laughing, and she couldn't stand it another minute. Everyone near them was talking; they had disrupted the entire performance. She climbed over Carson and ran for the front door. She made her way through the lobby and into the women's rest room. She stayed there for a long time, crimson to the roots of her hair. How could he? He knew better than to behave like that. He'd done it deliberately, and she knew it. He'd been trying to embarrass her, to humiliate her in front of what he thought was her own set. And that hurt most of all. That he'd done it to wound her.

Carson was waiting for her, his head down, glaring at his dress shoes when she came back out of the rest room. He heard her step and looked up.

His eyes were dark blue. Quiet. Searching. He took his hands out of his pockets and moved toward her.

"You've had your fun," she said with dignity. "Or revenge. Or whatever you like to call it. Now that you've ruined my evening, please take me home.'

His jaw tightened. "Miss Bush of Charleston, to the back teeth," he said mockingly. "Dignity first."

"I have very little dignity left, thank you," she replied. "And I'm through trying to civilize you. I know a hopeless case when I see one."

His eyes flashed. "Giving up?"

"Oh, yes," she said with a cool smile. "And I wish your woman joy of you, Carson. Maybe if she can put a bridle on you, she can tell people you're a horse and don't know any better manners."

The expression that crossed his face was indescribable. He turned on his heel and led the way out the door. She followed him stiffly, standing aside to let him unlock her side of the car.

It was a long, harrowing ride home. He turned on the radio and let it play to fill the silence. When they pulled up in front of her house, she was too drained to even notice what was playing. He'd told her in actions just how much contempt he felt for her.

"Mandelyn," he said.

She didn't even look at him. "Goodbye, Carson."

"I'd like to talk to you," he said through his teeth. "Explain something."

"What could you possibly say that would be of interest to me? You and I have absolutely nothing in common," she said with cool hauteur and a look that spoke volumes. "Do invite me to the wedding. I'll see if I can find something homespun to wear. And I'll even send you a wedding gift. How would you like a set of matching knives for your table? After all, you have to have something to eat your peas with, don't you? Just the thing for a savage like you!"

She got out of the car, slammed the door and marched up the steps. It took her the rest of the night to try to forget the look on Carson's face when she'd said that to him. And she cried herself to sleep for her own cruelty. She hadn't meant it. She'd only wanted to hurt him as much as he'd hurt her. He'd as much as told her that her world was shoddy and superficial. It had been the killing blow. Because she understood all at once why it hurt so much. She was in love with Carson. And she'd just lost him forever.

8

Mandelyn couldn't even go to work the next day, she was so sick about what had happened the night before. She shouldn't have behaved so badly, even though Carson had provoked her. She shouldn't have hurt him like that.

"I've got a migraine," she told Angie. She knew she sounded unwell from crying all night. "If anyone needs me, tell them I'll be back tomorrow, okay?"

Angie hesitated. "Uh, Patty came by as soon as I opened up."

"Oh?"

"Yes. She asked if I knew that Carson was in jail."

Mandelyn gripped the receiver hard.

"What?"

"She said he went on a bender last night and dared Jake to call you. Danny had to lock him up. They said he set new records for broken glass, and to top it all off, he ran his Thunderbird into Jim Handel's new swimming pool."

Her eyes closed and tears welled up behind her swollen eyelids. Because of her, she knew. Because of the way she'd hurt him.

"Is he still there?" she asked after a minute.

"No, ma'am. Patty bailed him out. She took him over to her place to look after him. He's pretty bruised and battered, but she says he'll be okay. She, uh, thought you might want to know."

"Well I don't," she said quietly. "I don't want to hear about Carson Wayne again as long as I live. See you tomorrow, Angie," she added on a sob and hung up.

He was at Patty's. He was hurt, and he was at Patty's. And she was nursing him and taking care of him and loving him….

Mandelyn burst into tears. Somehow, she was going to have to stop crying. Her heart was breaking.

She didn't eat breakfast or lunch. Around midafternoon she heard the sound of a car coming up the driveway.

She looked out the window and was shocked to see Patty's truck pulling up at the front door. Her eyes flashed. She wouldn't answer the doorbell. She wouldn't even talk to the other woman! Patty had Carson now, what else did she want?

Patty rang the bell and Mandelyn ignored her.

"Mandy!" Patty called. "Mandy, I know you're in there!'

"Go away!" Mandelyn called back, her voice wobbling. "I've got an awful headache. I can't talk to you!"

"Well, you're going to," Patty said stubbornly. "Shall I break a window?"

Mandelyn decided that another broken window would be too much trouble. Reluctantly, she opened the door.

Patty paused, shocked by the other woman's pale features.

"What do you want?" Mandelyn asked. Her voice sounded hoarse.

"I came to see about you," Patty said, surprised. "Angie said you had a migraine, and I thought you might want me to go to the pharmacy for you."

"You've already got one patient, just take care of him and leave me alone."

Patty moved closer, eyeing her friend closely. "Mandy, what's wrong?" she asked softly.

That was the straw that broke the camel's back. Mandelyn started crying again, and couldn't stop. Her body shook with broken sobs.

"Oh, Mandy, don't, I can't stand to see you like this,"

Patty pleaded, helping her to sit down in the living room. "What's wrong? Please, tell me!"

Mandelyn shook her head. "Nothing."

"Nothing." Patty looked toward the ceiling. "Carson takes his car into the swimming pool with him and you play hookey from work with a nonexistent headache, and nothing's wrong."

"You've got him now, what do you care what happens to me?" Mandelyn ground out, glaring at her.

"I've got him? Him, who? Carson?" Her eyes widened. "You think I'm after Carson?"

Mandelyn dabbed at her eyes. "Aren't you? He did it all for you, you know. Learning all about culture, and going to ballets and making fun of ballerinas and fixing up his house. You ought to be proud of yourself! He didn't think he was good enough for you the way he was, so he got me to give him lessons in etiquette!"

Patty's mouth opened. "Carson isn't in love with me!"

"Of course he is," Mandelyn said with trembling lips. "And I wish you every happiness!"

"Me? What about you?" Patty shot back. "You went away for the weekend with Jake!"

It was Mandelyn's turn to look shocked. "I went to Phoenix…alone."

Patty flushed. "Oh." She glared. "But you were all over him at my party."

"We were consoling each other," Mandelyn said wearily. "I suggested maybe he could learn to play a guitar and sing like Carson, and he said maybe I could go to veterinarian's school...."

"Jake was jealous?" Patty asked. "Of me?"

"Boy, are you dense," Mandelyn grumbled. "Of course he was jealous. Mad at Carson, mad at you. He asked me to dance so he wouldn't have to watch the two of you together. And when you kissed Carson, I thought he was going to go wild."

Patty's eyes misted. "Oh, my," she whispered.

A dawning realization made Mandelyn's tears dry up. "Patty...it's Jake, isn't it?"

"It's always been Jake," Patty confessed. She stared down at her jeans. "Since I was a teenager. But he wouldn't give me the time of day. I thought after I went away, maybe he'd miss me, but he didn't even write or call me. And when I came back here, I found all sorts of excuses to go out to the ranch, but he didn't notice. At the party I'd just about given up. I was hurting so much I couldn't stand it, and Carson knew and he played up to me to try to make Jake jealous. But I thought it backfired, because Jake wouldn't come near me. Last night, when I got Carson out of jail and took him home with me, Jake came to the front door and raised hell. I yelled back at him, and I thought it was all over. But now..."

"Jake loves you," Mandelyn whispered.

"Yes, I think he might," Patty faltered tearfully. "But why won't he admit it?"

"He's Carson's foreman. He isn't an educated man. And you've a degree. Maybe he doesn't feel worthy."

"I'll soon rid him of that silly notion, wait and see." Patty grinned. "I'll seduce him."

Mandelyn blushed wildly and Patty laughed.

"You might try that yourself," she suggested gently. "The way Carson lets you lead him around, I don't think he'd be able to stop you."

"I don't feel that way about Carson. I just feel guilty." The flush got worse. Mandelyn stared down at her shoes. "He hates me."

"Oh, sure he does."

"But he does!" Mandelyn wailed. She blurted out the whole painful story through a mist of tears. "I could just die! I hurt him and he could have been killed. I'd never have forgiven myself."

"Carson's tough," Patty said. "At least, he's tough with everyone but you."

"He's nice to you," Mandelyn reminded her.

"Oh, Carson and I go back a long way. We grew up together. I love him like a brother, and he knows it. But he's never been with anyone the way he is with you, honey. You must be the only person in Sweetwater who doesn't know that Carson's in love with you."

Mandelyn stared at her friend as if she'd lost her senses. Her eyes widened and her heart began to race.

"Didn't you ever wonder why he'd let you save people from him when he was drinking?" Patty asked, her eyes soft.

"Because I wasn't afraid of him," she replied.

Patty shook her head. "Because he would have done anything for you. We all knew it. And he'd sit and stare at you and have the damndest lost look on his face…."

"But…but he said there was a woman." Mandelyn hesitated. "He said she wouldn't have him the way he was, that he wanted to change and get cultured so that he could have a chance with her."

"He was talking about you," Patty said. "You, with your genteel background and your exquisite manners. It was like wishing for a star, and he must have known all along how impossible it was. But I guess he had to try."

Mandelyn felt as if someone had hit her over the head with a mallet. Carson loved her?

"Don't feel so bad," Patty said. "He'll get over it. He's almost back to normal this morning. Once he's realized what a silly idea it was, he'll come around, and you two will be friends again. Carson doesn't hold grudges. He'll thank you for having brought him to his senses." She stood up, grinning. "Imagine, you and Carson. That would be something, wouldn't it? The debutante and the outlaw. Wow!" She stretched. "Well, I'll never be able to tell you how grateful I am to know how Jake really feels. And don't you torment yourself about Carson. You only helped him see the light. He'll be okay. He's mostly just hung over."

"Would you…tell him I said I'm sorry?" she asked.

Patty studied her. "Wouldn't you like to come with me and tell him yourself?"

"No!" Mandelyn took a steadying breath. "No, I don't think so. It's too soon yet."

"Well, I'll relay the message. Feel better now? He isn't hurt. He's just dented."

Mandelyn nodded. "Thanks for coming by. I'm sorry I was ratty."

"No problem. I know what guilt can do to people. Say, you weren't getting sweet on Carson, were you?"

"Who me?" Mandelyn laughed nervously. "As you said, that would be something, wouldn't it?"

"A pretty wild match. What interesting kids you'd have. Okay, I'm going!" she laughed when Mandelyn started to look homicidal. "See you!"

Mandelyn sat by the window for a long time, thinking over what Patty had said. Bits and pieces of conversation came back to her, and she began to realize that it might have been true. Carson might have been falling in love with her. But whatever he'd felt before, he hated her now. He hated her for trying to live in the past with Ben, and for what she'd said to him at the ballet. He hated her for making him feel worthless and savage.

She fixed herself a light supper, trying to decide what to do. Her life was so empty now that she didn't know how she was going to survive. Perhaps she could go back to Charleston.

That thought appealed for only a few minutes. No, she couldn't leave Sweetwater. She couldn't leave Carson. Even if she only caught glimpses of him for the rest of her life, she couldn't bear being half a country away from him.

Several times, she went to the telephone and stared at it, wanting to call him, wanting to apologize. Or just to hear his voice. Finally, after dark, she dialed Patty's number.

"Hello," Patty said cheerfully.

"It's Mandelyn. Is…is Carson still there?"

"No, honey, he went home to nurse his bruises alone," Patty said. "He's feeling pretty low, though. You might try him there."

"Okay. Thanks."

"My pleasure," Patty murmured, and a male voice laughed softly in the background.

Mandelyn hung up, smiling faintly. It had sounded like Jake's voice, and she was glad that for Patty, at least, the long wait was over.

She dialed Carson's number and waited and waited until finally he picked it up.

"Hello," he said deeply, in a defeated kind of voice.

She was afraid he'd hang up on her. So she only said, very softly, "I'm sorry."

There was a long pause. "Why apologize for telling the truth?" he asked coldly.

At least he was talking to her. She sat down and leaned back against the sofa with her eyes closed. "How are you?"

"I'll live," he said curtly.

She couldn't think of anything to say. Except, maybe, "I love you." Because she did, so desperately. Patty had said that he loved her, but those days were gone for good. She knew she'd killed the delicate feelings he had for her.

"Do…do you need anything?" she asked hesitantly.

"Not from you, Mandelyn."

She knew that, but hearing it hurt. She swallowed down the tears. "I just wanted to see how you were. Good night."

She started to hang up, but he said her name in a way that made her toes curl up.

"Yes?" she whispered.

There was a long pause and she held her breath, hoping against hope for some crumb, some tiny clue that he still cared.

"Thanks for the lessons," he said after a minute. "I'll put them to good use."

"You're welcome," she replied, and hung up. Maybe Patty was wrong, she thought desperately. Maybe there was a woman neither of them knew about, a woman in Phoenix or some other town. And that thought tortured her long into the night.

9

The next few days were agonizing ones for Mandelyn. She lost her appetite for food, for living itself. For the first time, work wasn't enough to sustain her. And her memories of Ben, which had kept her going for years, had become nothing more than pleasant episodes from the past. She missed Carson. It was like having half of her body cut away and trying to live on what was left.

Once, she accidentally ran into him in the local fast-food restaurant. She'd stopped to get a cold drink as she walked back to her office after an appointment, and he was just coming out.

Her heart leapt up into her throat and she dropped her eyes. She couldn't even look at him. She turned around and went back the way she'd come without bothering about the cold drink. The look in his eyes had been chilling enough.

The second week, Patty stopped by the house to invite Mandelyn to go with her to the Sweetwater Rodeo.

"Come on," Patty coaxed. "You've been moping around for days. You need some diversion."

"Well..."

"You can go with Jake and me," she coaxed, grinning. "Things are going very well indeed in that department, by the way. I've almost got him hooked."

Mandelyn smiled. "I'm happy for you. I really am." But she couldn't bear the thought of driving in the pickup with Jake and hearing him talk about Carson. "I've got something to do earlier in town, though, so I'll just drive in and meet you there. Okay?"

"Okay."

She imagined Carson would be there, and she almost backed out at the last minute. But he'd be a competitor, as he usually was, and she wouldn't get close to him. She'd be able to see him, though. And the temptation was just too much for her hungry heart. Just to see him would be heaven.

She left her house fifteen minutes before the rodeo started and had a devil of a time finding a parking space at the fairgrounds. She managed to wedge her car in beside a big pickup and left it there, hoping she could get out before the owner of the pickup wanted to leave.

Patty waved to her from the front of the bleachers, where she was sitting beside Jake, his arm around her.

"Just in the nick of time," Patty said. "Better late than never, though."

"I couldn't find a parking spot. Hi, Jake," Mandelyn said as she sat down next to Patty. It was as if they had changed roles for the day—Patty was in a green print sundress and Mandelyn in jeans and boots and a blue tank top with her hair loose and sunglasses perched atop her head.

"Hi, Miss Bush," Jake said with a wicked smile. "I didn't know you liked rodeos."

"I like a lot of strange things these days," she returned. "Looks like you didn't need to learn the guitar after all."

Jake laughed and hugged Patty close. "Good thing, since I've got ten thumbs." He glanced toward her curiously. "Boss is riding today."

Her heartbeat faltered. "Is he?"

"In the steer wrestling and bronc riding. He's been practicing. We got two steers with permanently wrenched necks and one poor old bronc with a slipped disk."

"Nasty old Carson," Mandelyn said.

"I expect he'll take top money."

Mandelyn glanced around the ring, looking for a city woman somewhere. "Doesn't he have a cheering section with him?" she asked with barely concealed curiosity.

Jake and Patty exchanged amused glances. "Sure. Right here. We're it."

Mandelyn glared toward the dirt ring. "Amazing. I would have thought the object of his affections would be around somewhere. How's the house looking?"

"Just great," Jake returned. "He's kind of lost interest, though. Says it's no use anymore."

"There isn't any woman," Patty murmured under her breath. "I've told you already, it was you."

Mandelyn's face went hot and red. "Not now."

"Do you stop loving people just because you get angry with them?" Patty asked.

No, Mandelyn thought miserably. She'd never stop loving Carson. But what good would that do her? She'd just die of unrequited love, that was all.

The bronc riding competition was exciting. Most of the cowboys who participated drew good mounts, and the scores were high. But when Carson exploded into the arena on a horse named "TNT," groans were heard all around.

He rode magnificently, Mandelyn thought dreamily, watching his lean figure. His bat-wing chaps flew, his body whipped elegantly, gracefully, as it absorbed the shock of the bronc's wild motions. And by the time the horn blew, everybody knew that top money was going to Carson that day.

"Damn, isn't he good?" Jake laughed.

"I thought you'd be riding this time," Mandelyn remarked.

Jake looked down at Patty with a dreamy expression. "No. I've got more important things on my mind."

Patty blushed and snuggled closer and Mandelyn felt empty and cold and alone.

The sun beat down as rider after rider competed in bulldogging and calf roping. And then came steer wrestling. Carson was the last competitor, and there was a wild cheer as he came down off the horse squarely in front of the long horns of the animal. He dug in his heels, gave a quick, hard twist with his powerful arms, and the steer toppled onto the ground. Applause filled the bleachers, but Mandelyn was holding her breath as Carson got to his feet. The bull headed straight for him.

"No!" she screamed, leaping to her feet. "Carson!"

But it was all unnecessary. Lithe as a cat, he was onto the fence rail even as the animal charged. The rodeo clown made a great production of heading the steer off, finally leaping into a barrel and letting the animal work its frustration off by rolling him around.

Mandelyn managed to sit back down, but her face was white. Patty put an arm around her.

"Hey," she said gently. "He's been doing this a long time. He's okay."

"Yes, of course he is," Mandelyn said, swallowing down her fear. She clasped her hands tight in her lap and sat stiffly until the end of the competitions.

Later, she was about to head for her car when Patty caught her arm and tugged her along the aisle behind the pens. Carson was just loading his horse into the trailer behind the ranch pickup, and Jake went forward to shake his hand.

"Hey, boss, you done good." Jake grinned. "Congratulations."

"And you kept saying you were too old," Patty added, hugging him. "I was proud of you."

He hugged her back, smiling down at her in a way that twisted Mandelyn's heart. At least he and Patty were still friends. She hadn't wanted to come this close; she hadn't wanted to have to talk to him.

He looked up and saw her and his face froze. His expression went from sunshine to thunderstorm in seconds.

"We're going to see Billy for a minute," Patty called. "Be right back!"

She dragged Jake away, looking smug and triumphant.

Mandelyn twisted a knot in the necklace she was wearing while Carson glared at her.

"You...did very well," she said, hating the long silence.

Around them, animals snorted and whinnied, and there was a loud buzz of conversation among the milling cowboys.

"I didn't expect to find you at a rodeo," he said, lighting a cigarette. "It isn't exactly your thing, is it?"

"I like rodeos, actually," she returned. Her eyes went down to his opened shirt, and there was a red welt across his chest, visible through the mat of black curling hair. "Carson, you're hurt!" she burst out, moving close to him with wide, frightened eyes. "The bull got you...!" She reached out her fingers to touch it, and even as they made brief, electric contact with his skin, he'd caught her wrist bruisingly hard and pushed her away.

His eyes blazed like blue lightning. "Don't touch me, damn you!" he whispered furiously.

Her face went white. She could feel every single drop of blood draining out of it as she stared at him, horrified. So it was that bad. She was so repulsive to him that he couldn't even stand to have her hands on him now. She wanted to crawl off and die. Tears burst from her eyes and a sob tore out of her throat.

She whirled and ran sightlessly through the crowd,

crying so hard that she didn't hear Carson's wild exclamation or his furious footsteps behind her. She pushed people aside, jumped over saddles and trailer hitches and ran until her lungs felt like bursting. She wanted to go home. She wanted to get away. It was the only thought in her tortured mind.

She rounded the corner of the fence and squeezed by the pickup and into the front seat of her car. She was so blinded by tears that she could hardly see how to get the key into the ignition, but she managed it. She'd just started the car and was fumbling it into reverse when the door was jerked open and a lean, angry hand flashed past her to turn off the ignition and pull out the key.

"You little fool, you'll kill yourself trying to drive in that condition!" Carson said harshly. He was breathing hard as he stared down at her furiously.

The tears grew more profuse. "What the hell does it matter?" she asked brokenly. "I don't care if I die!"

"Oh, God," he ground out. He eased himself into the front seat beside her, facing her. His hands framed her face and he brought her mouth under his, tasting tears and mint and trembling lips. And the sob that rose from her throat went into his hard mouth, mingled with his rough breath.

He eased her head back against the seat with the pressure of his lips. His tongue caressed her, probed into the soft sweet darkness of her mouth. His sweaty chest pressed against her soft breasts and she could feel the hardness of muscle and the warmth of flesh and the wild thunder of his heart.

It was so sweet. So sweet, after all the long days and nights of wanting and needing and loving and pain. She slid her hands over his shoulders, up into the thick dampness of his hair and sighed shakily as her mouth opened and answered the tender pressure of his own.

His lips lifted, then came down again, kissing away the tears and the pain while she sobbed softly and tried to stop crying.

"Carson," she whispered achingly.

"It's all right," he whispered back. His hands trembled on her face. He kissed her again, so tenderly that it hurt, and she moaned.

"I'm so hungry…for you," she moaned. "So hungry… for your mouth, your…hands."

"Baby…" he protested.

She crushed her mouth against his, drowning in sensual pleasure as he answered the hard kiss. His arms slid under her, pulling, crushing, and she thought if she died now, it would be all right. Life would never offer anything more beautiful than this, than Carson wanting her.

A long time later, she felt his mouth lift, and the breeze

cooled her moistened lips. Her eyes opened, dark gray, still hungry, worshipping his face.

His nostrils flared. His own eyes were fierce and hot with unsatisfied passion.

"I want…to have you," she whispered softly, searching his eyes.

His eyes closed. His teeth clenched. "It's no good! It won't change anything!"

"It will give you peace," she said, smoothing his hard face gently.

His eyes opened again, searching hers, and there was pain and hunger and loneliness in them.

She managed a tremulous smile. "Patty said once that I should seduce you. That you'd probably let me."

His fingers traced her mouth, unsteady and gentle. "That would be one for the books, wouldn't it? A shy little virgin seducing an outlaw like me?"

"Would you like it?" she whispered, wide-eyed.

He trembled before he could get his body under control, and she touched his hair, his face, with hands that loved the feel of him.

"I'd be…very careful with you," she said unsteadily, on a nervous laugh. "I wouldn't even let you get pregnant, I promise."

He burst out laughing, but his eyes were solemn and quiet. "Mandy…"

"Please," she whispered, beyond pride.

His eyes closed and he mutterd a harsh word. "Look, it's no use," he said after a minute. "You and I are too different. Desire…it fades. So I want you. And you want me. But if we had each other, it wouldn't solve the problem. It would only make things unbearable." He sighed roughly and put her away from him. "No, honey. You go your own way. Someday you'll find some cultured dude with fancy manners and you'll live happily ever after. I was a fool to think anything would change. Goodbye, Mandelyn."

He got out of the car and left her sitting there, staring after him. She thought about what he'd said and a slow, easy smile came to her lips. That one tremor had given him away. She dried her tears and drove back to the house. She had things to do.

About midnight, she had a nice warm bath and doused herself in a faint, subtle perfume. She powdered her smooth, pink body and pulled on a button-up yellow dress, and nothing else. She brushed her hair until it shone. Then she slid into her sandals and got in her car and drove to Carson's house.

The lights were all off. She ran up onto the front porch, sure that the boys were all gone because it was Saturday night. She smiled wickedly as she thought about what she was going to do. Drastic situations called for drastic measures, and nobody had ever been this desperate, she decided. She knocked hard on the door, noticing that the woodwork was freshly painted. The porch looked nice. Very white and different, and there was a white porch swing and rocking chairs, too. She approved of the renovation.

There were muffled curses and thuds as she knocked again. The door flew open and Carson stood there, in the lighted room, without a stitch of clothing on his powerfully muscled, hair-roughened body.

10

Carson blinked, staring at her as if he thought he was having a dream. "Mandy?" he asked softly.

She was just adjusting to the sight of him. It had been a wild shock, although he was as perfect as a man could possibly be, and her eyes were only just able to drag themselves back up to his shocked face.

He stood aside, running a hand through his disheveled dark hair, just staring at her. She opened the screen door, her heart pounding, and walked into the living room. It was as much a shock as Carson. The sparse, worn furniture was gone, replaced by heavy oak pieces with brocade fabric in cream and chocolate. The brown carpet was thick; the curtains were of the same fabric as the upholstery on the chairs. And the beautiful fireplace had been renovated and was the showpiece she'd once thought it could be.

"The house is lovely," she remarked breathlessly, forcing her eyes to stay on his face.

"What are you doing here at this time of night?" he burst out.

Her eyes glanced down and up again and she flushed. "Getting anatomy lessons."

He glanced down, too, and smiled ruefully. "Well, you should have called first."

"I guess so."

"Want me to put my pants on, or is the shock wearing off?"

She searched his blue eyes, hesitating. It had seemed so easy when she was thinking about it. And now it was becoming more impossible by the minute. The longer she waited, the weaker her nerve became. He needed a shave, but he looked vital and exquisitely masculine and she wanted to touch him all over that bronzed skin.

She moved closer to him, watching the way his eyes narrowed warily.

"I...want you...to come to bed with me," she faltered.

He glared at her. "I told you this afternoon how I felt about that," he said curtly.

"Yes, I know." She reached out and touched his chest, watching the way he stiffened. His hands caught her, but she trailed her fingers slowly down his body and his hold weakened. His body trembled and jerked.

"Don't," he whispered huskily.

It was so easy. Easier than she'd dreamed. Heady with success, she pressed her body against his and reached up to coax his head down.

"Help me," she whispered. She eased her mouth onto his and kissed him tenderly. She loved his immediate response to her. He tasted of whiskey. It was a little disturbing at first, but the warm hardness of his mouth got through to her and she became accustomed to the strong taste.

His hands caught her shoulders. "Mandy, we can't," he breathed roughly. "You're a virgin, for God's sake!"

"Yes, you'll be my first man," she whispered. "The very first."

That made his hands tremble and she stood on tiptoe, brushing her body softly against his so that something predictable and awesome happened to him. She sighed and moaned.

"It's going to be so beautiful," she said at his lips. "The most beautiful night…"

She left him long enough to close and lock the door. Then she went back to him, where he stood frozen and waiting, and reached up her arms.

"Would you carry me?" she whispered.

He bent like a man in a trance and lifted her tenderly in his hard arms. She nestled her face into his throat, feeling the thunderous beat of his pulse there, feeling his taut body absorb the shock of his footsteps as he carried her into the darkened bedroom and laid her down on his rumpled bed.

"Honey..." he began in a strangled voice.

"Here," she said, drawing his hands to the buttons of her dress.

He muttered something, and his fingers trembled as he fumbled them open. She sat up, sliding the dress off her body. She lay back, her body pale in the patch of moonlight coming through the window. She held out her arms.

"Come here, darling," she whispered. She wasn't even afraid. She wanted him. She wanted a child with him. And tonight she was going to make sure she had that, if nothing else. If he sent her away, she wanted at least the hope, the tiny hope, of having a part of him.

"Mandy," he groaned. He lay down on the bed with her like a lamb going to slaughter.

"It's all right," she whispered. She trembled a little when his hands moved down her thighs and back up over her flat stomach and her soft breasts.

"You're afraid," he whispered.

"It's very mysterious right now," she explained quietly. "I…I know the mechanics, but I don't know how it's going to feel, you see. Will…Carson, will it hurt me very much?" she whispered.

"We don't have to do it," he said.

"I have to," she breathed. "I have to!"

"Why?" he asked.

His hands were fascinated with her body, and she stretched like a cat being stroked, loving their rough tenderness. "I want a baby," she whispered. "I want your baby."

He shuddered wildly. His breath caught and he buried his face against her body, groaning helplessly.

Yes, she thought, drawing him closer, yes, that had done it. Now he wouldn't be able to stop, or stop her. It would happen now, because she'd stirred him in an unbearable way.

His mouth found hers hungrily, and his hands began to touch her in new, shocking ways. She trembled and twisted and moaned, and still his hands tormented her. His mouth went on a trembling journey of exploration that left not one inch of her untouched, that made her cry out and whisper things to him that would have shocked her speechless in daylight.

When she felt his weight on her, she stiffened a little, and his hands brushed back her damp hair, calming her.

"I won't take you in a rush," he promised tenderly.

"Mandy, close your eyes for a minute. I'm going to turn on the light."

"No...!"

"Yes," he whispered, brushing his mouth over her eyes as he reached out to turn on the light at the head of the bed.

Her eyes opened, shocked, frightened and although she knew he was too committed to draw away, she was afraid the starkness of the light might make him stop.

His hands smoothed her hair, touched her hot cheeks. His eyes adored her, glazed with desire, bright with passion and hunger.

"I asked you this once before. Let me watch," he whispered shakily. "You came in here a virgin, and we're about to do something extraordinary together. Let me... watch it happen to you...please."

Her body trembled, but she didn't say a word. Her hands touched his broad, perspiring shoulders, his chest, his face. She felt him move and her eyes dilated. She stiffened, but his fingers touched her hair again, soothing, comforting as his hips eased down.

"No," he whispered when she tried to move away. His voice shook, but his smile was steady, his eyes were... loving her.

"Oh," she whispered sharply, staring straight into his eyes as his body locked with hers.

"Yes," he said, shuddering, his face clenching. "Oh, God, yes, yes…yes!

Something incredible was happening. She couldn't believe the intimacy of it. Her nails were biting into him and she didn't even realize it. Her body forgot that it had a brain and began to entice him, incite him. It arched and forced a deeper intimacy that began as pain and suddenly became easy and sweet and achingly tender.

"Now," she whispered mindlessly. "Now, I…belong… to you…!"

"Baby…was there a time…when you didn't?" he bit off. His mouth burned into hers, hot and wet and hungry, and his body began to find a new rhythm with hers. She felt his hands, holding her hips, showing her how. She closed her eyes and let her body teach her what to do, her hands touching, her mouth whispering into his. Storms. Sunlight. Wild breeze and sweet peace. Open fields and running feet. A surge. A scream. Hers. And all too soon she felt conscious again. Carson lay shuddering helplessly on her trembling body, his voice shaking as if he were in unholy torment, whispering her name like a litany.

She reached up to cradle him, to comfort him. Her eyes opened and there was the ceiling, the light fixture. She moved and felt his body move, and realized that they were still part of each other. She caught her breath at the beauty of it.

It took him a long time to calm down. She stroked him and soothed him, and wondered at the force of his passion.

"It had been a long time, hadn't it?" she whispered softly.

He levered himself over her and searched her misty eyes with regret and pain in his own. "I took you," he said jerkily.

"Not exactly," she murmured with a warm smile.

"For God's sake…!"

She arched up and kissed his mouth softly, tenderly, smiling against it.

"Don't,…"

Her hips twisted sensuously under his and something that should have been impossible, suddenly wasn't. Deliciously surprised, she closed her eyes and kissed him harder.

"Oh, God," he ground out. And then he stopped talking. She locked her arms behind his neck and held the kiss until the world exploded around them again. Finally, exhausted, they slept in each other's arms.

She awoke before he did, slipping back into her dress while she studied his long, elegant body on the bed. He was beautiful, she decided. Not cultured and citified and well-mannered. But beautiful and sensitive and he'd make the most marvelous father….

Her face burned as she recalled the long night. Well, it was too late for regrets now. He'd marry her. He'd have to. Because if he didn't, she fully intended to move in with him anyway.

She went into the clean, neat new kitchen and found an equally new refrigerator that had been recently filled. She cooked eggs and bacon and thick, fluffy biscuits and made a pot of coffee. When she'd set the table, she went back into the bedroom.

He was sprawled on his back, still sound asleep. She sat down beside him and bent to brush her mouth slowly over his.

"Baby…" he whispered hungrily, and reached up to kiss her lips. Then he stiffened. His eyes opened. He looked up at Mandelyn and his face went white. "Oh, my God. It happened."

"You might sound a little less horrified," she murmured drily. "You seemed to enjoy it enough last night."

His hands went to his eyes and he rubbed them. "I had a bottle of whiskey and then I went to bed. And…" His eyes opened. "You seduced me!"

She sighed. "That's what they all say," she said with mock weariness.

He sat up in bed and stared straight into her eyes. "You seduced me!" he repeated roughly.

"Well, you needn't make such heavy weather of it, Carson, I'm surely not the first woman who ever did," she reminded him reasonably.

"You were a virgin!"

She grinned. "Not anymore."

"Oh, God!"

She got up with a sigh. "I can see that you're just not in the mood to discuss this right now. So why don't you come and have breakfast?"

He threw his legs over the side of the bed and stared at her departing figure. "Why?"

She turned at the doorway, her eyes soft and possessive. "Don't you know?" And she walked out.

He made his way into the room minutes later. He was dressed now, in jeans and a brown patterned shirt and boots. But he looked half out of humor and bitterly regretful. He glared at her as he sat down.

"What a horrible expression," she remarked, handing him the platter of scrambled eggs.

"Aren't you even upset?" he burst out.

"Should I be? I mean, you did drag me into bed with you and...

"I did not!" he growled. "You did it, you crazy little fool!"

"That's no way to talk to the mother of your children," she said calmly and poured coffee into the thick mug beside his plate.

"Children…" He put his face into his hands. "You knocked me so off balance I couldn't even hold back. What if I got you pregnant?"

"I like children." She smiled softly. "Just think, Carson, if we have a little girl, I can teach her how to be a lady. And if he's a boy, you can teach him the guitar."

He looked up with bloodshot eyes, staring as if he didn't believe what he was hearing. "Mandy?"

Her fingers reached out and brushed over the back of his with an adoring pressure. She searched his eyes and all the amusement went out of hers. "I love you," she whispered. "I love you more than anything else in the world, Carson. And if you'll just let me live with you, I won't even ask you for anything. I'll cook and clean and have babies and you won't know I'm around, I'll be so quiet…!"

"Come here," he said in a voice that shook with emotion. "Oh, God, come here!"

She went around the table, to be dragged down into his arms and kissed to within an inch of her life.

"Love…you," he groaned against her mouth. "So much, for so…long. I was dying…."

"Darling, darling!" she whispered, clinging, loving, worshipping him with her hands, her mouth.

He couldn't seem to get enough of her soft, eager mouth. He tasted it and touched it and kissed it until it was tender from the rough pressure. His mouth slid down her body, against her breasts.

"It was me," she guessed, closing her eyes as she remembered the pain she'd caused him. "It was me you were being tutored for, because...because you thought I wouldn't want you."

His arms tightened. "Eight years, Mandelyn," he said unsteadily. "Eight years, I worshipped you. And it got to where I couldn't eat or sleep or live for loving you. I wanted to fit into your world, so that I'd have a chance with you."

"And as it turns out, yours suits me very well," she said humbly. "You were right, Carson. Your world is real and honest and the people don't put on airs. I like it better than mine." She clung to him. "Let me live with you."

"Always," he promised. "All my life. All yours. But first," he said curtly, lifting his head, "we get married. Pronto."

Her eyebrows arched. "Why the rush?"

"As if you didn't know, you little witch," he said. His big hand pressed against her stomach and he kissed her roughly. "Whispering that to me last night, when I was doing my damnest to keep my head, to stop myself. Whispering that you wanted my baby. And I went crazy in your arms. You were damned lucky I didn't hurt you."

"I wouldn't have cared," she murmured contentedly. "It was so sweet, so heavenly. Oh, Carson, I loved you and I knew, I thought, I hoped you loved me. And you were so tender, and I wanted to make it perfect for you."

"It was perfect all right. Both times," he added drily. "After we've been married a few years, remind me to tell you that what happened was impossible, will you?"

She grinned. "You said yourself you'd been a long time without a woman."

"That wasn't why," he said. His eyes held hers. "It was wanting you. Obsessively."

She kissed his closed eyelids. "I felt the same way. I could have died the night we went to the ballet. Those things I said…and when I heard about your driving the car into the pool, I got sick all over. I wanted to go down on my knees and apologize. I missed you and I loved you and I knew I'd die without you."

"I felt the same way," he confessed. He drew her close and held her securely on his lap. "Then yesterday, at the rodeo, you touched me and I wanted you so badly that…" He sighed. "I got the shock of my life when you started crying after I pushed you away. I was terrified that you were going to get in the car and have a wreck.

I trampled two people getting to you. And then I knew just how bad I had it—that I was going to waste away without you. I knew you wanted me, then. But I didn't think you loved me." His eyes searched hers. "I thought you came to me last night out of pity."

She shook her head. "It was love."

"I should have realized that you'd never give yourself without it." He sighed. "You're much too fastidious for love affairs. Even with wild men you desire."

"You're not wild," she murmured. "You're just a maverick. I love you the way you are, Carson. I wouldn't change one single thing about you. Of course, I'll never go with you to another ballet…oh!"

He pinched her and laughed uproariously. "Yes, you will," he murmured. "We'll take the kids. I want them to be polished. Not like their father."

"They'll have a lovely father," she sighed, kissing him again. "When are we going to get married?"

"Today."

She sat up, and he pulled her back down. "We'll drive down to Mexico," he said gently. His eyes searched hers. "It has to be done right. Making love to you without my ring on your finger doesn't sit well. Does it?"

She lowered her eyes to his broad chest. "No," she confessed.

He tilted up her chin. "But I don't have one single regret about last night. That was the consummation. That was the wedding vows. Now we make it right."

Her fingers touched his mouth. "I adore you," she whispered passionately. Her gray eyes searched his blue ones. "I want you so much."

His hand touched her stomach, flattened, caressed it. "Tonight," he whispered. "After we're married. It will be better this time. Slower. Sweeter."

She trembled and leaned toward him, but he shook his head with a tender smile. "First you marry me. Then you sleep with me," he said.

"We got it backwards."

"We'll get it right this time," he promised, smiling. "Up you go. I want to call Patty and see if she and Jake will stand up with us."

"They way things are going with them, it might be a double wedding," she laughed.

He looked down at her. "I was jealous of Jake."

"I was jealous of Patty. When she kissed you that night, I wanted to mop the floor with her."

He searched her eyes and smiled wickedly. "Yes. I saw that. It was the only glimmer of hope I had."

Her mouth fell open. She started to speak, but he bent and put his lips on hers. And since it felt so good, she gave up protesting and wound her arms around his neck. He might not be the world's most polished man, but he was the only one she would ever love.

They drove down to Mexico, and Mandelyn and Carson said their vows in muted, solemn voices while Jake and Patty looked on.

Mandelyn looked into his eyes while she spoke the words, and he couldn't seem to look away, even when it was time to slide the ring on her finger. He did it blindly, with amazing accuracy. And then he bent to kiss his wife.

It was a beautiful day, and Mandelyn felt like a fairy princess. She clung to Carson's lean hand, hardly believing all that had happened. When he suggested that the four of them stop by a bar on the other side of the border for a drink, she was too happy to protest.

"Isn't this nice?" Patty sighed as Carson and Jake went to get drinks. "I loved your wedding. Jake must have enjoyed it, too," she added with a grin, "because he proposed under his breath while you two were sealing the ceremony with that absurdly long kiss."

Mandelyn blushed. "I hope you'll be as happy as we are," she laughed.

"I hope so, too. Didn't it all work out..."

"What the hell do you mean, 'move over, Pop'?" Carson's deep, angry voice came across the room like a cutting whip and Mandelyn opened her mouth to say, "Oh,

Carson, don't," when the sound of a hard fist hitting an even harder jaw echoed in the sudden silence.

Mandelyn gritted her teeth. "No," she groaned, watching Carson going at it with a man just his size. "Not on my wedding day. Not just before my wedding night!"

"Carson's tough," Patty promised her. "Quit worrying. It will be all right."

Just as she said that, a man who'd been standing beside Carson's opponent picked up a chair. Mandelyn's mouth flew open. Her temper flared like wildfire. That was her husband that ruffian was about to hit!

"Mandy, no!" Patty called.

But Mandelyn was already bounding over chairs. She picked up a vase from one of the tables and threw water, flowers and all into the face of the man holding the chair.

He sputtered, wiped himself off and glared at her. "Women's libber, huh?" he said curtly. "Okay, honey, put up your dukes."

"Whatever happened to chivalry?" Mandelyn wondered out loud. She brought her high heel down on the man's instep and when he bent over, she brought up her knee. The blow was apparently very painful, because he went sideways onto the floor.

She grinned, heady with success. "Hey, Carson…" she began.

Just about that time, the man who'd been trading blows with Carson took one too many hard rights and careened backwards into Mandelyn. He rammed against her and she fell headfirst into a huge planter full of ferns.

Wet, covered with dirt, she heard the sounds of the brawl escalating all around her as she struggled to get up again. As she raised her head, Carson came flying backwards from an uppercut and landed against her, and in she went again.

Somewhere there was a siren. And minutes later, she was extricated from the planter by a heavyset, blue-uniformed man who looked as if he had absolutely no sense of humor at all.

"We can explain all this," Mandelyn assured him in her most cultured voice.

"I'm sure you can, lady, but I assure you, I've heard it all before. Come along."

"But we just got married," she wailed, watching Carson being led out between two burly deputies.

"Congratulations," the uniformed man said blandly. "I'll show you both to the honeymoon suite."

As they waited to be booked Mandelyn leaned against the wall staring daggers at her new husband. Her hair was thick with dirt and traces of green leaves; her dress was ruined.

Carson cleared his throat and sighed. "Well, honey,"

he said with a grin, "you have to admit, I've given you a wedding day you'll never forget."

She didn't say anything but her eyes spoke volumes.

He moved closer, oblivious to the noise and confusion around them. "Mad at me?" he murmured.

"Furious, thanks," she replied.

"My Charleston lady," he whispered, smiling with such love that her poise fell apart.

"You horrible, horrible man," she murmured, "I love you so much!"

He laughed delightedly. "My poised little lady, right at home in a barroom brawl. My God, you laid that cowboy flat! I've never been so proud of you…." He lifted his head and looked stern. "But never again, honey. I don't want you fighting, even to save me. Especially not now," he added. His gaze went to her waist. "We don't know yet, remember," he whispered tenderly.

She flushed and looked up into his eyes. She knew exactly what he meant.

He bent and kissed her very gently. She managed a watery smile.

"Oh, I hope I am," she breathed fervently.

His chest rose and fell heavily. "We can make sure, if you want," he replied in a voice hoarse with passion.

"Is it too soon?" she asked.

He shook his head. "Not at our ages. We'll just be spreading love around, that's all." He grinned.

She laughed. "You can sing lullabies," she said. "And I'll sit and listen."

"Remember that song I wrote—

Choices?" he asked, searching her eyes. She nodded. "I wrote it for us. That's right," he added when she looked stunned. "I thought someday, if you ever started noticing me, I could sing it to you, and it might tell you something."

She sighed miserably. "And I was too busy being jealous of Patty to listen to the words," she mumbled.

"I'll sing it to you tonight, while we make love," he whispered.

"And here we are in jail," she moaned.

"Patty and Jake will be here any minute to bail us out," he promised. He grinned. "Don't you worry, honey. Everything's going to be fine. Next time, I won't hit, I'll just cuss. Okay?"

She burst out laughing, loving him with all her heart. "Okay. But don't change, will you?" she added seriously, searching his pale, glittering blue eyes. "Darling, I love you just the way you are."

He looked at her for a long time before he spoke. "I'm no gentleman."

"I'm no lady. Remember last night?" she whispered.

He trembled and kissed her quickly again.

Nearby, two slightly intoxicated men were staring at them. Mandelyn thought she recognized them from the brawl.

"Ain't that the blonde who threw the vase at me?" one asked the other, who squinted toward her.

"Yep. Looks like her."

"And kicked me on the foot and knocked me out with her knee?"

"The very same one."

The burly man grinned. "Lucky son of a gun," he slurred.

Carson glanced at him with a slow grin. "You don't know the half of it, pal," he murmured and bent his head again.

Mandelyn smiled, feeling as if she had champagne flowing through her body. "Darling, about that brawl…"

"What about it?" he murmured absently.

She grinned. "Could we do it again sometime?"

And that was the last thing she got to say until Jake and Patty came along to bail them out. Not that she minded. She was already making plans for the night and whispering them to a glowing new husband.

★★★★★